Life Drawing

W/D SALE

Life
Drawing

ROBIN BLACK

PICADOR

First published 2014 by Picador
an imprint of Pan Macmillan, a division of Macmillan Publishers Limited
Pan Macmillan, 20 New Wharf Road, London N1 9RR
Basingstoke and Oxford
Associated companies throughout the world
www.panmacmillan.com

ISBN 978-0-330-51176-6

1 3 5 7 9 8 6 4 2

A CIP catalogue record for this book is available from the British Library.

Printed and bound by CPI Group (UK) Ltd, Croydon, CR0 4YY

For my children,
Elizabeth, David, and Annie
&
For my mother,
Barbara Aronstein Black

The greatest happiness of life is the conviction
that we are loved; loved for ourselves,
or rather, loved in spite of ourselves.

— VICTOR HUGO

Our dead are never dead to us,
until we have forgotten them.

— GEORGE ELIOT

Life Drawing

1

In the days leading up to my husband Owen's death, he visited Alison's house every afternoon. I would watch him trudge over the small, snowy hill between our two properties, half the time away from me, half the time toward me. And I would wonder what he thought about as he went. Wonder too if Alison watched him from a window of her own, and whether the expression she saw on his face as he approached was very different from the one I saw as he came home.

In the weeks that followed his death, I would stare out the same window, the one in our living room, nearest the fireplace, for as much as an hour at a time. Sometimes even longer than that. There was a huge blizzard on the day after his funeral. I watched as nearly three feet of snow fell to the ground, staying all through January, then much of February, picking up a few more inches now and then, drifting against anything in its way, flattening the landscape so the hill wasn't quite so distinct anymore and the trees all looked shorter, their trunks buried deep.

It was, I imagine, very beautiful. But imagining and remembering are not quite the same thing. I don't remember thinking it anything but eerie at the time.

Owen wasn't buried. I had known practically since the day
we met that he wanted to be cremated. We'd had the sort of
courtship—though the word would have seemed old-fashioned to
us both—that included a lot of talk about the meaning of life, the
prospect of death. We were young, very young, and undoubtedly
neither of us believed, not really, that we would ever die, which
made that sort of discussion, often late at night, often just after
sex, exhilarating. There was a beauty to be found in the transitory
nature of existence, we would say. There was liberation in the acceptance of mortality. Religion was for fools. Religion, along with
marriage ceremonies, Thanksgiving dinners, station wagons, pro-
creation, and so on. Burial was a perverse notion if you really
thought about it, without the assumptions of the culture blinding
you. All those dead bodies, taking up all that land. A peculiar,
fetishistic custom.

We were to be a cremation couple. It was established early on.

Except that we were never going to die.

I thought about so many things during those first snowy weeks,
including the fact that I too was mortal, that I too would disappear one day, leaving behind such things as panes of glass through
which other people could gaze, and cold that they could feel. Snow
that had to be shoveled, not just contemplated. Practical issues for
which I would no longer be a help or a hindrance. Relationships
abandoned like unfinished thoughts.

It isn't that no one close to me had ever died before. I was
forty-seven years old. Few reach that age unscathed and I hadn't
made it past toddlerhood before a brain aneurism took my mother
in a matter of hours; then my oldest sister, Charlotte, lost a filthy
battle to cancer when she was forty-six; and my father was wandering his solitary, demented way toward a graceless, profoundly
unjust kind of death.

But Owen was Owen. Owen was me. I was Owen. Anger and all. Betrayals and all. Owen would walk into a room and I might well want to kill him—so to speak—but at the same time, for much of my life, I couldn't really have told you where I left off and he began. And then he died. Leaving me standing at a window, staring into a landscape as though, well, as though he might just reappear one day. Of course.

I was certain about cremation, but in fact a lot of our other opinions had softened over the years. That is what happens. There was a marriage ceremony, eventually. There were attempts to procreate, which led to discovering that Owen could not, so when we bought the minivan we had sworn we never would, it was for hauling my paintings, not children. We never did get religion, either of us, but we started to value the idea of ritual. Still, no celebration of Thanksgiving with its intimations of smallpox-infected blankets and European domination, but on the second Saturday of April we threw a big party, invited old friends out to the country, cooked an insane amount of food, drank too much, and talked appreciatively of pagan celebrations of spring. And back when we were city dwellers, we went through a phase of lighting candles every Wednesday night. *"Ain't nobody's Sabbath but our own,"* Owen sang the first time that we did, so we played Billie Holiday every Wednesday after that.

But *softened* isn't really the right word. Our opinions didn't soften. More accurately, we reacted to life. And we reacted, time and again, to threats. To us. To us being us. Why did we finally get married? Because I had broken the promise that we had never made. Owen forgave me, or anyway, we moved forward, but we did it with a vow this time. Why did we try to have children? Because there was a period in there when the possibility—absurd five years before!—that we needed more than just each other, crept into our thoughts. Our fabric seemed to be wearing thin. And why this desire for ritual? To anchor us. *I will be here the second Saturday of every April. I will be here every Wednesday night.*

We never saw it that way, of course. I saw it that way later on. That's what happens when one of you dies. The clock stops. The story ends. You can make some sense of it all. Begin to see patterns. Begin to understand. Maybe you can only begin to understand. Maybe the patterns are only the ones that you impose. But the thing takes on a different shape. It takes on a shape.

Or, as one of my teachers used to say, you cannot see a landscape you are in.

But you do begin to see it when you step away.

This is me, just before my first glimpse of Alison: I am standing, hands on hips, staring at a patch of basil that has gone to seed, peeved at myself for having once again planted so much and once again failed to harvest it at the right time. It is one of those obscenely hot late July days when you walk outside and think there's been some kind of terrible mistake, because weather can't really be meant to be this oppressive. My hair, long and still close to entirely black, is tightly braided, pulled off my neck, clipped straight on the back of my head, so if the sun weren't too high for shadows, mine would look like I had feathers sticking up. I am wearing just a bra and shorts. My body, at forty-seven, is tan from gardening, mowing, walking. And I am strong, stronger than I ever was before I became a country dweller. My face? My face is broad, my Russian forebears lending me their wide, prominent cheekbones, their heavy square jaws. And my eyes, which are dark blue, are bluer still under thick black brows. If I am beautiful, I am not classically so; but at forty-seven I think I am beautiful. More than I ever did at twenty, at thirty. By this time I mind mirrors less. If I am honest, I will say I sometimes seek them out. I look at my face, at my body, with a kind of clinical detachment into which a strand of admiration inserts itself. I always wanted to be powerful. In this decade, finally, I look powerful. I feel powerful.

And I feel alone. Standing there in front of the house, knowing the mail has already arrived so there won't be anyone close again for another twenty-four hours, I am alone in a way that is familiar to me by this day, but that I never experienced until nearly three years before, when we moved to this otherworldly place. It is a kind of solitude that continues even when Owen is standing beside me. It is a solitude that includes him. We are apart from the rest of the world. We are invisible to it. We have become by this time a single being, a being that argues with itself from time to time—as a knee may ache, as a tired back might refuse to cooperate, so you say, *Oh for God's sake, could you stop being so difficult;* but you are saying it to a part of yourself.

While I am peering down at herbs, Owen is in the barn, writing—or trying to. For months now, he has been that weary back that won't cooperate. He imagines that his prose has wandered to a distant acre of our universe, curled up and died. He still spends days inside the barn but he comes out looking grieved. I feel this ache all the time, though my own work is going well, and it is probably this that has made me wander out into the garden, into the day, so horribly hot. I am restless for him. I am restless as part of him.

The basil I am eyeing with such irritation is rampant. The air smells of it and of lavender. Owen and I are enthusiastic, ignorant gardeners. We are inadequately attentive. We are perpetually amazed. We are innocents to nature, stupefied by its every trick. Even as I am annoyed with myself for letting the basil go to seed, I am also in awe of it. Magic! These beings that continue to grow, that know what to do next, and next, and next.

"Halloooo . . ."

I am not alone.

First, a British voice. Then a small woman in a violet sundress. With a mop of gray curls. "Alison Hemmings," she says, her hand outstretched long before I might reach it. "I've just rented the house across the way. I'm so sorry if I'm here at a bad time . . ." A smiling face. Round cheeks. A firm grip. Startling light gray eyes, almost silver to match her hair.

No one during our time has lived in the house next door, the only building within sight of our home. I have stopped thinking of it as having an interior. It has become solely a shabbily beautiful façade.

"Gus Edelman," I say. "Augusta, really, but Gus. Welcome."

My voice is riddled with question marks; and then I remember that I am only in a bra. Folded in among the thoughts of a neighbor is the thought that the bra, which is purple, may pass for a bathing suit; then the thought that it serves her right, barging in—though she hasn't really barged in. Then the thought that it's too late to say anything about my bra. We have absorbed the fact of it already. We have moved on.

"It's so lovely here, isn't it?" she says.

"Yes, it is," I say. "Can I help you out in some way?" It isn't quite right, I know. I sound like a salesperson at the end of the day hurrying to close the store.

She tells me she is leasing the place. "At least through September," she says. "Maybe beyond. Depending on how things go."

"I hadn't realized they were renting it out."

The owners, a young couple who inherited the property from distant family, have only ever visited once, maybe eighteen months before. They walked the land, several acres, had seemed to be arguing and then had driven off, never to return.

"You haven't seen the advert?" she asks. "Because you're in it. You and . . . is it your husband?"

I shake my head, frowning. "I had no idea . . ."

"On one of those rental sites. One of the features is the couple who lives next door. The writer. The painter."

"Oh. How strange. They never mentioned . . ."

She smiles. "I promise not to be a pest, but it did make the setting more appealing. I'm actually a painter too. And somehow the notion of a creative enclave . . . plus I figured if the ad mentioned you, you probably weren't axe murderers."

"Not recently," I say. "Not me, anyway." As we speak, I decide she's only a few years older than I, despite the gray hair. Early fifties. We look at one another a bit more, awkward, until she says she should be getting back to her unpacking. I tell her please to let us know if we can help her settle in, but I don't say it with much enthusiasm and as she steps away I lean down to pick some of the leggy basil, as though she has caught me in the middle of an important, pressing task.

"Many thanks," she calls back. "So good to meet!"

When I'm sure she's gone, I straighten up, my hands full of basil stems. I look toward the barn, and think of going there. A new neighbor is big news. But then I decide it can wait. Owen needs to be left alone to push the rock back up the hill. And I too need to get back to work, so instead of turning left, I turn right and go inside.

We'd moved into the farmhouse nearly three years before, after Owen's Aunt Marion died, surprising us by leaving a small fortune. Very small. But still, a fortune to us. It was enough money that we could think hard about what changes we wanted to make in our lives, enough money that we could afford to make changes without thinking too hard. For the first time in forever we had a safety net. We'd always talked about living the country life in a maybe-one-day kind of way, but once it was possible, we started to get serious, checking real estate online, driving beyond the suburbs to explore houses that we knew within seconds we would never want to own. Too new. Too obviously designed for families of four. Too close to other human beings.

But then we found the farmhouse, and as buyers we were sold right away. Built in 1918, it was exactly the kind of lovely we'd been looking for. We saw it first on a breezy day in May when the land shimmered with every leaf imaginable, from ground to sky. I thought we'd stumbled onto the hidden spot in which the universe tested out its most exquisite shades of green. The pond, perfectly round, had a fairy-tale look, frog princes poised to set themselves on its edge. I have fallen in love very few times in my life, and once was with those seven acres, our home, on that day.

I wanted to live there. I wanted to paint every vista.

Owen could write in the stone bank barn once we ran electricity, and I could set up a studio in the enclosed porch, with its windows on three sides. There was work to do, of course. The kitchen, set back in the house, was a horror show, its only saving graces a beautiful worn terra-cotta-tiled floor and the old glass-paned door out to what would become our garden. The roof was a joke—like the old dribble glasses, designed to leak. But the house itself was dirt cheap and we had more than enough money to fix it up.

Our friends back in Philadelphia, incurably urban, thought we were mad, and we both rather enjoyed that part. In our crowd it was hard to latch onto any eccentricity no one else had yet claimed. Overnight we became oddballs, objects of affectionate eye rolling and shaking heads. *They'll be back in a week.* We had set ourselves apart from the crowd. And in some other sense, some entirely literal sense, that was exactly what we needed to do.

Neither of us acknowledged that our move had anything to do with my infidelity two years before. It had been some months since our City Hall ceremony, the ritual that was to have been the punctuation-mark ending to the whole episode. But that didn't

mean the betrayal wasn't a lingering presence in our lives, a taunt-
ing little goblin in the shadows, daring us to call him out.

For Owen, I knew, there were reminders everywhere. When I'd
confessed to him, I had confessed fully—with all the misguided
passion of one who believes that she is cleansing herself and for-
gets that she may be staining the listener. Owen became the man
who knew too much. He carried in his head a map of meeting
places, of locations where we might run into Bill. He could envi-
sion us slipping into this dim café, slipping out, a few minutes
apart, from this hotel. He knew how to drive from our home to
Bill's. He knew where Bill's law office was.

I always half believed that Owen would have an affair one day
himself to restore balance of a kind. In certain moods, dark moods,
I even believed he was entitled, though the thought of it was hid-
eous to me. Sexual jealousy. Emotional jealousy. I couldn't bear
the prospect of going through what he had gone through. (What
I had put him through.) But a part of me believed that it was only
fair. A part of me thought maybe it would set us right again.

A couple of times, I almost convinced myself it had happened.
There was a student of his whose name seemed to come up too
often. Victoria Feldman. And a little later there was a young
woman, a girl really, who worked at a nearby coffee shop. I thought
I could catch a little atmospheric hum around each of them. I had
my hunches. But then, for whatever reasons, I changed my mind.
Maybe he said Victoria Feldman was *tedious,* a word I knew he
wouldn't use about a woman he was taking to bed, not even to
cover something up. Maybe I looked a little more closely at the
coffee shop girl and realized he would be appalled by her age,
closer to sixteen than I had thought. I don't remember the details
of how my mind first entangled, then disentangled him from
these nonexistent liaisons, but the point is that I was always on
alert.

When I was a teenager, long before any of this, my sisters and

I used to play a game, just between ourselves, that consisted solely of muttering under our breath, *there's a nice little friend for you,* whenever we saw a boy—or in my sister Jan's case a girl. Most of the time it was said sarcastically: *there's a nice little friend for you,* just as the most appalling skinhead cousin of the kid hosting the party walks in. Every once in a while, though, it was said appreciatively. *There's a nice little friend for you. No, seriously. By the door.* We were always on the lookout. All teenagers are, I suppose. We were human periscopes, scanning, scanning. And the fact that there were three of us, close in age, meant that there was never a time when at least one pair of eyes wasn't engaged.

The period between my affair and our move to the country was a bit like that. Is this her? Is this possible? *There's a nice little friend for you.* I hope he doesn't think so. I hope he doesn't see her. I hope he does. I hope he never tells me. I hope he does. It was never far from my mind.

We could move out to the country now, you know.

As we always told the story, the idea came upon us both at once, as though we had acted on it without either of us having to speak the words aloud. But in fact I was the one who said it, sitting in a diner, dawdling over late night pie and coffee, trying to comprehend the degree to which our circumstances had changed with our newly copious bank account.

"We could move out to the country now, you know."

This is Owen, on the day we moved in: He is pacing off the distance between the kitchen door of the house and the great doorway of the barn. Well over six feet tall, slender to the point of being skinny, as he places one heel to the front of the other foot's toes, and again, and again, he looks single-legged and as though he will blow over with just a mild gust of wind. It is autumn, mid-October, and the greens of our first encounter with this land have dressed up in fancy costume, orange, scarlet, yellow, to welcome us. It is almost too much to take in, all the beauty. And this is why Owen is doing what he is doing, measuring this line—which there is no reason to measure. Because this is what Owen does when he is overwhelmed.

Watching from what is to be my studio, I know he doesn't really need or even want to know how many lengths of his own feet it is from one building to the other. Except that it is a start. In this hurricane of incomprehensible loveliness, he begins with the ground, with his own feet on that ground. He begins with a count. And standing at the window, I remember how he first loved me, physically. What those earliest sexual moments were like when he counted the freckles on my belly, when he stretched his hand across my breasts, nipple to nipple, measuring my body with his own, so earnest, so strangely in his own head yet defined by the act of knowing me, all at once. It felt like a form of devotion I had never imagined, as he committed my body to his memory and so committed himself to me.

I could never match it, I was sure.

When he reaches the barn, his form relaxes. He turns and walks briskly, loosely, back to the house. He is still boyish at forty-eight. He is that boy with the just-too-long hair that falls into his face, wearing the sweater he must have borrowed from his dad. His limbs still seem as though he'll grow into them, with time. As he nears, I see the earnestness on his face. He has solved a problem. He'll move on now to the next one. Testing the depth of the pond. Or counting the steps to the basement. This, for him, is moving in, as for me painting walls and hanging pictures is. He is all about acquiring knowledge. I am all about recasting a place into what I want it to be.

These are the sorts of things you see when you step away. It doesn't mean you're right. It just means it's what you see.

2

The basil I picked that day ended up on our kitchen table in a mason jar where it looked more than a little sad, and I went back into my studio, back to work.

It is typical of productive artistic periods for me that they have their origins in something beyond my control. (That's true of the bad times too, of course, which is the hell of it—as Owen was daily experiencing.) My work that summer had started with a bathroom renovation we had finally gotten around to a few weeks before Alison's arrival. The second-floor hall bathroom was a wreck. It had never been used much, so we'd always ignored it, but that winter the tiles had started popping off the walls and somehow that made the sagging ceiling intolerable. In May, we took a few bids, all of which were low. Nobody had enough work, everyone was cutting their profits. We went with the man who seemed most amiable, and before a week passed he had a crew there doing demolition.

I spent an irritated morning listening to the bangs and shattering, to the too-loud, blaring radio, and then around noon went up to ask if they needed anything for their lunch. Something caught my eye. A pile of old newspapers, twisted and crumpled, in my hall.

"What are those?"

"From when the house was built," the contractor—Thad— told me. "People used those to insulate. Back in the day."

The first thing I did was iron them. (Owen laughed because in all the years we've been together neither of us had ever ironed anything. The iron had come with the house, as had any number of such odds and ends.) It took me a long time. It took me far longer than it had to because I got caught in watching the way the faces, the images, and the words came clear. The crumples themselves were like a blurred focus that I could manipulate. And there was also, inevitably, a sensation of moving backward in time. Not only because the papers were old, but because the act of crumpling a newspaper is a strictly forward-moving act. It isn't something one normally does, then undoes. The ironing process became all about restoration for me. Restoration, clarity. And then, also, loss. War. 1918. World War I. Crumpled newspapers with body counts. With surges of hope, documented. Defeats. Deaths and more deaths. Homecomings and more deaths.

I recrumpled some, to get the feel of doing that. Just the act of bringing the names of the slaughtered into focus and then obscuring them again; then back into focus. I began to jot notes about permanence and impermanence. I began to imagine the newspapers themselves in other forms. Things that could not be crumpled. Chiseled in stone. Etched into metal. I took one and burned it in a small copper bowl I had and saved the ashes. Why? I didn't know why. I'd stopped thinking sensibly—which is *not* how projects usually begin for me. But from the beginning, this was different. This was about ideas, about intuitions, something intriguing me that I didn't understand. And in the beginning, that felt right.

I took pictures of the bathroom still under construction, of the space between the walls where the papers had been entombed. I thought about the papers having been used for warmth and of the heat of the iron bringing them back. I tried to make something of that. I thought of the tiles popping off, of the pressures exerted not by the fluctuations of temperatures over years but by the words and images themselves.

There are moments in a creative life when you understand why you do it. Those moments might last a few seconds or maybe, for some people, years. But whatever the actual time that passes, they still feel like a single moment. Fragile in the way a moment is, liable to be shattered by a breath, set apart from all the other passing time, distinct.

But then it changes. And what seemed unimaginably exhilarating gets bogged down, even when a project is going well. It is a gradual, inevitable sobering during which your right to be passive diminishes. What the ether has given you, now in fact belongs to you. And then it is work. Then it is hard.

By the time Alison arrived, I had moved into that second stage. The one that requires not only that boundless sense of possibility, but practical decisions. What form was this project to take? All my life, even in childhood, I had drawn and painted views of one kind or another. Landscapes. Streetscapes. Buildings. Interiors. Whatever happened to be outside a window. Since we'd moved to the country, it had been mostly rural views, the occasional village street. To the modest circle of people who knew my work, my canvases were distinctive for their minute detail and precision. And I had always had a way with light, an essence that seemed to speak a language in which I was fluent, a vocabulary of projection and shadow. But I had never been much for portraiture. I could manage simple likenesses, as any decent art student might, but human forms, human faces, were not for me.

Yet it was these boys, caught in these obituary photographs, and the fact of their cannon-fodder deaths that drew me in. Not a vista, as usually inspired me; but something more like a story. Their deaths and then their utilitarian haunting of my home.

I didn't understand the project yet, nor what it would grow to mean to me over time, but I was already somewhat wary of my attraction to these stories of death, aware of my capacity to define myself by what I had lost when my young mother lost her life; aware that my sister Charlotte's death had echoed my mother's, compounding that capacity in me. Painting had always been a shelter from those wounds, my canvases both unpopulated and unapologetically beautiful, a salve for the uglier realities of human life. That those realities seemed now to be finding their way into my work unsettled me; but I could not ignore the pull.

These were the problems I was worrying about in the morning, just before I met Alison, problems on which it wasn't easy to concentrate after our encounter in the garden. *Halloooo . . .* The intrusion, as I thought of it, as if it were clearly a negative event, though underlying that peevish stance toward any interruption of our solitude lay a curiosity about her presence that bordered on excitement.

Unable to focus, I gave up and checked my email. And there, among the political petitions I might sign and the notices of gallery shows back in Philly I wouldn't attend, I found a note from Bill's daughter, Laine. Laine, who was the reason Bill and I had met. She'd been one of my private students, back when she was in high school. By the time of Alison's arrival, she'd just graduated NYU a few weeks before, staying on in New York, working at temp office jobs and taking a studio class. We exchanged emails regularly, every couple of months, a fact I kept hidden from Owen, though I didn't like to think of it that way. I had just never mentioned it, I preferred to tell myself. I was always happy to see her name there in my inbox, though always too, inevitably, her emails carried a wave of sadness back to me.

So, it's time for me to give you the summer report. Aren't you just dying to hear how my adventures in The Big City progress?

Our work together had started in the spring of 2005, soon after Charlotte's death. Just seventeen years old, Laine had been a handful then. It was her mother (Georgia, about whom I would later have emotions like battling weather systems) who'd made the first call, describing Laine as very sweet *underneath it all*. And artistic—they thought. They were looking for something for her to get into, something to keep her from becoming a completely disaffected, messed-up kid. She was about halfway there, halfway to fully checked out, her mother said; and I'd felt a lot of respect for Georgia's straightforward approach. Most of the kids I taught who were heading for trouble had parents with their hands over their ears, saying *la-la-la-la-la* dawn to dusk. I looked forward to meeting a mother who seemed ready to see her child for who she actually was.

But then it wasn't the mother who brought Laine that first Friday afternoon. It was the father. It was Bill.

It was always Bill.

Laine and I worked together for eighteen months, a time during which she grew from being a surly, hostile kid hell-bent on pissing off all adults, to being a hardworking young woman anxious to please; and a damn good painter too. And all that time, all those months, all those Friday afternoons and then later Fridays and Tuesdays both, Bill brought her and Bill picked her up—because Laine hadn't yet learned to drive and because this was their special time together; and because now and then the universe just insists on changing your life in ways you didn't ask it to.

This studio class I'm taking is totally worth it, even though approximately half the people in it are complete freaks—and not in a good way. But the teacher is really excellent though not as excellent as you, of course. . . .

Sometimes a teacher and student click, even though their work is very different, and that was our story. While I had never been drawn to figures, Laine saw herself, even then, as a portraitist of a kind. While I could find it oddly unsettling to stare at faces, Laine became increasingly aware that doing so both soothed and inspired her. And since the models most readily available were me, Bill, and also Laine herself, reflected in a mirror I had supplied, many of her paintings were of one or two or sometimes all three of us. She would also turn up occasionally with sketches of her mother, meaning Georgia watched over us all during some weeks. Once in a while, I would shift Laine's gaze out the window toward the skyline of Philadelphia, or take her into Fairmount Park and ask that she broaden her view, think more about the big picture, the interaction of light and something other than a face; but soon she would turn back to what she loved.

"It's the only thing that interests me," she would say. "People."

"Well, me too, I suppose. But there's more to people than the people themselves."

I just broke things off with Dean—whose real name wasn't even Dean, it turns out. Do you believe that? He had this James Dean fixation, so the name was some kind of homage and honestly if I had known that from the start I definitely would have spared myself three months of discovering what a pretentious wannabe hipster fool he is. But at least it was only three months. . . .

Over the time that she and I worked together and argued and grew—both of us—*something* developed between me and Bill though we never crossed any lines, never did any more than talk. And we never talked about anything even remotely inappropriate. I had blurted word of Charlotte's death early on, maybe using the fact to excuse some mistake in scheduling I'd made, my thoughts still scattered, my brain not quite functioning; and it turned out he too had lost a sibling—a brother, when they were small. A house fire, Bill in the home as well, but rescued in time. I remember how his telling me seemed to freeze the scene we were in, just for a moment, as if I needed a pause in reality to recast him, to reconfigure us all. I had been so quick to dismiss his suit, his briefcase, his clean-cut, lawyerly presence, and to mistake it for his real self. I had been so wrong. We didn't speak exclusively or even often about grief for all those months, not by any means, but we shared an intimacy with it that I did not with Owen. And we shared Laine increasingly too. His daughter, whom I was also rais-ing—in a way. Who needed me. Who had taken on some of my outlook, some of my being. I would never have said she belonged to us, together, but I felt it in my body, in my blood.

"Neither Georgia nor I has the least creative talent," he would say. And he would marvel at my work in a way I was unused to, traveling as I did in artistic circles where it was just assumed that everyone had talent of some kind. To Bill, the fact that I could fill a canvas with oily goo from tubes and have the result be both beautiful and—as he would say and say—emotionally compel-ling, was nothing short of a superpower. That I could help his daughter do the same he looked on as a miracle. There was an in-nocence to him, an innocence of my world, that ultimately at-tracted me enough to rob us both of any claim to innocence we might make.

Sometimes, when Laine used us for subjects, she would ask that we sit motionless while we spoke, and occasionally would insist that we stop moving even our lips—almost as though she sensed something might be happening that she should try to avert.

But nothing could avert what was to come.

Watching Laine over those months was like watching a slow-motion film of a driver who damn near swerves off the road, but then corrects course just in time. Watching me, I suppose, was like some kind of reversed reel. At the time, it felt like the rela-tionship that Bill and I developed was helping me heal—from Charlotte's death; from learning that with Owen I would never have the children I had decided I wanted after all. I felt not only grief-stricken then; I felt incapable. I had been unable to save a

sister. Unable to become a mother. What was I able to do? What
powers did I actually have? I was right up close in a staring con-
test with the undeniable fact that for all the little things over
which we have some control, for the most part we have none; and
I was at a loss to know how to respond.

It's a lesson I might have learned when I was two and my
mother died. It's a lesson that should perhaps have been etched
into me then, whatever my conscious memory of events, but it felt
newly true after Charlotte's death, after my own empty body remained unfilled.

*And to be honest, after faux Dean, I think I may be done with
relationships for a while. I mean, the whole "we're going out together" thing is kind of a joke. I know you've been with Owen your
entire adult life, but the truth is that basically no couples my age
make it past a year. So why even pretend it's some kind of lifelong
thing? I would much rather put that kind of commitment into my
work. . . .*

This is us on the afternoon of Laine's last lesson:

Bill and I are seated on wobbly old stools at the end of my studio, all rough-hewn factory space. And we are suddenly awkward
with one another. Because it has happened in a flash. A look has
passed between us, a sudden, irreparable change. And it has stifled
the flow of our speech. For weeks now, for months, we have been
engaged in excitement over Laine's next step. She got into the
school she wanted to attend. She put together a senior project of
paintings so eloquent they seemed eternal; they seemed like real
art. It is all so exciting. I am filled with pride, as though she were
my child. Maybe I exaggerate my own role—my push back to the
universe. *Look! Look, it does matter what we do. It does.*

But in all the excitement, in all of the pride, one fact has gone
unrecognized.

It shouldn't be hard to manage—not if we really are, as they say, just friends. It should be easy. *Well, we'll just have to meet for coffee from time to time.*

Except suddenly what should have been easy has become impossible. Everything has become impossible as we sit together, Laine painting her own portrait some thirty feet away. It is unacceptable to leave seeing each other to chance. But to make a date . . . there is no kidding ourselves. To make a date is to make a date.

And we do not make a date. But I know that we will make a date. Laine gives me a huge, heart-rearranging hug goodbye; and as I tidy up, forestalling going home; as I walk the six blocks, then add six more; as I eat dinner with Owen; moving through every activity of that evening, that night, the next two days, I am both agitated and disturbingly calm. Because I know what is going to happen. And it scares the hell out of me. But it also feels right. And good. And deserved.

> *. . . And my work is going well. At least I think it is. I hope yours is too and I hope the country life is still good. You have to tell me everything. It's been way too long. You owe me a full report.*
>
> *Love,*
> *Laine*

Deserved.

To what exactly had I felt entitled with Bill? There is an answer: Joy. Not happiness, which by that time seemed a fantasy one had to agree to give up in order to keep from going mad. By forty, is there anyone who hasn't had to recognize that happiness, as understood by youth, is illusory? That the best one can hope for is an absence of too many tragedies and that the road through the inevitable grief be, if not smooth, then steady? Daily life was a pale gray thing, it seemed, and to expect otherwise was to be a fool—at best.

But there could be moments of joy. And there had been something like joy in those afternoons with Bill and Laine. There had been hours for me so restorative, so critical to my vitality that the thought of *never again* felt like death. And it had been enough. As long as Laine was there and I could have her as my protégée, my girl, and her father for my partner, it was enough.

If only time had been forced to a stop.

We were a distortion of the married couple whose marriage collapses when their child leaves home—as Bill's to Georgia did not even two years later when their son went off to school. Our child left us and we fell in love.

By the day of Alison's arrival, I wasn't in love with Bill anymore, but I was tender still, tender the way a bruise is tender; and it wasn't a feeling I wanted that day, a day destined not for melancholy memories, but for the comic if also irritating potential of a new neighbor materialized across the hill. I typed a hasty response.

So good to hear from you, Laine. The class sounds good. The boy like a good one to dump. Much more soon, I promise. Lots of funny stuff going on here, along with some less funny stuff. I will have to catch you up. All love . . .

And then I stopped, just for a moment, before signing *Augie,* Laine's nickname for me, born of her refusal when we met to do anything asked of her. "Why call yourself by your second syllable? People should call you Augie. Has anyone ever called you Augie?" No. No one ever had. And no one ever did—except for Laine and Bill.

"*Augie,*" I wrote, and pushed send, then returned to my work.

As if to shock myself back into the project, I picked up an obituary from the pile of papers, John "Jackie" Mayhew, killed at seventeen, in action in France; and I began to sketch his face in charcoal. I got the shape, the wide forehead, balanced by a wide

jaw. And I could replicate his eyes, round and a little close together; the small lips, set for the photograph in that serious,
straight line. All correctly copied. All distances between the features accurate. But as I drew, I felt the familiar sag of mediocrity
travel down my arm, through my fingers, into the charcoal, onto
the paper, stiffening my lines, emptying him of life.

"Of course," I said out loud, as I viewed the result. "What did
I expect?"

The western wall of my studio faces the pond. The eastern faces
our front lawn. If you stand at the corner where east meets north,
you can see scraps and pieces of Alison's property about an acre
away through the trees; and as I drew I knew that she was there,
that I might see her carrying boxes and who knows what, if I
looked. I also knew that if I looked, I wouldn't stop looking. So,
instead of crumpling the sketch, my first impulse, I pushed forward, softening a line here and there with a finger, using my reliable companions, light and shadow, to create more interest in the
composition, if not in Jackie Mayhew's emptied face.

Owen spotted Alison's car as he walked back from the barn at
around five. I saw him coming, and I stepped away from the studio, through the living room, into the kitchen, to fill him in on
the news.

"What you don't know," I told him, "is that she's a painter who
came here in part because apparently we are one of the features of
the home. The artist couple next door."

"Oh great. That's just what I want to hear. Maybe we can
charge people admission to watch me stare hopelessly at the
walls." He turned on the tap. His afternoon drink of water. I was
never sure whether he knew that he filled the same glass each day
when he came back from the barn. I stayed silent while he downed
it, as though neither of us could speak with his mouth full.

At fifty-one, Owen had finally lost some of that boyishness.

His face, well defined by a long straight nose, a sharp, just barely cleft chin, was acquiring an unmistakable cragginess. The lines on either side of his mouth had deepened, and the light brown of his eyes shined now from below a lowered brow. Though still lean, he had become more substantial in the way some men do, almost as though their bones, not their flesh, have gained heft. His hair, which I had been cutting for years to a running stream of Samson and Delilah jokes, was graying gradually, all over. No creeping silver sideburns, just a lightening from year to year.

"It's hotter than hell out there," he said, as he put the glass down. "We could use a thunderstorm."

"We really could," I said.

By then it had been about ten months that Owen had been unable to write anything he thought worthwhile. Since his early thirties he'd authored five quirky little books, all published by small presses, all embraced by whatever critics took notice, and, for the most part, all eschewed by all but a couple of thousand readers. His was the sort of career that earns you descriptions like *underappreciated* and *a writer's writer,* serious, significant praise that presents itself tinged with an aura of befuddled disappointment. In the great race of professional life, he saw himself as the ultimate tortoise, waving on multiple hares while hoping for the eventual victory. His share of our income over the years had come from juggled adjunct and lecturer jobs, a bounty of which exist in the greater Philadelphia area—though the word *bounty* seems wrong to describe something with returns, of money, of prestige, that are so slight. But through it all, for years and years, he kept at it, the teaching, the writing, all with a calm and a confidence that made me feel like a broken barometer as I careened over highs and lows of hope and despair over my own extremely modest professional life.

But then, the fall before Alison's arrival, everything for Owen came to a screeching halt.

The only time I'd felt that sort of vise grip of creative empti-

ness was the year after I told him about my affair; and it had been
easy for me to connect the two occurrences. Over those months,
pain had blossomed in me at every waking, a physical sensation in
my gut, as though I had swallowed a malevolent flower, respon-
sive to the rise of the sun. Nearly all of my energy, creative and
otherwise, went into contending with that ache.

And my unspoken fear was that Owen's blockage, years later,
also related to that time.

When I'd told him about Bill, he was already embarked on
two simultaneous projects, books four and five, one a collection of
essays about his itinerant childhood as the only child of a pair of
married archaeologists, the other a novel that used related material, reimagining a particular summer afternoon of his mother's
life, early in her career, on a dig in Morocco. Both projects were
shelved for some months while we thrashed through whether to
stay together, but then, once the decision was made, though I
found myself creatively stilled, he went right back to work. Those
books kept him busy through our sudden affluence and our first
years in the country. When they came out they were praised to the
sky by critics in obscure literary journals, and barely sold—just
like all of his previous work. I never understood it. I loved it all.
The gentle, acute sensibility, the quiet passion for getting things
right; while at the same time, evidently, poignantly doubting that
such a task is possible. Whenever I read his work, I thought that
all his readers must fall in love, and maybe all of them did, but for
reasons that eluded me there never were very many in that group.

Then, soon after the double publication, it became clear that
he was struggling to come up with something new. It made sense
that there would be a transition lag, but from the start this felt
like more than just needing a break between projects. I saw panic
in his eyes when he came back in from the barn. Occasionally, it
would seem as though he was onto something, for a few days,
maybe even a couple of weeks, but then he'd walk into the house

with that unmistakable expression on his face. Another project revealed to be hollow. *I doubt I'll ever do anything worthwhile again.*

I was keenly aware that this was the first time he'd had to generate anything new since my telling him about Bill, and it was all too easy for me to believe that a piece of what I had shattered then was a necessary component of his creative being. The betrayer doesn't get much sympathy, not even from herself, but it is in fact a heavy weight to have hurt someone you love, and it can be difficult even years later, to detect any impermeable boundaries around the damage you may have done.

We didn't discuss writing or painting on that day of Alison's arrival—nor, of course, Laine's email to me—as together we made a meal of grilled lamb, salad, and rice. By then I knew better than to talk about work, his or mine. Earlier, in the spring, he'd told me it wasn't helping to have to *report in* to me every day—his term. So I'd stopped inquiring. And I forgave him the irritation in his voice, the nasty phrase, because I understood the terror that it's all just disappeared. I felt tempted at times to try and encourage him, to say things like *I've been there and I came back. You'll come back too.* But I knew it would only irritate him, as it would have me. And it was simply impossible to discuss my own projects, however well or poorly they were going, in the context of a prohibition on mentioning his.

"Did she say how long she's staying?" he asked, as we ate.

"That seems to be unclear," I said.

This taboo created a huge chasm in our days, a terrible change in our rhythm. So much of our shared life together, a life that began when I was only twenty-two, had involved processing our work, comparing sorts of creativity, commiserating through lousy days and celebrating triumphs. But that dialogue depended on our both wanting to have it, and he no longer did.

This wasn't my first experience living under a regime of unspeakable subjects. I was well practiced. After my mother died, my father mandated that she not be mentioned, so by the time my conscious memory of childhood kicks in, I was already trained to short-circuit the flow between my thoughts and my voice.

There were very few ways in which Owen reminded me of my father—at certain points just the idea of any similarity would have horrified me—but in fact both had played this censoring role in my life, rendering my speech a kind of topiary, trimmed and trained and shaped to please.

"I have a terrible headache," he said, as he put down his fork. "But I don't think we can blame the new neighbor for that."

"Why not?" I asked. "Why not blame her for everything from this point on?"

Why not, indeed. By then I was more than ready to cast someone else in the role of guilty party.

3

⁓

During the first week or so of Alison's tenancy, if we hadn't known she had moved in, we would barely have noticed she was there—except for the car in the drive. True to her word, she left us alone, and we didn't hear a sound. The only practical change I made to accommodate her presence was no longer traipsing around my own yard half undressed, and though I complained to Owen about that, it wasn't, in fact, a big deal.

But then, one day, she appeared at the kitchen door.

"Knock, knock," she called in. "Hallooo?"

She wore the same purple dress. She looked so exactly as she had, it was as though she hadn't actually existed during the intermittent days. An apparition. She apologized for intruding, and I shook the apology off, saying something about having meant to check in on her, but . . . I gestured at the air as if it were crowded with unfinished tasks and obligations. "I'm afraid we haven't been very welcoming. It's been an oddly busy time for us."

"Actually," she said, "I've come by to ask if you and your husband might come over for drinks one night. Even tonight. Or any night. But please don't hesitate to say you're busy. I realize . . . I know what it's like to want quiet and solitude. I just thought . . . Well, I thought I would ask . . ."

"And so it begins," Owen said at dusk, as together we crossed the hill between our homes.

And so it began.

Two women and one man, middle-aged, reclining on gaudy, sunflower-patterned vinyl-covered chaise lounges. The porch supporting them is redwood, and has been smacked, ugly, against this dainty old farmhouse. The day is thinning into darkness, the light evaporating, so the fat, green midsummer trees not fifty feet away seem to be receding, excusing themselves from the scene. Only two patches of brightness remain. The spill from the lighted kitchen, some two dozen feet down the porch, and the fluid, silver hair of one woman, oddly immune to the dropping sun, glistening, glowing, like a fallen, restless moon.

On a table nearby are bottles, alcohol, enough for a party of fifty, as though the other guests have all left. Or as though they have never arrived.

"I wasn't sure what you drink, so I just set everything out on the porch."

The three people speak quietly, earnestly. They occasionally laugh—but not too heartily. They laugh knowingly. As though they have stumbled over a clue or a bit of evidence or a coincidence. *Oh, yes!* A laugh of recognition. *That is so true.*

Their reclining bodies add an air of intimacy to the scene as the conversation murmurs on.

"I was twenty-eight when I had Nora. I thought I was very grown-up, which of course I wasn't at all."

"We did a lot of work on the house. We are still doing work on the house. We will always be doing work on the house."

"Before my marriage, I planned to be a doctor, but then life had other plans. For better and worse so to speak."

"Owen uses the barn. I have a studio inside."

Soon, they begin to slap at their skin. Bare ankles. Necks. Occasionally the man claps the air. One of the women makes a quick fist, opens her hand and examines it. The rhythm of this becomes more frequent, until the clapping and slapping, the odd skirmishes with the invisible, are drowning out the conversation. But still no one rises. Not for some time, as the sun drops more decisively and the last traces of color fade.

"I suppose we could go inside," the silver-haired woman says. The others look at one another, a question passing between them. "Or you two probably need to get home," she says. "I don't want to keep you."

"We really don't need to leave," the other woman says. "But we don't want to impose . . ."

"Oh no. I would love it if you could stay."

They begin to rise, each taking a few bottles from the table, a couple of glasses. They go inside, their arms filled.

Sometimes, when you do something for the first time, you're aware it will be the first of many. When I first slept with Owen, I knew. I thought to myself: this will always have been the first time, even when we have had sex a thousand times, a million times, this touch will always have been the first. And this. And this. (With Bill, two decades later, I never had that thought. Every time was to be the last—especially the first time, when I was still comparatively innocent. *Just this once. This was a mistake. Never again.*)

"We'll just go this once," I had said to Owen, when conveying Alison's invitation. "Just to get it over with."

But I had been talking about a reality that evaporated right away.

Her kitchen floor had the same terra-cotta tiles as ours, but cracked and broken along the edges. And her appliances looked very much like the ones we had replaced. Too old to be in good working order, too new to be vintage. We'd dumped the electric stove in favor of propane, but she still had those awful black coils. Yet there were some nice things about the room, things more intrinsic than old appliances or shoddy tiles. The windows were much larger than ours, and I spotted a massive walk-in pantry that I immediately coveted.

"How much of the furniture is yours?" I asked as Owen and I sat at the oak drop-leaf table.

"Almost none," she said. "Nothing in here. It's an odd array too. Some very nice pieces and then some absolute bombs."

"This kitchen is lovely though," I said. "Great bones."

She made us spaghetti as we sat bemoaning the bug bites we now had, all of us saying what a lovely evening it had been, meaning the beauty of the fading light and the mild air, meaning that the beauty had seduced us from worries about being eaten by mosquitoes; meaning too, how surprising, how fun.

We all offered more scraps of information about ourselves. A quilting circle of sorts, putting it together. We knew by then that Alison had been divorced for two years—and that there was something ugly there, though she didn't go into detail. We knew that she had lived in Boston for the past nineteen years, but was originally from London, and had spent some of her twenties in DC. "I hear this is a big country, but I only managed to get from one end of the Northeast Amtrak corridor to the other in nearly thirty years."

We learned that she worked as a high school science teacher at a private school, initially for the tuition break for her daughter, just graduated from Tufts—Laine's age, I realized.

"I always assumed I'd stop teaching when she was finished with high school, but then my marriage ended. Empty nest, empty marriage. So I needed a way to support myself." She stirred the sauce she had concocted of tomatoes, basil, garlic, as she told us she was on sabbatical from her job. It was the kind of school with a fund for its teachers to take sabbaticals, a wealthy school, for wealthy children. "The timing was perfect. Ran away to the woods to be an artist. For a time, anyway." Her former husband was a philosophy professor. "But not what you're picturing," she said. "Not the tweedy, muddling sort. Not at all." Her daughter—Nora—was traveling in Europe for the summer, and would be visiting for a few days at the end of August or maybe over Labor Day. "She's hoping, well, she was a creative writing major in school, and I suppose she's hoping to follow through with that. But for now she's got to be looking for work," she said. "Some sort of nonprofit, I suspect. She's a bit of a do-gooder type."

"Nothing wrong with that," Owen said. "Or with creative writing, of course. Unless of course you plan on being happy."

"No . . . Though . . ." She looked over at us from the stove. Her face was damp and flushed, some combination of the boiling water's steam and the several drinks we'd each had by then. "I should ask. I don't know if either of you is religious?"

We assured her we were not. "Heathens, through and through," Owen said.

"Well, that's a bit of a relief. So I can be frank . . ."

The daughter, it turned out, had become a churchgoing Christian. There had been a boyfriend, sophomore year. "I never liked him, but I had no vote." The relationship had ended, but the influence remained. "It's terrible to complain because your child believes in God, because she goes to church. People deal with so much worse than that. And it hasn't changed her politics. I mean, she hasn't become some, well . . . I should probably ask about your politics too."

"We're exactly what you would guess," I said. "Look at us."

"Right. Well, I was going to say she hasn't become a right-wing maniac. She just believes in, from my perspective, in a fairy tale.

And it's the first thing that's ever come along that makes me feel we're really different. But there are reasons, she's had a lot to deal with . . . it makes a certain kind of . . ."

She let the sentence fade into the pantry as she withdrew a box of spaghetti. Owen and I exchanged a glance. Stitched together another fact; took note of another unknown.

And what did she learn about us that first night? Truly, a marriage is a paltry, skeletal thing when both members are present, talking to someone whom neither knows well. Whatever little leaks and blurts one might make if alone, are censored out. How many years had we been married? *We've been together a quarter century.* Any children? *No.* Where were you before the move out to the country? *We were in Philadelphia. (We were in limbo. We were in hell.)*

"We'd been teaching a lot," Owen said. "Especially Gus, who was always in more demand for individual work, which can actually pay more than the adjunct stuff. And she's a better teacher than I'll ever be. But we were just making ends meet. Not quite living in a garret, but not far off. Then my aunt died and we had a little money and suddenly this opportunity came up."

We didn't talk much about art that night. In Owen's presence Alison seemed embarrassed to have described herself as a painter. "I was just trying it out, saying it like that. Being brave. Really I'm a biology teacher who likes to paint." And Owen and I observed our well-honed practice of silence on the subject of our work, of course, so beyond the brief mention of the daughter's writing aspirations, the whole subject of creativity was set aside.

We did talk about the land around us. Alison had been for walks in the woods along both properties. She'd also walked the nearly two miles into town. We told her which stores we preferred—not that there was much choice.

"We don't know how the pharmacy on the corner survives," I said. "Patterson's. I've actually done a painting of it, of that whole block. Last summer, I set up across the street for nearly two weeks, and I don't think I saw ten customers go in. No one under eighty.

I'm certain they still grind their own pills in the back. It's the drugstore that time forgot."

"Yes, and that the Rite-Aid over in Lowry replaced," Owen said. "Just nobody informed the Pattersons."

Nothing of much importance was said, but that seemed unrelated to what took place.

When I first began gardening, uninformed, I was shocked by the impact water could have on a thirsty plant. Of course I knew that plants needed water, but I didn't know the miraculous impact a good soaking could have. I would notice a perennial, often sage—we grew a lot of sage, for its color and its hardiness—practically shriveled from thirst and heat, and I would get out the hose and then half an hour later would see it revived, its leaves unfurled, its very being seeming healed.

Owen and I had sex when we got home.

We got into bed at the same time, unusual for that summer. Most nights, I would head up with a book, often about World War I, and he would wander out to the barn to bang his head on work for a while more. Or I would wake in the wee hours and find him sitting downstairs, a drink in hand. But that night we climbed the stairs together, leaving the darkened house below.

At what moment had we each begun to feel the erotic charge? Walking home over the hill, a little drunk, we'd been laughing together. I had bumped against him with my hip, flirting, teasing, like a teen. Once in the house, switching off the downstairs lights, checking the leaky kitchen faucet, I felt a charge in the air. Unmistakable.

Nothing coy, nothing subtle, no nuzzling against one another in the bed, finding the comfort of familiar sex that's half about pleasure, half about the start of falling asleep. I sat on the edge of our bed, still in my jeans, and spread my legs, unzipped the zipper, lay back, waited to feel his hands on my hips tugging the denim down, waited to feel his mouth on me. Didn't wait long.

Sex. We had always had so many different kinds. Like different sorts of music. Sometimes sweet. Sometimes just edging on violent. No whips and chains, but teeth a little too sharp, the occasional slap. Rough play. Sometimes in public, half hoping to get caught. Owen would get me off under restaurant tables, in backs of taxis. Before we lived such secluded lives.

And then there was the other sex, the sex that's like the decent enough music you listen to because the drive is so long and it's the only radio station you can pick up.

There are points in every marriage, maybe in every long relationship, at which you have sex with your partner not because you are so drawn to that person, so turned on that you want to have sex, but because you want to have sex and that's who you can have it with.

By the time we met Alison, we weren't having sex frequently at all—not by our old standards. And what sex we had was mostly of the radio station, long-drive sort. One or the other of us would feel the need. The other would oblige. We could go weeks without.

But then that night, after our dinner with her, we tore the bed apart. Hungry. A little tough, a little rough. The sort of sex where you feel both slavish and mean, tuned in to the tension of desire, the gratitude for the moment, the anger at the power those moments hold. Hands, mouths everywhere. Skin tingling. Unbearable.

"God, I needed that," Owen said, afterward.

"Me too," I said. "God, I needed that."

There are often two conversations going on in a marriage. The one that you're having and the one you're not. Sometimes you don't even know when that second, silent one has begun.

4

One of the unanticipated impacts of our life in the country was that time had taken on a different feel. As Philadelphians, we had been teachers, shoppers, socializers, therapy attenders, bus catchers. And all of these things require an awareness of the clock and of the calendar. You have to know it's Monday, and you have to know it's noon, if you are going to get to your Monday 1 p.m. appointment. But even after only a month or two in the farmhouse, we started shedding that awareness. It was so rare for it to matter much whether it was Tuesday or Sunday. We stopped our Wednesday night candle lightings. The rhythm was wrong. We weren't living in seven-day cycles anymore. Not in cycles at all. Even my body gave up its cycles, my reproductive potential stuttering to an early stop as if in acquiescence to its pointlessness. I still kept track of daylight, of course, noticing, as painters must, when each day dimmed, but that is a gradual, unpunctuated sort of way to measure time.

Occasionally, though, there was a reason to keep track. The morning after we had dinner with Alison, I realized it had been two weeks since I'd visited my father—though it was a funny thing to measure. He was far enough down the road into his own private reality that time had taken on yet another quality for him.

When I appeared, if he knew who I was, he might think I had been there the day before. Or not for a decade. On the previous visit, he'd greeted me with the news that I had just missed my sister Charlotte, dead for six years. It was a shame, he said, as she'd brought cookies with her and I could have had some.

There were many ways in which I loved my father more in his demented state. We'd sat there, on that earlier day, and talked a long while about Charlotte's visit. It had been strange and lovely to think she had just left the room a few minutes earlier. That her not being there with me was a matter of a missed connection, a failure to coordinate our plans better. In the moment, it had soothed me. My father had soothed me, as he rarely had when he was still my real dad, tight-lipped and stoic, and not this otherworldly mystic receiving social calls and cookies from our dead.

Owen offered to go with me but I knew he wanted to be home and I didn't want to be the cause of his missing a chance for the breakthrough that was bound eventually to appear, so I set off on my own.

It was my other sister, my younger sister, Jan, a doctor, the practical one, who had found the place where my father was to dwindle, then disappear. (I sometimes pictured a star doing the same thing over millions of years, slowly, slowly losing its bearings in the universe, finally flickering out.) The home is just west of Philadelphia, not far from where we grew up, about an hour from me, a little closer to where Jan and her partner Letty live. And it was an awful place but also as good as such a place can be. Jan and Letty are generous people. It hadn't always seemed that way, because Jan has a certain harshness to her, or anyway she does with me; but they were certainly generous financially when it came to this. Jan chose the place knowing that our father's schoolteacher pension would never be enough to cover it and that my sporadic teaching income wasn't worth thinking about, but that they, a doctor and an investment banker, wouldn't even notice that the money was gone. When Owen and I suddenly became flush, I offered to chip in more, but flush to us was still marginal to them and they were quick to say no.

The drive there always made me feel grateful for where we lived, but also primed me for all the sadness to come. I passed seven strip malls—a number I knew because Owen had counted them. There wasn't a single one that didn't have at least one store that was also in another, and a couple of them, the closest to us and the closest to my father, were pretty much identical. This unmistakable decline into homogeneity invariably depressed me. At some point in every drive to my father, I would catch myself thinking: *what exactly is the fucking point?* And maybe I didn't really plummet because by then I had passed two Bed, Bath & Beyonds, two Lowe's, two Home Depots, two Michael's, and three Taco Bells. I know there was more to my despair than that. But I always told myself that the dismal scenery was the cause—every time.

My father was in what Owen called his *high-quality science fiction mode* that day, meaning that nothing he said had any bearing on reality but it all made a certain sense. Whatever universe he was in had solid, logical underpinnings. He had been on a sailboat and was angry because the man in charge—"The captain?" I asked as if clarity on this one point might be meaningful—had told him he could drink the ocean water, but it wasn't true. The man hadn't been lying, but he was wrong. He was mistaken.

Every once in a while, the schoolteacher in my father would come shining through. Like when he used the word *mistaken*. As in: *I'm afraid you're mistaken, young man. The American Civil War was not started by Napoleon.* The schoolteacher, and the father too. As in: *You may think I am going to support you, Augusta, if you leave college to draw pictures all day, but you are sadly mistaken.*

I wasn't paying the sort of attention I'd paid on the visit before when he'd told me about my long-gone sister's baked goods. Mostly, as I sat in the small chair across from an identical chair that he barely filled with his dwindling, flickering starlight self, I watched his facial expressions, trying to translate them into something having to do with him. When he got stern like that, was he, somewhere in the folds of his consciousness, actually back in front of a class, giving in to the temptation to make a stupid child look even stupider? Or was he, as his better self, giving holy hell to the bully picking on the skinny kid who at thirteen still had trouble tying his shoes? Could there be this other narrative, the one he'd actually lived, playing out in the core of him? Could the smile he suddenly flashed have sprung from the Father's Day when all of us, Charlotte, and Jan and I—under Charlotte's direction, of course, she being the ringleader of all such activities—put on a little sketch, about who knows what? I couldn't remember. But maybe he could. Somewhere.

"A man in charge of a boat," he said, "should know about water."

An old painting of mine hung behind him and I glanced at it while he spoke. A streetscape I'd done in New York, when I was twenty years old. Fourteenth Street. About six months before this visit, I'd found it stuck behind his bed. One of his nurses, not knowing it was mine, told me he'd said it was boring. "Of all things," she said. "Boring!" But he hadn't been wrong. It dated from before I had learned to use my natural precision to my advantage and it had that kind of technical strain for correctness that makes just about everything dull. I had been going to take it from behind the bed, bring it home, throw it out, hide it away, but Owen said I shouldn't. Because what if my father ever wanted it back? What if he woke up one day and said, *Where's that old painting of mine? The one my daughter Augusta did?* Which he may well have done, because during the spring the painting reappeared. Though it was also entirely possible that a different nurse had just found it and thought it belonged on the wall.

I stayed about two hours. I didn't kiss him goodbye, as I hadn't kissed him hello. We weren't a kissing family. Not the three thorny ones of us who were still alive, anyway. My sister Charlotte had spilled over with affection, and I always imagined my mother being the same, but not me and not Jan and surely not our father.

The sun was low as I pulled into our drive. There's a line of tall spruce on the western edge of our front lawn. They mark the place Owen stops mowing, leaving all meadow beyond. When the sun is at a certain point in the sky, summer afternoons, the shadows from those trees lie across the grass like felled giants. "Why not just sleeping?" Owen asked me, when I told him that.

"Because they're too still for sleep," I said. "They're too untroubled."

All the drive home I had felt age settle over me. No more the daughter. Not even the forty-seven-year-old woman. Certainly not the seductress tossing the bedcovers into chaos with her lover the night before. But an old, tired soul. Aching from the heart outward. I sat in our drive for a few moments after turning off the car. I sighed as I looked at those heavy shadows on our lawn. When I opened the door, creaking my newly ancient body into the day, I found Alison standing in the drive. Her face took in my condition even before we could say hello.

"I've been visiting my father," I said. "I think I told you? He's in a home. He has Alzheimer's. It's been a long day."

"How terrible. I imagine it has been." And then, "You look like you could use a drink. Maybe even two."

I smiled—barely. "I can see you're going to be a bad influence," I said. "But I think you're right." I looked over to the barn. "Why don't you come over this time, though. We have a good bottle of red . . . Let me just tell Owen I'm home, then we'll go inside."

She said she would be over in half an hour. She reached over and gave my hand a squeeze before turning away.

When Owen's work was going well, I would never knock. I'd just barge in. Even when the doors were closed. I knew he wouldn't hear a knock if he was really absorbed. He would be far, far away, in another place and time.

But I had learned during those months of his frustration to pause at the door and at least give him a warning shout. Not because there was anything happening that I might derail with an interruption, but because he felt ashamed. He needed a moment to arrange his expression or maybe to set himself up at the computer as though he were engaged. We'd never had that conversation, he'd never asked that explicitly of me. But I had learned. And so, that day, at the top of the great wide ramp to the open barn doors, I knocked and I called, "I'm back."

"Oh, good. Come on in."

Without question, the barn is the most spectacular space on the property. Cleaned of all trace of the livestock it once housed, all that remained was the shell. Pennsylvania bluestone floors. Wood walls of horizontal planks, heavy beams, a vaulting ceiling into which we had cut four skylights that we'd framed in old weathered barn wood. It had the cool hush of a church.

"How was it?" he asked.

"It was the same. It was sad. I'm tired." I walked over and touched his shoulder, gave it a quick kneading. I didn't ask him how his morning had gone. "Alison stopped by," I said, stepping away. "We're going to have a glass of wine. Or something. Two glasses of wine. She rightly diagnosed my need."

He looked at me, a smile hovering there. "Tell her I said to get you good and drunk. I wouldn't mind an afternoon like last night."

"You and me both," I said. "Feel free to join us. For drinks that is."

"Very funny. But I think I'll keep at this a while more."

"Sounds like a plan," I said, never quite sure how to respond when I sensed Owen digging himself deeper into his seemingly endless futile pursuit. And then, "See you in a bit."

We sat in the living room, Alison on the pale, slipcovered love-seat that had come with the house and I on the pumpkin-colored wingback chair we'd chosen from the relics in Owen's aunt's home. I poured us each a large glass of wine. Very large.

Alison commented on the beauty of the house, the old random-width floors, the stone hearth, and I thanked her. She asked if the room beyond the French doors flanking the fireplace was my studio, and I said it was.

"I'm sorry if I seem a bit out of it," I said. "The visits to my father . . . they never fail to upset me."

"No, I'm so sorry," Alison said. "It does seem like a terrible . . . passage. A terrible way to travel through the final years."

"Yes. Yes, it is."

I asked her how her morning had been; but then, as she answered, I felt her words floating all around, not quite finding their way into my consciousness, my attention riveted elsewhere, a million miles away, back to my father, back to my childhood—and then finally fixed on a painting of mine above our mantelpiece, an oil of an old milliner shop in South Philly, facing out from inside, looking through the window filled with finished hats on mannequin heads. The first painting I did after Bill. The painting that marked the true start of my recovery from all that heartache. I stared at it as if it might steady me, like a spinning dancer finding a single focal point.

"Is that one of yours?" Alison had followed my gaze.

"Yes. I'm sorry. Yes. From a few years ago. But I don't mean to zone out . . . I'm afraid I really am tired."

"I like it very much. And you should just relax. Don't mind me. Unless you'd like me to go . . ."

"No, no, not at all. I'm just sorry to be a bit out of it. But very glad for the company."

"I love the hats," she said. "Every detail is so . . . so vivid. Even the netting. You must use a single-haired brush."

I laughed. "Not quite, but close. I thought I might paint just the window, from the outside, I mean. It was so . . . so beautiful and I've always been drawn to exteriors. But then . . . then I ended up not finding the hats as interesting as the scene behind them. Also, it was very cold outside."

Cold outside. And cold inside of me. A full year after Bill. Eleven months after my confession to Owen. My heart like a single tooth, sharp and useless; my ability to paint, frozen, perhaps forever stilled. I'd found Steinman's one afternoon on a directionless, miserable walk that had promised nothing beyond freedom from the frustrations of my studio. I had stumbled across this tiny store, a bright red door, gold lettering, the elaborate hats, beautiful, fantastical against the dingy gray of Fourth Street.

"It seems like a long time ago." That wasn't entirely true. At moments, it seemed like I could stand up, turn around, and walk right back into that time. "I loved it there," I said.

That part was true. The place had been run by an older pair, a brother and sister, Len and Ida Steinman, both in their early seventies. Neither had ever wed and they had an intimacy like that of a couple, so at first I had thought them married. He was tall, taller than Owen—which, coming from my family of short Jewish men, surprised me. She was tiny though. Birdlike. And beautiful. She had such an elegance to her. The shop itself was a mess, the sort of chaos only the owners of such a workshop could navigate; but she was anything but. A polished gem among the filmy fabrics and odd forms on which the hats were built, she was breathtakingly complete in a sea of aspiration.

"The light is incredible," Alison said. "Why am I sure it was winter?"

"It was. Winter light. It's got a certain clarity. Also, through the window, see? That tiny tree way down the street is bare. It doesn't jump out, but it registers, I think."

I'd sat in that store for weeks, doing sketches, then setting up an easel, bringing in paints, hoping no one would complain as the air took on the new smells. Neither Len nor Ida appeared in the painting—except for one of Ida's arms. I'd wanted to paint all of her, a rare impulse for me. But I had felt too daunted to try. Even apart from my poor portrait skills, I was sure that her essence contained an element of perfection I had no right to try and channel. Me, in my fallen, repentant state. So I spent all those weeks with my eyes on the rolls of tulle and the fabric flowers, the light slipping around the gold lettering in the window; and I stole long, inexplicably hungry looks at Ida Steinman. I could detect it in the painting still, the way that she was neither in nor out, that navy serge jacket sleeve, child-sized, hovering at the edge of the canvas, at the edge of my consciousness.

"It isn't one of my favorites," I said. "Owen loves it though. He more or less insisted we hang it there."

But I didn't want to discuss the painting anymore. It was like hearing the ocean, waves crashing, the memories beginning to pound against my thoughts as we spoke. How often had I sat with Owen just like this, in the aftermath of my time with Bill, my heart breaking, my energy all directed toward hiding that fact? I had been well practiced then at secret oceans, secret waves, adept at splitting myself in two. Now I just wanted to move off that subject, that time.

"Are you painting yet?" I asked. "Are things set up?"

She told me she'd been shifting things around, still trying to work out which spaces were for what. "But I think I know which room will be the studio. And I heard from Nora today," she said, her voice brightening. "Just a note, but that was nice. She's zeroing in on when she'll be here. Probably early September. She's in Florence now, and I have a hunch that there may be a boy, though she didn't say so outright. I am reading between the pixels—or whatever they are."

"You must be very close. If you can read what she isn't saying." I wondered if I could do that with Laine, though it was hard to imagine Laine leaving much unsaid—a thought that made me smile.

"Oh, we are close. We truly are, which is such a gift, I know. Not to say we don't have our moments, but isn't that the case with all mothers and daughters?"

"I suppose."

"It's hard for me to believe she's so grown now. Gallivanting over Europe. It's a cliché but I think she'll always be a child to me. In my mind, she froze somewhere around five."

"I imagine it's hard to keep up."

"It is. You just blink and they're adults." She took a long sip of wine.

"We wanted to have children," I said—something I hadn't said out loud in years, a sentence gathering dust among all the other unspeakable ones. I could barely believe the words had slipped out, escaped while I had been busily pushing other subjects out of mind. "But it would have meant all kinds of interventions. And complicated decisions and then there was the thought of adopting, but . . ."

But Charlotte had been so ill then. Charlotte, who had never married and had only her sisters to see her through. The two crises had somehow collided, competed for space. Dying had won. "We didn't do it. Obviously."

"I'm so sorry." Alison kicked her sandals off, tucked her feet up under herself. "Do you still talk about it?" she asked.

"Not really." I hoped she wouldn't ask for more details. Owen would have been horrified at my chatting to the new neighbor about his negligible sperm count, and I didn't have the imaginative energy just then to make something up. "Owen . . . well, Owen is very much one for just moving forward. He doesn't really do regret."

"Perhaps I'm a bit that way too," Alison said. "Not doing regret—which is good. Because I could easily waste decades if I did."

It had been so long since I'd had this sort of talk with another woman. I had forgotten how smooth the glide into intimate subjects could be. "Do you mean your marriage?" I asked. "You said that was difficult."

"That. Yes. My husband, Paul, well, it was all very turbulent. Awful, actually. I suppose the phrase is 'anger management issues.' He has anger management issues. So it was very hard at times. To put it mildly. Though without the marriage there's no Nora. So nothing's simple, is it? Least of all regret."

"I'm so sorry. That sounds terrible. You stuck it out a long time."

"Just about twenty years." She took a sip of wine, the last in her glass. I pointed to the bottle, and she nodded. "Yes, thanks. Some of it was just Nora, I suppose. Not wanting to put her through the whole broken-home thing. And also . . ." She hesitated. "Also, I didn't want Nora alone with him when she was young." She shook her head. "That came out wrong. I don't mean anything lurid. Paul's not that sort at all. I just knew from years of experience that if I was there, his anger got directed to me. And if she started spending lots of time with him, alone . . . I worried. Maybe without reason, but I felt better having her under my roof. Even if it meant having him there too. But then once she went off to school, it was just . . . just untenable." She closed her eyes briefly, shook her head. "Awful," she said. "I'd thought I was the witness holding the worst of him back, but then it turned out that Nora had been."

"How horrible," I said. "I can barely imagine."

"Yes, it is. It was," she said. "Which is why I don't look back too much."

"Owen and I don't really dwell on the past, either. Maybe because we're so alone here. There's no one to talk to who didn't live through all the events." But I knew it wasn't our solitude that had shut down so much of our history. It was our history that had produced our solitude. "We . . . we talk our way through the facts of each day. It's raining. The garden needs weeding. Look what's in the paper. We rarely get into the past. Though I think that's more Owen than me."

I was making a choice. I could feel it. Maybe the wine was fueling that choice, but I would confide in Alison about Owen. I wouldn't divulge our real secrets, but I would say things to her that I wouldn't say in front of him. About him. About us.

"No marriage is entirely easy," I said. "Even the ones that last."

"Well, I wouldn't know about the ones that last." Alison laughed a little. "I might have settled for one that was only difficult."

I asked her if she was still in touch with the ex.

"Not at all," she said. "Nora sees him. I do not. Emphatically. Do not."

"It must be strange," I said. "Being that intimate with someone for so long and then . . . Nothing." Bill entered my thoughts, again. We had been so intimate. And then nothing. I took another sip of wine.

"Oh, I am big on fresh starts. Second chances. Third, if necessary." Alison looked at her glass, empty again in her hand. She put it down and stood. "I'm now going to wobble my way home and probably pass out. And after that, I need to get back to setting things up."

At the kitchen door, I thanked her. "It was a tough day," I said. "This made it a much better one."

She smiled. She said, "For me as well."

When she'd gone, I returned once again to the painting over the fireplace—as if it and I had unfinished business, as perhaps we did. I stared at Ida's arm. Navy blue serge. Two brass buttons at the cuff. Her hand obscured by a cascade of lilac taffeta. Her elbow, just beyond the painting's edge.

How often had I wished I could pull on that sleeve? How many times had I ached to tug at the cloth, as if to get her attention; and guide the woman herself to the center of the scene.

A painter looks. That's what she does.

But she doesn't always look in the right direction.

5

Within a matter of days, having Alison next door felt close to normal—except to the extent that the novelty of her presence was itself a positive. Any early irritation at being intruded on had dissolved. And though she and I didn't immediately form a habit of lengthy visits back and forth, or take the walks that would later become regular in our days, we chatted in the yard a bit now and then and waved from one porch to another. When she picked up her mail, she left ours on our step; and when I got there first, I did the same for her. And during that time, I felt the strangely unfamiliar pleasure of making a friend. How long had it been since I had last done that? It had been years. Maybe it had been my entire life—in a way. Charlotte had always been my closest friend, the girl and then the woman in whom I could confide anything. But there was a difference here, because in part that had been because Charlotte knew me so well. And with Alison, some aspect of the pleasure was that she didn't know me at all. The air around us was clear, unfilled with history. I had a chance to recast myself afresh. Or anyway I believed that I did, and weary of my own prior mistakes and missteps, I reveled in that.

Over those same days, I continued to push myself to understand what I wanted from the newspaper soldiers—or what I wanted to give to them. It didn't matter how inherently interesting they were, or how their entombment in my walls resonated with my own obsessions; if I couldn't find my way into the project, it was about nothing more than a curiosity found during a bathroom renovation.

But then, one morning I woke up with an idea. Like spontaneous generation, this sudden certainty about what to do.

The first canvas I envisioned was of two soldiers, WWI soldiers, in my living room, on my furniture, playing chess. The pale brocade couch, the old orange armchair, all of it ours. The trees through the window, our trees. Our house. And them. These too-long-dead boys released from my walls, set back into motion. I imagined one leaning forward, intent on his next move. Jackie Mayhew, learning how to play chess. The other boy grinning from ear to ear.

I rose and went downstairs, leaving Owen still asleep. As the coffee brewed I grabbed a sketchbook, a few pieces of charcoal from my studio. By the time Owen shambled down, an hour or so later, I was lost, a half-empty, cold cup of coffee by my side. He didn't say anything to me and I didn't expect him to. I was working. Somewhere in my consciousness it registered that he went back upstairs; and then that he came back down. I may have smelled hints of his shower, soap, shampoo. I heard the kitchen screen door, the wooden clatter as it closed. I knew without knowing that he had gone to the barn.

I wandered the house like a restless ghost myself that first day— a ghost with a sketchpad and charcoal. In each room I let myself imagine what these boys, these young men, might be doing. I didn't have a particular idea in mind, not any one kind of activity. I didn't think: *It needs to be ordinary.* Or: *It needs to be childlike.* In the guest bedroom, I sketched a boy opening the window. Just a very rough sketch. In the kitchen, I put one at the refrigerator, one at the stove, frying eggs. Another, sitting, his boot-heavy feet up on the table. I didn't begin to think then about the level of logic involved in these works. Was I trying to depict an actual household? A strange barracks of a kind? Were these things all going on at once? At the same time of day? Would a single face appear in more than one room? Those were all questions I would ask in the weeks that followed, but then I just drifted from one space to the next.

I pushed aside another question too: how I was going to do paintings in which human figures played so prominent a role? I never had. But I would manage somehow, I told myself. My instincts couldn't be this strong and also be wrong, I told myself— as if I had never made a passionate mistake in my life.

By dinner, I was bursting, but the sight of Owen's somehow sunken face silenced the excitement I wanted to share. I have always been an artist who talks through her projects. I like having conversations with people about what I'm doing. It helps me think. But with Owen in the state he was in, I knew it was wrong to crow about my breakthrough and my sudden conviction— necessary at the start of every project—that I was about to do the best work of my life. When he finally got around to asking me how my day had gone, I just said, "I think it's moving forward." And when he let the subject go at that, I tried hard not to resent his failure to detect the insincerity underlying my casual tone. A rich man has no business expecting a starving man to ask him how his four-star dinner was that night.

"I think I'll do some shopping tomorrow," he said, as we ate. "We're out of stuff and I could use a change of scene."

I heard the invitation, but giving up the next day's work was unthinkable. I said nothing and after a bit he said, "So make me a list if there's anything you want."

"I will," I said. "Thanks." And then, "Shampoo, I think. And toilet paper too. Definitely toilet paper."

"Just make a list," he said.

I don't know at what precise moment it occurred to me that maybe I could talk to Alison about work—mine *and* hers—but the next day, while Owen was on his shopping trip, I walked over the hill and knocked on her door with that in mind.

"Hold on . . . ," I heard.

"It's Gus," I called through the glass panes, watching her emerge from the kitchen, a dishtowel in her hand. She wore a dress, as she always seemed to do, this one pale blue, and glasses, great round ones with black rims. They were large enough that they might have looked ridiculous, but instead, by contrast they made the delicacy of her features even finer. She had lipstick on, a bright coral, something I found vaguely disconcerting since she had been alone.

Once I knew she'd seen that it was me, I tried to open the door, but it was locked.

"Hang on," she said, turning one knob and then another. "How nice of you to come by." To my surprise, she leaned to kiss my cheek. I wondered if any of the coral had stayed on me.

"It's been three days since I did any dishes." She folded the towel. "It's tricky living by oneself, isn't it? You think there's nothing to clean, no one to do it for, and the next thing you know, there are fruit flies everywhere."

"Oddly enough, I've never lived alone." I was wondering whether I too would keep my doors locked in broad daylight, if I did.

"Well, I never had either, until I left Paul, but now I do, blissfully so, except for missing Nora. And the odd touch of loneliness, now and then. Which will get some relief when she visits." She smiled, delight at the thought immediately evident. "Are you here for a reason? Have I been too loud?" she joked.

"Yes, that's it," I said, looking around. "Too many wild parties." In the time since our dinner there, she had made the house seem much more like a home. There were books in the bookshelves, throw rugs on the floor. "No, I just came by to say hello, to see how you're settling in."

"Shall we sit out back?" She shook out, then refolded the towel as she spoke. "A bit early for drinks, but I could brew some coffee . . ."

I noticed a narrow streak of paint, yellow paint, on her arm.

"Actually," I said, "I would love . . . if you feel comfortable . . . I would love to see your paintings."

"Ah." Her sudden nervousness was visible, as was her quick resolve. "Well, in that case, why don't we head upstairs?"

The work reminded me of Beatrix Potter right away. Not Potter's bunnies and mice, but her botanicals. They were watercolors, gouaches, and some ink drawings, works only a scientist could do. Or anyway, the mind that could paint plants and minuscule parts of plants at this level of scrutiny and detail was a mind that would also be drawn to scientific studies. Though Alison was no miniaturist. That was inherent in the impact the paintings had. They were enormous, the petal of a flower spanning two feet. Nature writ large. But they weren't wholly clinical. There was something oddly affectionate to them, which was perhaps what brought Potter to mind. The focus loving rather than cold, despite the obvious scientific bent. The mood warm, rather than grand.

"They're wonderful," I said, meaning it—and relieved. "And to think that you called my work precise!"

"Well, I make tiny things huge. You paint such tiny details. Different kinds of precision, I suppose." She walked around the room, touching the canvases. Still nervous. On a long, narrow table half a dozen microscopes sat, lined up beside another row, jars with flowers and leaves in every one. "I'm just an amateur, I know. But I do so love doing it."

"If you sell me a painting, you won't be an amateur."

She laughed. "No, I think then I become a dilettante. And you become an enabler. But you know what I mean. I'm not a trained artist."

"Maybe not, but you're obviously a trained something. Observer. Which is more than half the battle. And I barely am either—only a few college courses ahead of you, I'm sure. We're all faking it half the time, don't you think?" I walked closer to a large pencil drawing of a pinecone. "How long have you been at this?"

"Oh, you know. Forever. In one way and another. I had an aunt who gave me my first microscope when I was small. Nine or ten. She was appalled by the fluff of my upbringing. All princess pink and ballet class. My mum constantly telling me not to speak so much, as boys disliked it. The microscope got me interested in biology, or maybe in observing, as you say. The drawings followed quite naturally from that. In many ways, my life has been a chaotic one. These . . ." She indicated the pictures. "These have always been the calm at the center of the storm."

I told her that surprised me, her description of a chaotic self. She seemed so pulled together to me, so orderly.

She laughed. "Well, you know those people who are better at living other people's lives than their own? Wise about everyone else's problems? But then a bit suspect about how they go about things themselves? I think I'm one of those. The tidiness is deceptive covering."

"I guess that makes the rest of us the lucky ones." I still wanted to talk about work, probe the depths to which we could talk about our respective processes. "I don't know if this happens to you," I said, "but there are moments when I'm so . . . I don't know, so excited by a project, not that it's going to be genius or even great, but just that it has me so by the scruff of my neck. I'm almost too excited to do it then. I can't sit still. I have to calm down first."

She seemed to think that over. "No, I'm not sure I've ever had that exactly. As I said, my work is . . . not the exciting part of my life. More of a centering activity. But really just a hobby."

"So you keep insisting," I said. "But I'm sure there's more to it than that."

"I'm afraid it's really true. I'm a dabbler. I just . . . I just do it. I don't much think it through."

"Well, we're all different," I said. "I have certainly been accused of overthinking it. And Owen is . . ." Saying his name out loud, I felt a wave of sadness; then of anger; distinctly both. "Owen is in a very rough patch now," I said. "With work, I mean. But when he's working well, he isn't manic at all. Just calm. And happy. All smiles. Not me, I'm like a windup toy that's been overwound. Of course, I haven't seen that mood of his in a very long time."

She asked me why, and I told her more about Owen's bad months, about the muse that had abandoned him, the ways I had to tiptoe around his fragility, the stress of that, the tension. I could feel myself abandoning my intention to speak to Alison about work, and creeping further into an area in which I might share secrets about my marriage instead; and as I crept there, I felt accompanying twinges of guilt and of entitlement. But Owen had left me bereft of meaningful conversation, and in the presence of that vacuum entitlement won out.

"Do you think Alison is very beautiful?" I asked him over dinner, a juicy spit-roasted chicken he had picked up in town.

His face was unreadable. "Have we already established that she's beautiful?" he asked. "So you're only asking about the very?"

I rolled my eyes. "I think she's very beautiful," I said. "I was just wondering if you do too."

He waited a moment before speaking. "Yes," he said. "Yes, I do too."

"It's her eyes, isn't it?"

He shrugged. "She has nice eyes," he said. "There are an awful lot of very beautiful women in the world, Gus."

And if I had wanted to marry one . . . He didn't say it, but I said it to myself.

"She wears lipstick when she's home, by herself. I think that may mean she and I are of different species."

"But you like her." It wasn't a question.

"I suppose." I wiped my mouth with my napkin. "Don't you?"

"I'm getting used to the fact of her. I'm not sure I like *that,* but yes, I like her. I'm just not sure I like having someone so close."

I didn't say anything beyond "Huh." I couldn't bring myself to agree and it seemed insulting to say I was glad for the company. "So, are you heading back out to work?" I asked.

"You mean, to try and work?" He nodded. "Yes. I am."

"Excellent," I said—just a little too brightly to sound genuine. "Don't worry about the dishes. There's not much and you did all the hunter-gathering stuff today."

"Hunted rotisserie chicken and gathered toilet paper," he said.

"My brave one," I said. "Yes. You are definitely off dish duty tonight."

Later, as I looked out our bedroom window toward the barn, I thought: maybe this is what a mother feels like at times. When she can't help one of her children. When she has to just stand by and watch her daughter strike out on the softball field, watch her son fail at math despite whatever effort he may put in. This ache. This defining double bind of roaring, passionate protectiveness and its equal, weighty, leaden uselessness. And even the impatience with it all; and then the guilt about feeling impatient, about finding it a bit oppressive despite the immeasurable love. Maybe this is what mothering sometimes feels like, I thought.

6

For the next week or so, as I made more rough sketches of scenes in the house, I didn't cast them with specific soldiers—aside from Jackie Mayhew, who had emerged as a kind of emblematic figure. I left room only for the boys in the scenes. I wasn't yet taking on the task of *humanizing* the figures, as I thought of it; I was just placing them there, these empty people-shaped placeholders, postponing the task about which I was most anxious.

But the postponing itself wasn't without its unsettling qualities. I fidgeted a lot through those workdays, taking frequent breaks, for walks, to weed patches of garden, to visit Alison, and to check my email—where one afternoon I again found Laine's name, newly arrived.

Hey, Augie, Do you remember you owe me a full report of your summer? I'm going to bug you until you send it. And you know I will be relentless. So consider yourself bugged. Also, I HAVE to tell you about the critique I had last night because I think it's such a good example of how MORONIC people are when they think it's their job to tell you how to do your own work. Especially boys who are convinced that they are the next great artistes of the world. . . .

It went on like that for a good while, a full account of her long night of fools and pretenders. *But none of this is surprising, I suppose,* she wound up. *We both know that many people who paint are idiots. And there were also some decent points made, so all in all, for all my whining, I'm glad I've taken this class. But mostly I am sick of talking about myself and really you do owe me a better email than the last one. Please!*

And then:

Looks like I'll be back in Philly for the wedding at the end of October. I did tell you Dad's marrying Miriam, right?

I deleted it.

I went into the trash folder and opened it again. Reread those words. Then closed it and restored it to my inbox. Then signed out of my email, shutting my laptop, keeping my hands pressed there, as though it might just pop open again.

I hadn't known. I hadn't even known there was a woman in his life. Laine may have thought she'd mentioned it, but she had not.

Miriam. Jewish presumably. Like me.

But not me.

Laine knew nothing, of course. Our affair had lasted just beyond the span of her first semester at NYU. Georgia never knew either. No one knew. No one ever would have known had I not told Owen in a fit of guilt that March, just over a month after I broke it off. Guilt. And also fear. Fear that it would start up again. That without making myself accountable to someone beside myself, I would run right back to Bill and accept what he could offer—which were moments. Moments that seemed apart from all the harsh realities of my life. But still, only moments. He had his son at home. He wasn't going to be that guy, he said. That guy who breaks a family up, who tears a family down. It was bad enough discovering that he was willing to be the man he had become.

Almost two years later, when he and Georgia finally threw in the towel, he phoned. But I had already put Owen through hell, already watched him turn his heart inside out, like some sort of great deep pocket in which he might just find enough of some quality I could barely imagine: generosity, compassion, forgiveness, love. And like a miracle, he had.

I told Owen about the call. So scrupulous had I become. I told him that Bill's marriage was over, and that he had phoned about picking up where we had left off. And that I had told him I was 100 percent in my own marriage—a marriage, as we had finally exchanged vows—and I had no interest. *Not* that I felt too guilty to do it or that I was afraid of getting caught. But that I had no interest. And I told Owen I had asked Bill never to call me again.

Along with whatever scruple I felt to be forthright, I'd also expected Owen to view my unambiguous dismissal of Bill as a gift of some kind—which he did not. That phone call cost us about two weeks of misery. What I thought would mark an end, for Owen just dredged it all up again. Bill still existed. Bill was now single. Bill had the ability to pick up a phone and dial. If I had ever thought of telling Owen about my contact with Laine, those weeks put an end to that thought.

Laine. Laine who had no reason to predict the impact of what she had written me.

Sitting with my palms still on the lid of my laptop, I felt dizzy, slightly ill. I didn't think I would cry, though I wondered. But I didn't even know yet if sadness was in play. At that moment, it felt more like being slapped.

Eventually, I stood up and walked to my easel, where I stared at a drawing for some time, or maybe at a few drawings, before realizing I couldn't possibly focus on work.

Alison, in her doorway, said yes, of course, she would come for a walk.

"How's the pond?" I asked. The pond was fine. "Seven times around is pretty much exactly a mile," I said. "Owen measured absolutely everything when we first moved in. He can tell you the precise distance between our houses, I'll bet."

Alison laughed. "I doubt I'll ever need the information," she said. "But in case I ever want to build some sort of walkway, I'll know who to ask."

We made our way past the barn, through the thicket of spruce at the lawn's western edge. The day was cool and cloudy. No threat of rain, not anything serious, anyway. Maybe it would spit a little later but nothing like the downpours to come later in the summer.

"If you stay about four feet out from the edge," I said, "there's less mud."

"Is something wrong?" Alison asked, as she adjusted her path. "Or is this really just a walk around the pond?"

"Points for perception," I said. "You're pretty good."

"Maybe you haven't seen your face, Gus. I'm not that good. You look like someone's died. Has someone died?"

"No. Nobody's died." I took a deep breath, filled my lungs with soggy air, thick with grass and mud. "It's a long story, Alison."

I had never told anyone. Whom would I have told? Charlotte was already gone. Jan was many admirable things, efficient, practical, intelligent, and generous, of course; but all of it held together with wires too barbed for her ever to have been the right confidante for my ribbon-sliced heart. And all of my friends back then were Owen's friends too, back when we had friends whom we saw more than once a year, back before we ran away into the supposed safety of our solitude. I'd had no right to tell them anything so personal about us both.

And maybe I still had no right, but I couldn't help myself. "I learned today that an old . . . an old . . . a man I once . . . I should begin at the beginning, I suppose. Five years ago, I had an affair . . . and Owen knows," I added quickly—there still being a touch of pride in having fessed up, even though if I'd had it to do over, I might well have chosen to spare us both my unburdening myself.

Alison said nothing.

"It's been over for a long time. And it didn't go on that long. I mean, it wasn't a weekend fling but it wasn't years either. It was just one fall—in both senses, I suppose. One autumn though, is what I mean. And then into January, too."

Because we were walking side by side, I couldn't see her face. Maybe that was why my instincts had brought us outside, though it had felt more as though it would take all the vast sky, all that infinite space to make my disclosures feel small enough to bear.

As I told her the story, I sensed an elasticity to its form, realizing how very malleable a thing I needed my tale to be, how much emphasis I wanted on the terrible emotional state I was in after Charlotte's death; how little I wanted to linger on the degree to which I knew exactly what I was doing. (That week between when Laine stopped taking lessons and when Bill finally called, how absolutely certain I had been about what was going on . . .) I could make it so much more comfortable a story with just a little stress here, a small elision there. It didn't even matter that I knew I was editing, it felt good hearing it that way.

And then I told her what I had not told her before.

"Owen couldn't have children. We'd just found out. A few months before Charlotte's death. And that news, I didn't handle it well. I mean, I said all the right things, and I felt terrible for him. I always did. I still do. But I just felt so bereft, and so confused.

No excuses, I know. But everything was such an unbelievable mess."

"It sounds like a lot. A lot of hard stuff all at once."

"And today," I said. "Laine wrote me today that Bill's remarrying." We took another couple of steps. "I have no right to . . . to have any reaction to this. I know that I don't. And I don't even know really what my reaction is."

But it wasn't quite true. By then I did know. He was in love. That was it. That was the truth exploding again and again. He was in love. He was having *it*—the fresh start, the moments of joy, maybe even the children, for all I knew; and not the tired, battle-weary, tattered and stitched-together love I had settled back into with Owen. Bill had fallen in love. Again. And not with me. With a woman named Miriam.

"I can see why this would be hard," Alison said.

"I honestly don't know why it's upsetting me so much. We haven't so much as spoken in years. And I should tell you, I can't let Owen know I've heard this, and definitely not that it's got me all riled up. And truly not that you know a thing. This really has to be just between us. The fertility stuff, too. All of it."

"No, no, I understand. Of course. And as for why you're so upset . . ." She took my arm, a gesture that felt both awkward and welcome. "I'm not sure who wouldn't be, Gus. You fall in love with a man and want to run off with him. He stays with his wife, and then, however many years later, he marries someone else. It doesn't help that he ran back to you after his divorce. You never came first. That's the thorn in the rose right there. The wife didn't exactly come first either, but now . . . I can't imagine who wouldn't be upset."

It was difficult to hear. *You never came first.* But it was true. Maybe it had been temporary insanity on my part, but he *had* come first for me. I would have thrown it all over for him. "I didn't have children to think of," I said out loud. "We had completely different situations. Owen and I weren't even married at the time. Maybe that did make it feel easier for me."

"I don't know about your heart," Alison said, "but mine has never been particularly logical."

"No," I said. "Nor mine."

We were on our fifth time around the pond by then. "I have always been a little irritated that Owen paced this off," I said. "It . . . It takes some of the wildness out, some of that sense of just wandering in the countryside."

We walked a bit more, still arm in arm.

"My husband hit me," Alison said after a time. "That year after Nora went to school. He started hitting me. I became one of those women fidgeting with heavy makeup to deal with covering bruises."

"Jesus, Alison. I'm so sorry. And here I am complaining about a paced-off pond."

She shook her head. "That's not why I'm telling you. You're supposed to find Owen irritating. You're his wife. But I wasn't supposed to put up with being hit. Or before that. Even then, I shouldn't have put up with being afraid of him. It's just . . . it's just so terribly difficult to admit that someone doesn't really love you. Not in the way you thought. Not in the way you'd hoped. There were a lot of reasons I stayed as long as I did, Nora, of course, and also fear, but in part I just wanted to think he loved me." She stopped walking, so I did too. We faced each other, and against the backdrop of tall marsh grass, her lips lacquered coral, her eyes that silvery gray, she seemed oddly vivid, a silver-haired figure from a surrealist painting.

"I'm so sorry, Alison. I had no idea you'd been through that. I knew about the temper. Not the hitting though."

"I rarely mention it. I don't like remembering, I suppose."

"Does your daughter know?"

"Oh, that's a long story," she said. "For another day. The real point I'm making, the only reason I raised all that, is that I know how heartbreaking it is to lose belief in another person's love. It's devastating. However it comes about."

"That's what I did to Owen. That's what I put him through."

"Maybe. But then Owen chose to stay. And he's an adult, yes? He could have done otherwise."

We started to walk again. "I couldn't have, you know," I said. "Done what Owen did. If it had been reversed, I would have been out the door. I couldn't have borne it."

"Trust me, Gus. One never knows what one will endure."

A rabbit, neither baby nor fully grown, scampered across our path some ten feet ahead. Alison asked, "Do you want advice? Or just a shoulder? Because I can give you either. I can even give you both."

"What's the advice? I mean, all I can do is just try to forget Laine ever wrote. Not act like some kind of moony teen around Owen. Seal my heart back up."

"That. Yes. But . . . maybe this is presumptuous of me but . . . Don't try to get in touch with him. You may . . . you may feel tempted."

"No." I shook my head. "Not tempted. Not tempted at all."

But it wasn't true. I was already composing coded, chilly messages to send through Laine. *Please do tell your father how thrilled I am that he has found real love at last. Please do give your father my love—assuming he even remembers who I am.* "No," I said. "I can see why you'd think so . . . but no. I have no temptation to be back in touch."

"Well, that's excellent, then." Alison took my arm again. "So, do you feel as though you have to go the full seven laps? Because I confess, there's something about knowing it's a mile that makes me feel that. As though we'll be shirking if we stop at five."

"Bingo," I said. "That's exactly why it irritates me so."

"But we're going to do those two more laps, aren't we?"

"Yes," I said. "We are going to do the two more laps."

At her porch, she hugged me. And I thanked her, meaning it. Two hours later, when Owen came in, he asked me what that had been all about.

"One minute I'm contemplating the indefatigable nature of a squirrel out my window, the next I'm watching my undemonstrative wife embracing our neighbor."

"Oh, we had been walking around the pond. She had . . . she had told me some things about her marriage that were pretty terrible. I think she just needed a hug. Shocking, I know, but even I can be compassionate at times."

"Shocking indeed. We'll keep it to ourselves. I wouldn't want your reputation ruined."

It was an old joke between us. Or an old routine I suppose, since calling it a joke implies humor. And maybe there was humor there for Owen. For me, it was something else. I'd always doubted that Owen understood that slightly standoffish manner of mine, the motherless part, the part that didn't know what to do with Alison's arm in mine as we walked. The part that could accept that sort of affection only like an ill-fitting garment, a hand-me-down I suspected wasn't truly meant for me.

"I'm thinking of putting a moratorium on work," Owen said, reaching for his water glass. "On what passes for work, I should say. For a few days, anyway. I think I have reached the point where I'm just spinning myself into deeper mud. I need a holiday." He looked at me and laughed. "You should see yourself, Gus. Don't panic, I'm not suggesting we go anywhere. I know that you're mid-project. I just think I may forbid myself access to the barn for a week. Work in the garden. Take long walks. Paint the front hall. Stop pushing so fucking hard—since clearly whatever it is can push back with greater force."

"I think that sounds right," I said. "God knows there's always

more work that can be done around here. And you must need a
break by now. I know I would. I think that's very wise of you."

"There must be a saying to cover this situation. Desperation is
the mother of common sense? Something along those lines." He
began to drink, and I walked across the kitchen. I kissed his cheek,
the glass still to his mouth.

"It's a good move," I said, thinking that it was good timing too.

What followed was a more relaxed week than our home had been
witness to in months. Owen was a creature of great will. When he
decided to do a thing, he did it. And having decided to set his
worries aside for a time, he seemed able to do exactly that. And
while I didn't stop working altogether, I slowed down, gave it less
space.

More than once over the years, I'd wondered whether people as
close as Owen and I were indeed telepathic. Was he responding to
a distress call I didn't know I was sending and that he didn't know
he was answering? Something grabbing his attention just in time
to remind me of why this life of ours was no mere consolation
prize?

We lingered over our meals. We played Scrabble after dinner.
I wandered out to whatever patch of garden he was weeding, and
would end up staying an hour, more, just talking to him, laughing. A couple of times we ended up in bed together, daytime sex.
We never quite matched the drunken near-brawl of that night
after dinner at Alison's, but we rolled around and teased each
other and we played. The only thing missing for me that week
was that he still didn't want to talk about my work. I tried once
and he sank into an awful and eloquent silence. But I didn't mind
it so much. Because in many ways our house felt like home again
to me. No longer like a place defined by paucity—paucity of happiness, of shared enjoyment, of conversation. It felt like a second
spring had come.

But then, after exactly a week, he announced he was going back out to the barn again—*I can't really just quit*—and before another week was up, we were right back where we had been.

"I suppose I should be grateful for the days we had," I said, sitting on the floor of Alison's studio, surrounded by her paintings, those botanicals so outsized, each detail so vast, that I felt miniaturized among them all. The old, uneven pine floor, filthy and ridged, had produced a splinter in my palm that I picked at as I spoke. "I feel terrible for him. I know how this can just rip you up."

"I wish I had some helpful experience." She was standing behind her easel and I could only see her legs, tanned and muscular, her feet, bare, her toenails painted the same coral perpetually on her lips. "What do people do?"

I shrugged. "They suffer. They make bargains with gods in whom they don't believe. They wait it out."

"Maybe I should be glad I'm just a hobbyist."

"If it makes you feel better to keep calling yourself that . . ." I looked at a painting I particularly liked, a four-foot-high watercolor of a broken piece of marsh grass. "Your work is good, you know. But if that's going to make you all self-conscious, I take it back."

"Thank you."

"Alison, how do you not have splinters all the time?"

"What? Oh, I don't know. My feet are probably too calloused. All those ballet classes I was forced to take." Then, after a moment, she said, "You seem better, Gus. About that other thing, I mean. I hope you don't mind my saying. I'm guessing the time with Owen helped."

That other thing.

Was I better?

For all that I'd loved that week with Owen, for all that it might have minimized any lingering emotions about Bill, I still hadn't

been able to bring myself to answer Laine's email. Every time I
tried, I reached the point at which I either would or wouldn't acknowledge Bill's marriage and balked at completing the task—as
though my doing so would be giving it a closure I couldn't bring
myself to give. That news had reopened a landscape of memories
from which I could not easily look away. A place unlike any real
place on earth, where fertile hills abutted jagged glaciers, and
deathly crevasses invited icy falls from sumptuous, sunny lawns.
A place of beauty and danger that I pined for and despised and
couldn't bring myself to push back out of view.

"Yes," I told Alison. "I am doing better. Thank you. It was a
bad day or two, but in the end," I said, "that was a different life.
Years and years ago. I'm really okay with it now."

I took her silence, just the few too many seconds before she said
she was glad, to mean that she'd guessed I was only saying what I
wanted to be true.

When Owen had gone back to work, so had I. But while he had
just walked straight into the old familiar misery, I was excitedly
engaged with the process of using my sketches to block out some
canvases. After visiting Alison, I turned to one I liked especially
of an individual boy—Oliver Farley, dead at seventeen, in a hospital in France—sitting on our front step, elbows on knees, chin
in hands. Just waiting. The image of a waiting boy. That's what I
wanted to convey, once I fully painted him in. All the time in the
world. This was the theme that kept coming up for me, the strand
I hadn't quite grasped right away. It wasn't that the boys were all
engaged in childlike activities or in the adult ones they had missed
by being blown from their own lives so young. It was that they
moved in these rooms of ours, occupied this space, as though they
had all the time in the world. *Let's play a leisurely game of chess. Let's
linger over a breakfast cooked under the lolling gaze of a friend whose feet
are up on the table. Maybe I'll just sit here and do nothing much.*

Time. And calm.

As I painted, not just that day, but throughout that whole period, I thought a lot about the atmosphere of my own childhood home. My mother, of course, had been the lost soul, the dead woman walled off, immured behind my father's edict that she not be brought up. Brought out. Into the light. I don't know if he thought of that as smoothing something over, the least unsettling course, but what I realized as I craved calm for these boys was how much hysteria lay behind my father's extreme approach.

That night, as Owen unloaded the dishwasher, I readied the next load. Always looking for topics to fill the void, I told him about Alison's strangely impervious feet, and he said, "Good to know. I'll add it to the list."

"What list?"

He reached up to shelve a stack of plates. "You really don't know that you come home every day with little factoids about her?"

I shut the faucet off.

"It's called getting to know someone, Owen, and I recognize we're a bit out of practice, but it really isn't so very strange. Is it?"

"No," he said. "I guess it's not. I was just teasing you, Gus. Trying to make some sort of joke."

"Well, it was hilarious," I said. "Everything's rinsed clean, here. Mind if I go do a bit of work?"

"Not at all," he said, as I left the room. "I'm glad one of us can."

There was no mistaking the envy, nor the unfair resentment directed my way. I almost turned around to ask if it would help somehow if I gave up, sat shivah with him for both our creative lives. But I pushed down my anger, rehearsing for myself again, again, what misery he must be feeling, how awful that sensation of emptiness; and I went to work.

7

Usually, when there was a problem with my father, the home would call Jan—a doctor after all, a family doctor who had treated her share of elderly patients. And there really hadn't been many emergencies. He wasn't one of the aspiring escapees and his dementia had never included a violent side. But every once in a while he would spike an odd fever, a simple cold blossoming into pneumonia then treated with the sort of medical zeal one might think reserved for a man whose continued existence is undeniably a gift to him. Any ambiguity about the quality of my father's life was banished with every technical skill available, by all professional valor. And so the drugs and tents and fluids were brought in until the fever was conquered, the lungs cleared, the battle won; the war still raging on in his brain.

There had also been a different sort of incident at the end of that spring, when he had fallen into days of inconsolable tears, a river with no source, no destination point. Flood, flood, flood, unholy, torrential flood. During that time—four full days, as many nights—Jan and I took turns sitting by his side consoling him, or not consoling him at all but trying to. And I had tried too to console the young nurse, Lydia, who believed she had somehow caused this deluge—impossible to imagine from so dried up an old man.

She had asked him about his life, she said. About his wife. He had split open in response, become a lake.

"It could have happened to anyone," I told her. "It probably didn't matter what you said."

She couldn't have been much more than twenty. I watched the argument taking place in her expression, the desire to be freed of blame pushing against the conviction, the hope, that her words should have meaning.

"It's not your fault," I said. "It's none of our fault."

In the third week of August, Jan was up in Nova Scotia with Letty for their annual vacation up north, so the first report of a violent outburst came to me, an early morning call—from a nurse I'd never met whose knowing voice, gravelly, deep, seemed somehow at odds with her optimistic statement that this might well just be a one-time event.

"What happened?" I asked. "Exactly, I mean."

He had grabbed the shoulders of the nurse helping him button his pajamas. "It's often something simple like that. Something for which there's no real explanation. He shook her. Pretty hard. Your father is a very strong man still. Surprisingly so."

"I'm so sorry," I said—though I knew an apology wasn't quite right. Sorry for what? For my father being ravaged by a disease? For his having worked so hard all those years to stay strong and well for his girls? Running those endless laps around the school field every afternoon. Pulling himself up on the bar tensed across the door to the bedroom he and my mother once shared, stopping often at that threshold, on his way to grab his wallet, to change his shoes, and just lift himself once or twice. A devotion, I'd thought unexpectedly, when home from college one time. A little act of remembrance, a piety. What had seemed so peculiar, so irritating—*Hurry up, Dad! Oh for God's sake, just go in and find your keys!*—had struck me that day as something beautiful.

"It was almost sexual," I told Owen, not many years after. "But not in an icky way. Like he was still physically devoting himself to her. And of course it was all about being sure we had at least one healthy parent left. I just think it was also about more than that . . ."

But of course I had been perpetually desperate for signs that she still mattered to him, that the door he'd slammed after her death had panes through which something still shone through, maybe something of her that I would one day see.

The nurse said, "It's easier with the ones who have grown physically weak. Though, as I say, this may well have just been a one-time event. We like to report all such incidents right away. Then if we do have to move him into a different level of care, you'll understand . . ."

"Yes. Of course." Something occurred to me. "Which nurse was it?"

"Lydia. She's fairly new."

I told her we had met. I rolled my eyes to the inexplicable heavens. Having their cruel little laugh. Poor girl.

"I'll come check in on things today," I said. "Maybe a familiar face will help."

At Alison's door, I was like the girl hanging out by the locker of her latest crush just hoping he'll ask her out. "And so, that's why I won't be around today . . . or anyway, for the morning."

She asked if I wanted company. "Or is Owen . . . ?"

"I'm letting Owen work."

"Well . . . I could actually use a change of scene," she said. "Unless it feels too . . . I don't mean to intrude." She knew better though. She would be ready in ten minutes. We would meet back on her side of the hill.

She drove. "It will do me good to be behind the wheel," she said. "Otherwise I'll never learn my way around this part of the world. I'm hopeless at maps. And anyway, you look like you could use an hour in the passenger seat."

This is us on the road to the finest private hell that money can buy:

We are seated close together, or so it seems to me, used to my van as I am. Two middle-aged women. I am in a jean skirt and black T-shirt; and with my arms inactive on my lap I am aware of the paint that clings to me even when I believe I have scrubbed it off. My hands, my wrists, seem covered in a translucent extra layer of skin, almost reptilian, adhering to the pores and fine lines beneath, pulling the texture of me into view. I feel grubby, overly conscious of this sheath. And Alison is in one of her bright colors again—a teal dress. Her car smells like her. As we pull off the property, out onto the road, I realize there is a scent I now associate with her. Spring flowers. Lime. For a moment, I close my eyes and breathe in, trying as I do to pull apart the strands of scent.

"I knew it," she says. "You're tired."

"Yes." I open my eyes. "Tired. But I'm not sleepy."

"That's good. Because I'm . . ." She laughs. "I should have warned you. You're in no danger of dozing off. I'm mildly famous for driving like a . . ."

"Maniac?" I ask. "Is that how that sentence ends?"

"That sounds about right. I may have heard that word tossed about before. Once or twice." She takes a curve with a gusto that lands me right against the door. "I'm very good though," she says. "I just . . . I just enjoy myself . . ."

"Okay." I sit up straighter, braced. "So, what about your par-

ents?" I ask. It isn't a subject change—the car is full of our mis-
sion, of my concern.

"My parents?" she asks, as though I have inquired about a pair
of unicorns. "Oh, they're just fine. Young. Mid-seventies. Fit.
They require no care and . . . and that's probably just as well, as I
can't imagine myself back there. My sense of filial duty is . . ." She
slams us to a stop. "My sense of filial duty is not all that it could
be. And impossible as this now seems, I fell so madly in love with
Paul there was no chance I'd stay over there. He was a student in
London, that's how we met. Now of course there's also Nora. It's
unimaginable being that far from her, especially with her father . . ."

She lets the thought go unfinished. It's often unclear how much
she wants this subject pursued, so for some time I say nothing,
just sit, holding on, thinking how strange it is that this road I
have driven dozens of times, so sorrowfully bland, is now mined
with near misses and jolts.

"I'm sorry," she says at a particularly sharp swerve. "But you
were warned."

If she were Owen, I would answer, "Well, I was warned when
it was too late—which technically isn't a warning at all," but I
don't quite feel the closeness yet for that. And so instead I say, "It's
not bad having a little excitement in my life," and she says, "No
indeed. It's not bad at all."

Her cell phone chirps. "Not while you're driving," I say, and
she tells me to extract it from her bag. On the screen there's a text:
"Labor Day weekend's good. Heather can drive."

I read it to Alison, whose demeanor suddenly shifts. What I'd
thought was enjoyment, even happiness, was nothing compared
to what she looks like now.

"Nora," she says, unnecessarily.

The mention of one young woman has brought another to my
mind. Laine. To whose email I have yet to reply. "Well, here we
are," I say, as Alison slides into a space marked *Family.*

As a child, I had been only vaguely aware that my father had served in World War II, just at the tail end, stationed in England—doing what? I never asked. My mother's death, barely mentioned though it was, seemed so much the focal point of all personal history in our lives, it was as though time began for us when it stopped for her. Maybe this is what happens to everyone—not necessarily sudden deaths, but certain events that create distinct before and after lines, walls really, requiring a great effort to climb, discouraging doing so.

That was what I thought about as I sat in my father's room, having introduced him to Alison, whose British accent had spurred him to say, "Oh, I remember you. You're that girl my buddy had the big crush on. Kenny. He cried on the boat all the way home. Did you know?"

Maybe we do move from one era of our own lives to another, the way we change residences. Doors shut, no key left in the mailbox, only the uncanny slippage of my father's mind allowing him to sneak back in.

I could imagine, as I listened to them "reminisce" about the war, that the death of his thirty-one-year-old wife might so have redefined him that even memories of war had felt out of reach. Another life. But how had I failed to be aware of that whole era of his history? How had his role in World War II not entered my consciousness? All the work in which I'd been immersed, Jackie Mayhew, Oliver Farley, others, and it had never struck me that my father too had been an American boy sent over to Europe to fight?

It was stunning how successfully he had cut us off from his past.

His face showed no more sign of the struggles of the night before than of the great conflict of sixty-five years earlier. I had been cautioned not to mention the incident. To the extent that he was shifting into a phase in which agitation might spur on violence, it was counterproductive to confront him, I had been told. And so I just sat there, relieved that for once I could visit and allow someone else to carry the conversational water. And Alison, for her part, turned out to be remarkably good at following the odd turns of his thoughts. She was perfectly content, it seemed, to play the part of a girl, resurrected, the long-lost love of a long-lost friend from a long-lost time.

As they chatted, it crossed my mind to ask him the questions I never had. *What was it like going to war? What was it like being a Jew in Europe then? What was it like fearing death? Losing friends? Being so far away from home?* But I couldn't bear the prospect of discovering that the memories had all fallen through the holes in his brain.

"Betty!" A coughing fit followed my father's proclamation. "That's your name," he said, his fist still up to his mouth, catching more sputters. "You're Millie's friend. Kenny's girl. Betty."

"I knew you'd remember!" Alison said. "You were always good like that. So clever!"

I had imagined they might find common ground as high school teachers. I had thought that was to be the surprise of the day: that she would be able to draw him out on those years when he taught, help me locate the father I could remember though he could not. I had thought briefly too that he might cast her as my mother; though the fantasy made me feel a flash of childlike shame. But no, she was to be Betty. Betty the British girl. Not some figure from my life with him, but flesh-and-blood evidence of a story that had nothing to do with me.

As if on cue, as though he had caught a whiff of my melancholy, he turned and asked, "Were you there too?" his eyes rheumy and full of concern.

"I wasn't," I said, standing up. "But how nice that the two of you can catch up." I touched the back of his chair. "I just want to go speak to the . . . the . . ." I let it go unfinished, as I left the room.

At the nurses' station, I peered over the counter, my head between the two enormous, unchanging displays of plastic flowers, and I asked if Lydia was available; but of course she'd gone home after working the night shift. I considered jotting something down, leaving her a message along the lines of: *It isn't you . . . don't feel bad . . . it isn't you;* but what might be said casually in person felt clunky and presumptuous as a note.

"Would you please tell her that I thanked her for her care of my father?" I said. "I know he hasn't been the easiest . . . I know she got the brunt of it last night."

The duty nurse looked at me with genuine kindness. "Oh, we're used to those things," she said. "Your father's a lamb. He can have a bad night once in a while. He's no trouble at all."

"You called me this morning, didn't you?" I asked.

"That's right," she said. "We have to make the calls. But please don't worry about us."

Looking at her, I thought Laine would have liked to paint her face. She was maybe ten years older than I, bright strawberry blonde hair, unusually dark brown eyes. Clipped, combed eyebrows. And her nose was asymmetrical, one nostril round, the other pinched—defying definition, just as the depth and gravel of her voice argued with the chipper sentences she spoke. Her face seemed like a collection of features hurriedly thrown together, not a coordinated expressive instrument. I could never capture that. But Laine, I knew, excelled at just such challenges.

"He goes to lunch soon," the nurse said. "Will you be staying? You and your friend?"

I looked up at the big clock behind her, identical to the clocks that had graced every classroom I had ever been in. Every classroom in which my father had ever taught. It was past noon. "No," I said. "We'll be heading out now." I thanked her again, and made my way back down the hall.

My departure from my father's room was barely a footnote to "Betty's" farewell. He seemed so sad to see her leave that I feared another deluge of tears, but her repeated promise to return soothed him enough that we could extricate ourselves without a flood.

We were silent as we walked through the air-conditioned, fluorescently lit halls to the door, just murmuring a simultaneous *thank-you* to the guard who opened the door. We were silent as we stepped into a world that seemed to have been set on broil during our hours inside. It was only as we approached the car that Alison spoke.

"I can't imagine how difficult that is for you," she said. "If it were me . . . Honestly, it must just be impossible to manage . . . Though . . ." We had reached the car. "Though he seems to be a nice enough man."

A nice enough man. Yes. That was what he had become— when he wasn't throttling nurses or drowning in his own tears. "Well, he was pretty damn stern when I was a kid," I said. "It's hard to see now. He seems so mild, I know. But he was . . . he was very tough with us. We weren't . . . we weren't an affectionate kind of family. We were never . . . never soft, I suppose. Never tender." I groaned as we slid into the stifling air. "Jesus Christ. And people leave their dogs in cars."

"Only people who want to kill their dogs." Alison pressed both buttons so our windows opened at once. "This sort of heat absolutely never happens in England. Not like this. Once in a century." She began backing out of the space.

"That's the most I've ever heard him talk about the war," I said. "By a long shot. It was strange to think of him having this whole . . . this whole era of his life that he just erased. Or buried. And then it comes rolling back. When you're old. And mad as a hatter." I looked out the window. A long stretch of office buildings passed, low-lying, sand-colored. A regular rhythm of For Rent signs. "It's a very funny business," I said. "This whole life thing."

"Well, that's certainly true. There's little doubt about that. When you were out of the room? He was talking. I don't know if you know this, maybe you do. About some woman? When he was in England?" She stopped at a light; and I realized that her driving style had changed, had become almost stately by comparison.

"Betty?"

"No. Not her. I gather there was another girl? You probably know this." But I could tell from her tone that she didn't really think I did.

"A girl in England? No. I never heard about that. I barely even heard he'd been there."

"Millicent," she said. "Millie to her chums."

"Oh." I laughed. "Of course. An English girl named Millicent. What else would she be named?"

"Well, Fiona. Dorothea. Dotty. Gladys."

"So, what about this girl named Millicent? Millie."

"Oh, it just seemed . . . at one point he seemed to think I was her. I gather they were quite an item."

"Is this where you reveal to me that I have an older brother living in England with Millie, his mum?"

Alison laughed. "No. I think at most it's . . ."

"Did he say he was in love?"

She took a curve with the same notable care. "Not in so many words. He told me, well, he didn't exactly tell me anything, since he thought I already knew. He was just talking over old times. Something about the pub and the walk home. And what a shrew Millie's mother was. My mother, I suppose. I wouldn't even have mentioned it . . ."

"No, I'm glad you did. That explains why he was so distraught when you left."

"It just felt peculiar to me. Him telling me. And me not telling you."

"Peculiar," I said. "Yes. That would have been peculiar. For my father who thinks you are his girlfriend from 1945 to tell you a story and you not to tell me." I looked at her. "What part of life isn't peculiar, Alison? Seriously? At what point, really, do you stop and say, well, *this* is really strange? *This* part. Not *that* part. But *this* part."

She didn't say anything in response, and for a time we just drove on. Past first one strip mall to the left, then its twin to the right. And I thought about Millicent. A girl in England. Just an hour before, less than that, I had been theorizing that the war must have been blown from my father's memory by my mother's death, and thinking myself so insightful. Life and its walls, its before and after events. But maybe the war had always been a taboo subject—because of Millicent. Maybe he had promised my mother never to bring it up. Maybe his proposal to her had included a confession that there had been another love. "Her name was Millie and until I met you I never thought I'd love again. . . ." Maybe he'd been doing all those pull-ups all those years to be ready to reclaim his British rose once his daughters were all out of the house. But then she too had died. Or she'd run off with the greengrocer. Or they'd carried on in secret and he never told us, lest we feel our mother betrayed. Maybe dear old Millicent was the answer to the puzzle of why my father never settled with anyone else for all those many decades of widowerhood.

As we drove, it crossed my mind that if I'd ever had children and then became demented enough to blurt, they would be asking each other, *Who the hell was Bill?* on their drive home. Except the chronology was off. If I'd had children, there wouldn't have been a Bill. For a moment, I thought that with great conviction— as I had for many years. If my sister had lived. If my uterus had filled with life. If everything had gone according to plan, then I wouldn't have . . .

But who knew?

"It really is amazing," I said, "how little we understand about anything."

"Yes." Alison raised both our windows. "Tell me if it gets too cold. I often think that about newborns, you know. That we're always focused on how much knowledge they acquire. But then there's also the business of learning how much cannot be known. Knowledge acquisition on the one hand and ignorance acceptance on the other."

"I suppose that's right." I thought then of launching into a whole theory about the role of religion in providing a story one could tell oneself; but I didn't want to be rude about Alison's child, now officially due to visit over Labor Day. And truly, my tired, unsatisfied heart wasn't in the project of pointing out how badly other people were managing their lives or what illusions they needed in order to get by.

"This is the best mall around," I said, pointing. "If you run out of paints and need an emergency supply. There's a craft store there. It's not top-line stuff, but it's okay if you're desperate. Though I probably have anything you need. I tend to stock up for years at a time."

"I'll keep that in mind," she said, then she lightly touched my arm. "You look so tired, Gus. Why don't you close your eyes. I promise not to drive like a lunatic. Why don't you try and get some sleep."

"Your daughter," I said, "she really believes in it all? I mean, the heaven part? We're all going to just keep on? A great big reunion one day."

Alison sighed. "Something like that. I haven't questioned her too closely on certain things. Like the afterlife. Heaven. Hell. It would be hard for me to know how to deal with her believing in hell, I think. Much harder than just telling myself to be glad she thinks we're never really going to have to say goodbye."

"Right," I said. "I can see that. Never having to say goodbye."

I thought of Charlotte. "It's easy to scoff," I said. "But I do understand the appeal. I would like to never say goodbye. Ever, I mean. Never again," I said. "There have already been too many goodbyes," I said, as I closed my eyes.

"Sweet dreams," Alison said, with another pat on my arm. "Sweet dreams, Gus, and no more goodbyes."

8

had imagined Nora small. All through Alison's chatter about her, I had assumed she would be shorter than her mother—for no good reason at all. Small, but with the same round lines, soft curves of Alison's figure, face, hair, even her personality. And I had also imagined her mousy—an indescribable quality, but a distinctive one nonetheless—doubtless because the most interesting thing I knew about her was her religious belief and my mind ran too easily to some absurd stereotype. All of it was a far cry from the lanky young woman in shorts and a tank top who appeared with Alison at my kitchen door Friday afternoon of Labor Day weekend.

"This is Nora!" Alison said it as if she had pulled a rabbit out of her hat, rather than welcomed her daughter from Boston. *Ta-dah!*

I said hello, and we shook hands. I ushered them in. "You had an okay drive?" I asked, noticing the gold cross, barely half an inch, on a near-invisible chain around her neck. "It's a pretty day for it, anyway," I said. "Long trip though."

"It was good," she said. "Just under six hours." She shrugged in the way only young people do, as though her shoulders were first pulled by strings, then dropped. "We talked. It didn't seem too long." I could hear a trace of her mother's accent in and around her own Boston one.

"Her friend Heather drove her. They've known each other from diapers."

"Heather has a boyfriend in Philadelphia," Nora said. "So it's pretty much on her way."

"Well, it's very nice to have you here. And I know your mother is excited. I hope she'll share you with us a bit." To my own ear, I sounded false, like a character on TV. Next, I would be talking about *us girls* going out to do a little shopping. "Would you like to sit, have a drink? It's early but I always feel like on holiday weekends the rules don't count. I could mix a pitcher of something light. Sangria?"

They exchanged a look. "Actually," Alison said, "I promised Nora a dinner out, with a couple of detours along the way. We're on our way now . . . I want to show her the area."

"Oh," I said. "Well, that sounds wonderful. Perfect. Another time then. Maybe tomorrow night. Why don't we all have dinner here?" Alison said that they would, and I told them to have fun. I didn't ask where they were going. I just smiled and waved goodbye at my door.

How had it not occurred to me that I would feel left out?

I set to work right away, my go-to response to any such ache.

On the canvas, the chess game and my living room were vivid. It had been years since I'd painted a space in which I lived, and I was enjoying the process of re-creating my own home in miniature. At heart, I thought of myself as a miniaturist, though my paintings were often of vast landscapes, and even this canvas was three feet high by nearly four long. I had spent hours on the loveseat's faded brocade, mixing shades so close to each other it was impossible to see any difference, until one became background and the other the pattern woven in. Each stone of our fireplace was like a universe to me, those odd shadows, those irregular shapes.

To paint a thing had always been a way for me to love it. And I was deep into a love affair with my own home; but not yet with the boys whose occupation of that home, of those pictures, was still only sketchy, who were themselves just blocked-out figures, bare, human-shaped white emptiness.

While I worked all that late afternoon, my thoughts drifted often to Alison and Nora. When I was actually painting, mixing colors, focused on a small task, I had no room in my head for anything else. But when I stepped away and tried to think through the larger scheme, the concept rather than the execution, my mind wandered to the house on the other side of the hill.

I tried to recall if there had been any resemblance between them. The eyes maybe? That same startling light gray? How could I not have noticed? But the differences were so overwhelming, the straight-lined body, the hanging blonde hair. All elongated. Nora, a Modigliani of her mother. I drew her, just a pencil sketch on a sheet of butcher's paper that I kept unfurled to my right. *Nora.* I wrote it beside the picture, then erased the name, then erased the drawing too.

Only later did it occur to me that I had sketched a human figure with no self-consciousness, no hesitation, for the first time in many, many years.

Dinner was stew, thawed from the basement freezer where I stored double portions of everything I cooked in big batches—something I did every couple of months. The giant cooking day. The stew was in honor of the first breeze of fall. It wasn't cold out, not even close, but there was a noticeably different quality to the air. Owen, after drinking his end-of-day glass of water, inhaled appreciatively. "Excellent choice," he said. "That was the daughter, I presume? Out there with Alison? The evil ex-husband must be very tall. She has almost a Viking look to her."

"I guess." I ladled stew into our bowls, the same red stoneware we'd had for fifteen years, though we were down to only two from a set of twelve. "She wasn't what I expected, for sure."

"How long a stay?"

"I don't know. The long weekend, maybe? A few days? Alison looked happy."

"They came by?"

"Briefly," I said. "Just for introductions."

"Huh." He sat across from me, ripped off a chunk of bread, dipped it in his bowl. And then we were silent for a while.

That one week of ease we'd had a month before seemed like years ago.

"It's supposed to stay cooler like this for a few days," Owen said.

"That's good. It's been a beautiful week. Nice for their visit, across the way."

"How's your dad doing? I keep meaning to ask." He broke off another piece of bread. "No new episodes, I gather?"

"I spoke to one of the nurses yesterday. I should go back soon. But there's nothing new. Not really."

"I should go with you," he said.

"It doesn't matter to him. I promise."

"Fucking nightmare," he said.

"That's for sure."

After a couple more minutes passed, he asked, "So, what's Alison like as a mother?"

"She seems . . . just as you'd think. Very maternal. Very happy. Beaming."

He nodded. "That makes sense. She seems like a motherly type. You see it when she talks about the daughter."

"Nora."

"Right. Nora."

We ate for a few more minutes.

"Things have changed a lot, haven't they?" he asked; and for a strange moment I thought he meant between us; but then he said, "Since Alison got here."

"I suppose. I don't know. What do you mean?"

He frowned. "I mean, there's obviously a big difference. Since for two and a half years we barely spoke to a soul and now we . . . we have a . . ."

"Neighbor?"

"Come on, Gus. There are neighbors and there are neighbors. I'm not sure you see how much time you spend with her. How much she occupies your thoughts."

I took a bite of stew. "I don't see the issue here. It's time when you're working—"

"Trying to work," he said. "Let's not elevate the activity."

"I really don't understand your problem with her. She doesn't take away from us."

"She doesn't take away from our time together," he said. "That's true. Pretty much." He stood, refilled his water glass. "Don't make more of this than it is, Gus. I'm not attacking Alison. I just miss the days when we were out here all alone. There's a part of me that's looking forward to when her lease runs out. Except I'm afraid . . ."

"What?"

He turned from the sink and faced me. "Oh, you know," he said. "How you gonna keep 'em down on the farm, after they've seen Paree? I just hope that when she's gone, our solitary, rural life is enough for you."

"Don't be ridiculous," I said. "I couldn't be any happier with what we have. Yes, I like Alison. I like having her here. And if every two years, a nice person moved in next door for a couple of months, I'm not sure that would be the end of the world."

"I'm not blind, or stupid," he said, sitting down. "It's been a difficult summer. I just feel . . . I suppose in a way, I should be glad you've had someone to spend time with. I know I've been . . ."

I reached across the table for his hand. "This will get better," I said. "I promise you."

He looked at me with an expression so familiar I could almost feel it gather across my own face, a combination of disbelief and hope. "I promise you," I said again.

"From your mouth to . . ."

"I promise you," I said one more time.

In bed alone, around eleven, I heard them coming home, laughter slicing the country silence from all the way across the hill.

Owen was back out in the barn. I had been reading, but after their return, I switched off my light and rolled over to wait for sleep.

He hadn't been entirely wrong. I couldn't quite imagine myself returning to our solitude. Or rather I could imagine it all too well. Alone again in paradise with Owen. And his inability to work. And his need for me to tamp down my own excitement about my work. And his perpetual right to hate me for what I had done—a right he never seemed to exercise, a fact that somehow didn't make it go away.

Had I been lonely for years? If I had been before Alison's arrival, I hadn't known it. There had been such a feeling of relief when we'd moved. And a feeling of safety. Until Alison brought me companionship and loneliness all at once, a package deal of some mean-spirited sort.

If Alison had never arrived . . . If Laine had never stopped being my student . . .

The only thing you are allowed to take from an affair is wisdom.

You can't say you are glad you did it or had moments of joy, but you can say that you learned a lot from your mistakes. And I did say that—to Owen and to myself. But in truth it was never clear that I had learned enough. After Bill, I spent so much time thinking about regret. Regret and its accompanying conviction that there is a perfect, placid life, one's own alternate existence, pristine and simple, existing in a neighboring reality in which certain turns in the road were never set upon. And it isn't true. Any of it. I knew that. I had learned it. But it is an irresistible fantasy, if only because it implies we have some control over our fates.

Owen came downstairs the next morning an hour or so after me. I was in the studio, but left my paints to join him. It was a cloudy day and in the kitchen, a space that tended toward dark, it could easily have been evening.

"Good morning," he said, as I approached.

"You're down later than usual." I sat, keeping my paint-smeared hands and forearms away from the maple table, a local flea market treasure that I had somehow managed not to ruin in nearly three years.

"I had a visitor last night," Owen said, turning down the flame under the kettle.

"What do you mean?" I imagined an animal of some kind. We had a fox once in a while, the occasional raccoon.

"The daughter. Nora. Alison's daughter. It turns out she's a fan. You want tea?"

"Yes. Wait. I don't understand." I watched as he took two mugs off their hooks. "She went out to the barn? She was in the barn?"

"She's read my books. After her mother told her about us. She looked me up. And I'm a genius according to her. An inspiration.

Underappreciated. Destined to be lauded after my death, you'll be glad to know."

"She couldn't wait until morning?"

"By my best estimate, she was at least three sheets to the wind. Maybe four."

"Jesus." I hadn't seen this coming. Weren't churchgoing girls a little more reserved than that? "Well, I just hope Alison drove. Assuming she wasn't also smashed. Was Nora making a pass at you? Was this some kind of move?"

He shook his head. He poured the water. "No. This wasn't that."

"Don't sound so disappointed."

"I don't sound disappointed. Because I'm not disappointed. This was more like the impulsive act of a young girl who fancies herself a writer." He brought over the mugs, then sat across from me and yawned. "Honestly, I don't know what it was. I just hope the poor girl doesn't explode from embarrassment when she wakes up. And I hope she doesn't make a habit of dropping in any time the fancy strikes."

"Well, it's always nice to be admired. And *in vino veritas* and all. It sounds like sincere admiration."

"Oh, it was sincere all right. It was, if anything, a bit too sincere."

"I thought you said it wasn't a pass."

"It wasn't a pass. It was . . . just very sincere. That's all. That's all I mean. It was possibly embarrassingly sincere. Sincere in the way that a reasonable, adult person might regret in the cold light of day."

"Well, she's young," I said. "She may not yet have a sense of how embarrassing a thing like that should be. She may not even remember it, if she was drunk as all that."

"Maybe not," he said, but in doubting tones.

"According to a certain extremely hung over young woman," Alison began as soon as we crossed paths outside that afternoon, "it seems your husband may have had a late night visit from an aspiring author and fan. Needless to say, I didn't know anything about it at the time. Please apologize on both our behalves."

"Oh, he didn't mind," I said—which was true enough. I had been more put out than Owen. "He could use a little ego boosting these days."

"Well, she wants to die. Of course. Though mixed in there is all kinds of stuff about being thrilled to have met him."

I laughed—part of my newly devised strategy for dealing with any crush Nora might be developing. I would make the whole thing out to be a joke. Ridiculous. "Tell her she doesn't have to die. We're artists, tell her. We're old bohemians. We're used to odd behavior. She didn't even register on the odd behavior scale. He was very flattered I'm sure. In fact . . ." I glanced toward the barn as if to consult. "In fact, aren't we on for dinner tonight? Ten seconds at our house and she'll know not to feel bad. We'll all have a good laugh together."

"It may take some convincing Nora," Alison said. "But assume we'll be there." She reached out and squeezed my arm. "She's already been punished with a wicked hangover. Poor thing. Stupid of me to let her get like that. Terrible mothering to let her drink so much."

I surprised myself by wondering if there wasn't some truth to that. "I'll admit I don't expect that kind of traipsing from true believers," I said.

"That, of all things, is no defense."

"I guess that's right," I said. "I shouldn't assume that everyone who believes in God is . . ."

"Well behaved?" Alison laughed. "Well, she is, at heart. I

mean, I do think the religion steadies her, not that she needs special steadying. But it surely doesn't mean she never gets drunk and acts idiotic. That would have taken better parenting, not more piety."

"Hardly," I said; though again, I did wonder if she wasn't right.

Owen greeted the news that Alison and Nora would be joining us for dinner with mock horror, but I wasn't convinced that the prospect of an admiring young woman at the table upset him one bit.

"Why don't you go put on your most dashing pair of shorts?" I called as he climbed upstairs to take a shower.

"Excellent idea," he called back. "The dress cargoes tonight."

Life. It begins and begins and begins. An infinite number of times. It is all beginnings until the end comes. Sometimes we know it and sometimes we do not, but at every moment life begins again. Nora. Young. And elegant—shockingly so, something that hadn't quite come through at our hurried first meeting. Young and elegant with a single pearl in each earlobe, the cross nestled between her collarbones. She wore a simple black sundress. And she was very beautiful, another surprise, as though it were a switch she had turned on since arriving the day before. Green eyes—bright like her mother's but a different shade. Straight blonde hair, fine and shining, lines of light shifting through it with her every move.

"I feel like such an idiot," she said, leaning against our refrigerator. Owen was not yet downstairs. "When I drink I have horrible impulse control and the people who love me have to deal with that, I'm afraid."

The people who love me.

Also the people who don't, I thought, but did not say. "We all have our shortcomings," I said, instead. "Anyway, I think you probably made his year."

She groaned. "I don't even remember what I said." She was playing with a clay palette-shaped magnet from the fridge, an ancient gift from Charlotte. I had to restrain myself from taking it from her lest it somehow break.

Alison said, "I'm sure you're far too well brought up to be rude."

"I think you just told him nice things about his work," I said. "There isn't a writer on earth who wouldn't enjoy that." I walked past her, a platter of baked chicken in my hands. "Why don't you put that magnet back and come sit down," I said. "We'll pour some wine and we'll eat, and you'll forget it ever happened."

Our dining room table, an inherited oval of no particular distinction, came from my childhood home. I had covered it that afternoon with three overlapping cloths, set at angles so some of each color showed: white, then pale gray, and then a dark rose one, on top. And I had gotten out the good china too—which meant an array of mismatched but very fine pieces we had picked up at garage sales over the years. I'd cut wildflowers and set them in green glass jars, one at each end of the table, with half a dozen candles randomly arranged. Long ago, back in the city, I had painted our chairs, also mismatched, all the same shade of dark gray, and lacquered them. They looked like shadows in the candlelight, shadows in sculptural form.

Stepping through from the living room and seeing it all gave me a flash of great pleasure. It wasn't often that Owen and I bothered to eat in surroundings that honored the activity. For the most part we sat in the kitchen, which I also loved, but which was dark and hardly celebratory. Or we shared the couch and stared together into a fire. And all of that was good, it was companionable and certainly convenient, but I had almost forgotten the pleasure of giving a room a magical aura like this one now had.

"This is lovely," Alison said.

"Cool chairs," Nora said. "I love how nothing matches but somehow everything does."

"Thanks. I like to think I was shabby before shabby was chic."

When Owen appeared, he stopped at the door to take it all in, the table and the three women then sitting at it too. He smiled at me and nodded just once, barely at all, a private tip of his hat to the tableau.

"No one makes a table like Gussie does," he said, as he sat.

"I've made baked chicken, nothing fancy, but lots of garlic. And salad. And there's some bread that's just the frozen stuff from the grocery store that you throw in your oven but is actually surprisingly good." As I spoke, I noticed Nora briefly close her eyes and lower her head. "So eat up," I said. "It's simple but it's plentiful."

We began passing dishes, and it was obvious even in candlelight that Nora was blushing her way through meeting up with Owen again. She, who hadn't struck me as the least bit shy earlier, was suddenly bashful and stiffly formal as she apologized to him for her visit. He assured her it had been absolutely fine, but an element of discomfort hung in the air until Alison intervened. "There's clearly only one way to manage this," she said. "So we can all move on. Each of us has to tell an embarrassing story about something we did when drunk or otherwise impaired."

Owen laughed. "I don't think we have enough time," he said. "There was a good two years in there where I mostly made a fool of myself, full-time. Right before I met Gussie. Not that you made a fool of yourself," he added to Nora. "Anyway, luckily, I've forgotten most of those days."

I took some salad and passed the bowl. Every embarrassing episode I could remember had something to do with throwing myself at someone, flirting outrageously with a professor, kissing the boyfriend of a friend. I couldn't see how parading a series of disinhibited-crush stories was going to help. "Nora, why don't you tell us what you have planned, now that you're back stateside? Are you working? Do you have a job?"

"Well, I'm looking," she said. "It's not a great time to be your basic generic English-major college grad. It used to be if you were willing to work for pretty low pay, you could get a job, but it's not that easy now. It's really hard."

"I'm sure you're underselling yourself," I said.

"She is," Alison said. "Nora's got all kinds of things she could do."

"And you'll never regret having read all those books," Owen said—which I thought sounded a little pompous and not really like him, even though it was a sentiment he doubtless believed.

As we ate, the conversation continued to revolve around Nora. We heard about her trip to Italy and, prompted by Owen, she talked about the writing she had done in college—blushing again, all through that topic.

"I did a modern take on *The Decameron,*" she said. "That was my thesis. A reconsideration of the stories, as if they were in current-day America. I read Italian, so that part was fun."

"That sounds ambitious," Owen said. "You must have something like a book."

"Well, maybe it's like a book, but it's definitely not a real book. They're pretty bad. I mean, it was a good experience, but it's not anything I'd want to work on ever again."

She didn't remind me of Laine—not at all, Laine with her tattoos, her exploding enthusiasms, and her longing for badass creds—except in the unself-conscious way the young can talk so obsessively about themselves, sometimes charmingly, sometimes tediously. I wondered if Alison had any impulse to redirect the topic or nudge her daughter to ask us some questions about our lives, but she seemed entirely happy just listening. Occasionally, she would beam my way, as if to say *Isn't she just amazing? Isn't she lovely?* And I would beam back, all the while feeling a steadily growing emotional pressure in myself. What must it feel like to be so adored? To be able to change how a parent carries herself? To produce such expressions of joy? My father had rewarded our accomplishments and expressed a quiet pride in us. But was he ever blinded by love? Would he ever have just basked in the sound of my voice? Heard every word I spoke on a flattering frequency?

And then, as the minutes passed, the inevitable, ancient question: Would my mother have? Would she have given me this devoted attention, this unchallenged right to center stage? It was easy enough to think so, sitting there. Charlotte, all of seven when our mother died, had often told me stories about the fun we all had baking cupcakes, singing in the car, playing in the park. *She loved pushing us on swings,* she would say, trying to slip her memories into my soul. *She kissed us goodnight every night, in bed. She woke us up with kisses, too.* In a sense it had worked. I carried distinct images to go with every story Charlotte told, each snippet hovering in the generous space where imagination and memory blur. *She sang songs in French sometimes.* But since Charlotte's death, I had felt those images fade as well. And my father was now incapable of having the conversations that he had always refused to have— unless his roulette-wheel mind happened to spin that way one day.

Watching Alison and Nora, smiling at them when appropriate, asking questions as needed to keep the conversational flow, I realized that there was no one left who could remember my mother. Maybe a cousin somewhere, an old neighbor. But not anyone close to me. Not anyone I could find. It had turned out to be a three-stage death: first hers, then Charlotte's, and then this horrifying slow leak taking place in my father's brain. And then there were none.

"You looked preoccupied at dinner," Owen said, as we lay in bed later in the dark, both of us just too drunk to consider trying to work. "You looked a little blue."

"I may be a little blue," I said. "It will pass."

"Anything I can do?"

It turned out that there was, though until he had asked, I hadn't known. Darkness and sex. Desire poured from me in a way I didn't expect and I'm sure he didn't either as I wrapped my arms around his back, pulling him close enough that at moments the goal became barely sexual, but only an embrace so intense that I could feel nothing else.

My dear Laine, I wrote the next morning. *Huge embarrassed apologies for taking so long to respond. It's been a difficult summer here and I've been waiting for time enough to give you a full sense of things, but then of course that time never does come. Owen has been struggling with work and my father's health is deteriorating. And we have a neighbor! This is such a huge change. I like her— which is a blessing because at these close quarters if she were awful it could be a disaster. But even that, just making a new friend, is strangely disruptive. You know what a hermit I can be if left to my own devices.*

Mostly, though, I am so happy to hear that the summer has been a productive one for you. (And I hope that's still true . . .) And by productive I mean both art and dumping any poser boyfriends. It's been productive for me too, in spite of all these distractions. I'm at work on a project, a series of paintings that are exciting me in a way I haven't felt for years. But of course I'm also thrown right back to where we all get thrown with anything new: the whipsaw of imagined greatness and certain failure. You would think after all these years there would be some way to moderate the extremes, but apparently not. So I am pinging around in a distinctly bipolar way, but I am being productive, so I don't really care that I feel a little unhinged.

I stopped then. Because I had surprised myself with that word. Did I feel unhinged? Not at that moment. But I left it in.

I hadn't known your father was marrying. I hope it is a fun event.

I deleted that.

I hadn't known your father was marrying. Please give him my best.

I deleted that.

I hope the wedding is wonderful. My best wishes to you all.

I settled on that and went on,

Please don't hold my slow reply against me and please let me know what you're up to, soon. And next time, ahem, a few pictures of your work wouldn't hurt. I want to see what you're doing! I am certain that it's wonderful.
    Love,
    Augie

I might never receive the adoration I'd watched young Nora receive all night, but I didn't have to ignore the one person alive on whom I could lavish it.

9

From my studio, all that Sunday, I caught glimpses of activity by Alison's house and toward the barn and on the path between, but I tried not to keep close track of the comings and goings—of anyone. The two women out in the car. The younger popping in to ask her new favorite author for some advice. The man crossing over the hill, a book in hand. I tried not to keep track. I didn't altogether succeed. Not at first. But gradually it all faded into background.

When I was a child, long before it occurred to anyone to be sensitive about such things, my sisters and I had special parent visiting days at our school. *Celebrate Mom!* It wasn't always that bad; but we were almost always the only children without a mother, and in the 1960s, the '70s, a visiting parent still meant a visiting mom. Each of us dealt with it differently. Charlotte, the ultimate lemonade-from-lemons girl, would try to share a friend's mother for the day, and when asked at dinner how it went would say, "Fine. It was fun," as though there were no reason to imagine otherwise. Jan, the youngest and probably the smartest of us all, would announce matter-of-factly that she would be staying home, interrupting our father's gruff offer to wander over from his own classroom, before he could get all the words out. And I would take the middle path, the compromise solution that so often means misery. I would go to school. And feel sorry for myself. Not pretend I had a mother. Not pretend my father was an acceptable substitute. Not pretend at all. But tough it out.

That was the idea anyway, but we can be more self-protective than we intend. I don't remember the earliest events, first grade, second grade, not clearly, not beyond the regular pulse of self-pity and jealousy beating through my heart. But I do remember a parents' day when I was eleven or so and realized that I could be there and still not be there at all. I only had to draw. Or paint. Or not even do either of those things, but just imagine doing them; think about what my next picture would be; and look around me, no longer seeing mothers and children, only objects, subjects, surfaces. Light.

During the second day of Nora's visit, I retreated again to that place.

I worked on the boy on my front steps again, Oliver Farley, using my drawings for early reference, continuing to paint around the empty canvas I thought of as him. Our rarely used front door is black, and I worked a good long time that day defining the raised panels, catching the gleam of the large brass doorknob, then muting it, as in real life, showing it worn and softened with age. That doorknob, barely a third of an inch on my canvas, took me the better part of two hours—and I knew I might need to change it later if another look outside revealed any missteps.

I sometimes think of such visual details as deep, private pools of water into which I dive alone. I am oblivious at those times to anything beyond my sense that there is a way to communicate to others exactly how the world appears to me. This is the precision for which I strive. Some kind of commitment to accuracy, my belief that the appearance of a thing can flow right through me and out to another set of eyes. And not just the appearance, but the beauty to be found—even in things not inherently beautiful.

There is an urgency I feel, maybe with its roots in those early childhood days of using art as an escape, but maybe not. Maybe just a part of me, whatever the history of my life.

I went through a period, in college, and for a while after then, of accepting that my work was old-fashioned—and fretting over the condemnation of that term. I had friends who were conceptual artists, of course, friends who did bizarre, socially disruptive installations, friends who were blessed—I believed—with the conviction that they could reinvent not only art, but thought. And I could do neither, I knew, which knowledge deflated me. But in the end I understood that I had no choice. I knew what I was, this vessel for taking in, holding, and then releasing again the facts of what I saw.

And there were arguments of course, late-night debates with our ever-present artist friends, since that word, *facts,* is not itself an accurate one. Each observation I have and then try to convey— always, that word, *convey,* always that desire to communicate— was warped and altered by my perspective. But it was an accurate enough way to describe what I understood myself to be, and an accurate enough way to describe the sensations that created the isolated trance into which I would fall while at work.

At some point that morning, Owen leaned in to say he was taking the women into town for lunch, asking if I wanted to come along; and I said no, but thanked him and told him to have fun. I didn't add that I'd had enough for a twenty-four-hour period of watching Alison worship Nora and Nora worship Owen, but I had.

By the time they came back, though I heard the car and then voices, it all seemed distant again. This was the power I had discovered as a motherless child, and could still access—sometimes. The power to make the unreal real, and make the real world go away.

But then in the late afternoon, while my focus was set entirely

on the diamond-shaped leaded glass windows on either side of our
front door, reality asserted itself. The phone. My father, out of control again. He had broken a mug and used it to threaten a nurse.
There were going to have to be some changes after all. Could I be
there the next morning for a consult?

It wasn't a question. I would go.

Owen would go too. That also wasn't a question. For a moment,
I'd thought he wouldn't offer, that the lure of an admiring young
acolyte would keep him home, but I had underestimated him.
There wasn't a breath of distance between us as we sat at our sor-
rowful dinner and talked through the coming process. Winnowing, winnowing. When we'd first moved my father, we'd winnowed
the old house into his new efficiency apartment; and now we
would winnow again. But even the winnowing had been winnowed. It wouldn't be a big job this time. No kitchen for him—
too dangerous to have breakables that could be hurled, knives,
even forks. And barred windows from now on too. Winnowed
windows. Winnowed windows for my winnowing widower father.
As I fell asleep my mind was filled with such phrases, nonsense,
surrendering to the nonsensical nature of life.

We met the doctor at eight in the family conference room, fur-
nished like a mid-level hotel, decorated with posters of worse-
than-mediocre art, pointless, meaningless washes of pastels,
framed in gold. We sat at a lacquered mahogany table that shone
in ways that struck me, ever obsessive about shine, about shadow,
as artificial in some way. The doctor was a youngster, an unfamiliar face who must have started there over the summer, almost
Owen's height with coarse red hair through which he ran his enormous hand at regular intervals. He looked nervous and not up to

the job of telling us what he had to tell us—even though we already knew what he would say and he knew that we knew. A necessary relocation. A different protocol. There was a three-strikes policy, he said. I pointed out that there had only been two strikes.

"It's possible no one told you about the first, in case it was a one-time event."

I wondered if the young nurse, Lydia, guilty still about provoking his flood of tears, had spared me a report.

Inexperienced and filled with more rules than wisdom, the doctor then went into unnecessary detail about the policy itself—about how sometimes it turned out that the nature of a single episode might be enough to trigger a change and in other cases the three-strikes policy could be suspended and on and on, as Owen and I raised our eyebrows at one another and widened our eyes but managed somehow not to be rude while we brought the conversation back to my father and his care.

"Has he been told what's going on?" I asked.

No. He hadn't. They always preferred to have family there to help explain it all to the patient. "Though in my experience," the doctor said, the notion of experience hanging around him like a too-large overcoat, "that can actually sometimes make things worse."

"How reassuring," I muttered to Owen as we trailed down the hall.

My father had always had a temper, but of a quiet, steady kind. It was part of what made him so effective as a teacher, I thought, that he knew when to be angry and allowed himself to be, but not in a dramatic way. And certainly not with any threat of violence. Clarity. That was one of his defining qualities. He would never yell and scream but he didn't buy the idea of calling anger by euphemistic names. When Owen and I were still in Philadelphia, surrounded by young families, we would hear the same parental spiel over and over: *I'm not angry, I'm just upset; I'm not angry, I'm just frustrated; I'm not angry, I was just worried about where you were.*

"I am furious at you both," my father would say if Charlotte and I came home late. And it meant a week of grounding or extra chores or both; and it also meant a day or so of palpable, lingering anger, detectable in a lack of interest in whatever we had to say, the failure to involve us in deciding what dinner would be for a while. We were ignored as he went into the backyard, lit a cigarette, and sat by himself, or disappeared into his bedroom—a couple of pull-ups on his way.

But what I saw in his eyes the day we walked into his little apartment was something new. A wild animal had slipped beneath his skin.

"Hi, Dad," I said.

"Hi, Sam," Owen said.

He didn't know us. And he didn't like us. I looked at the doctor for guidance and was surprised to find a transformed man. In this setting, he exuded authority. Later, in the car, I would tell Owen that should I ever be in a demented, disoriented rage, *that* was the doctor I wanted him to phone. He called my father Mr. Edelman, which alone seemed to soothe him—in a way that neither "Dad" nor his first name had. Here was a young fellow calling him Mr. Edelman. Could he feel himself becoming the teacher again?

"It seems like you've been having a tough time, Mr. Edelman."

"This black woman . . ." My father gestured toward the door. I felt the blood rise to my cheeks. "She won't let me go out."

"Yes. That's right. Those are my orders. I asked the nurses to make sure you stay put. We don't allow our patients to do anything unsafe."

"Ha!" My father looked at me. "Any time a Jew is locked up, you want to watch for that. Any time they start talking about their orders . . ."

"Your daughter . . . ," the doctor began; and my father frowned.

"That's me," I said. "Augusta."

He shrugged a little, made a face, not arguing the point but not entirely accepting it either. "And this?" he asked, with a shift in gaze.

"My husband. Owen. You like him."

He looked doubtful.

"You used to like him. I promise."

The doctor cleared his throat. "We have to make a few changes, Mr. Edelman. Starting with your room. We're moving you to a different part of the facility. You'll have some of the same nurses there with you, at least for a while, so it won't be all new."

"And I can visit you much more. If you want."

"In general, you'll be getting a more steady level of care . . ."

The unfamiliar rage in my father's eyes had been replaced by a look I did recognize: utter bewilderment, filmed over with an attempt to hide it. He nodded, as if comprehending, while clearly not comprehending. The doctor explained that though he would be moving that day, we'd have a little while to move his belongings. "Your daughter will make sure you have the things that matter most to you."

"And the rest, I'll keep just at my house," I said—for all the world as though the second half of the sentence were: . . . *so someday you can have it all back.*

When we emerged from the home, the sky had opened up, a perfect rumbling thunderstorm. We were drenched as we ran to the car. Owen drove, and any possible conversation was lost to the attention he had to pay as the windshield wipers struggled against the deluge.

Jan would be back from Nova Scotia in three days and the place had agreed to let us wait to clean everything out together. I had picked half a dozen items to go with him, transition objects, like little children use. I wavered over my own painting as if it were some sort of symbolically important decision, and then put it with the other things on his bed. That painting. A picture of me, Charlotte, and Jan in our teen years, all looking like he had told us to stand up straight and think about brussels sprouts. That was my one smile as I packed: that this sourpuss lineup was his favorite shot of us. I tried to include a porcelain figurine of a dog that had belonged to his mother, but was told that nothing that could be thrown, broken, or in any way rendered sharp could go with him, so I wrapped it in a washcloth and put it in my own bag.

When we got home, I ran through the rain, but got soaked again anyway. Upstairs, I stripped everything off, put on a bathrobe, lay down in bed and soon fell asleep—as though the events of the day were like a fever that had left me weak. I woke to find Owen sitting beside me. "I didn't think you'd want to sleep all afternoon and then be up all night." His hand was on my shoulder. I turned over, away from him, knowing he would rub my back.

"I feel like someone dropped an anvil on me," I said. "Me and Wile E. Coyote."

"Life dropped an anvil on you."

As he kneaded my shoulder, I closed my eyes. "It'll be better when Jan gets home. She's so competent. She makes everything feel manageable."

Neither of us spoke for a minute or so and then he said, "We've been invited for dinner—by the neighbors. The daughter leaves tomorrow. But only if you're up to it. I told Alison I wasn't sure, that you might just want to hunker down tonight."

"That actually sounds fine," I said. "I can't just lie here in the dark all night."

"You can do anything you want."

I stretched out some more, arching my back. "Right there," I said. "Right next to my spine. That's what I want."

At Alison's we ate in the living room, Owen and I on her couch, each of the others on a chair. She'd made chili and rice. It was all very simple and should also have been comforting. But the shift in dynamics since our dinner just two nights before unnerved me. During the day when I'd absented myself working, and maybe also during my sleeping hours that afternoon, Owen and Nora had moved well beyond the polite talk of strangers. Somehow. It was as though a thin pane of glass had shattered between them—but stayed intact just enough to keep me on the other side.

Alison was solicitous, offering every imaginable kind of help. She would drive me to visit my father. She would make us dinners. She would be a shoulder. "You deserve some coddling right now," she said.

"What Gus really needs," Owen said, "is to get back into her work. Gus is always at her happiest there."

"It's true," I said, though vaguely irritated at the claim.

"Well then, I can also leave you alone to work. Whatever you need. This is such a difficult thing to go through."

And so the evening wore on, worries about me alternating with more talk about the sorts of jobs Nora should be looking for back in Boston. She thought maybe something to do with early education—*those jobs are still pretty available*—though she really wanted to work in publishing, at least for a while. Owen, a whiskey or two in, proclaimed that that would be soul-destroying, unless she could find a small press filled with people who did it just for the love. She asked what he thought about people applying right after college for graduate programs. He said he thought it was a shame that she couldn't just take some time to write *before all the vultures set in*. Alison thought she should consider whether she really wanted to be around little kids and their germs all the time. . . . And then someone would ask me how I was doing; and I would say fine, and that it was so interesting to watch someone teetering on the cusp of adulthood; or something equally inane. And as an hour passed, then another, I felt as though I were being aged, rapidly, like the beautiful princess in the fairy tale who is suddenly revealed to be an old crone, every aspect of me having to do with repair, while across the table from me sat the embodiment of potential.

Yet I didn't hate Nora that night. Even if I envied her youth and her devoted mother and the amount of attention she seemed to accept without noticing. I felt I owed it to Alison and even to myself to get past all that. Yes, she was self-absorbed, but now that she had relaxed, it seemed less as though that was the result of ego and was instead entirely appropriate for a young woman excited about her life and also excited to have met someone to idolize. She was a bit short on boundaries, but to be otherwise at twenty-two might have been off-putting in its own way. For all her elegance and beauty, she clearly didn't have her life figured out at all, and even the drunken barn episode, I decided, could be folded into this larger picture, as a typical overstep of youth. I noted that she stood to help her mother, clearing plates, wrapping food, slicing the pound cake, brewing the coffee. Alison had joked about her being well brought up and I'd had my doubts; but in some ways she clearly had been.

On the walk home, I said something nice about Nora to Owen, and he made a sound, an *umhmm* or a *yep,* which seemed a little distant, as though his mind was elsewhere. And then he put his hand on my back and said, "It's been a long day, hasn't it?"

"Yes," I said. "It's been a very long day."

Later, as I lay awake, sleep playing hard to get, it occurred to me to wonder if there had been anything in that sound he made, the *umhmm* or *yep,* to which I should have been attentive, whether in its indecipherable, preoccupied quality, there lay a clue to something worrisome. I had spent so long fearing that a young woman, adoring and beautiful, would make easy any need the universe might feel to even scores. And now one had shown up as if sent from central casting. But she would be leaving in the morning, I knew. And my tired mind longed to be at peace. So I shook the worry off.

10

The shouts from Alison's yard drew me from my studio and Owen from the barn. A man. "Maybe if you weren't such a FUCKING selfish cunt . . ." I could only see his back. Alison stood facing him, one step up on her porch. The ex-husband. Paul. It had to be. I thought Nora must be inside until I saw the window of the strange black car go down. "It doesn't matter," Nora yelled, her head leaning out. "Stop it. Just stop it! None of it matters anymore. Please . . . please just stop it. I want to go. Can we please just go?"

Owen and I, fifty feet apart, exchanged a look. Should we intervene? But then the man slammed his way into the driver's seat and with more noise, more havoc, drove away; and Alison went inside.

"Jesus," I said, as Owen and I met up. "That was . . . I thought someone else was picking Nora up. The friend. Martha. Or Heather. Heather, I think."

He was still staring at Alison's yard. "I thought so too."

"I should go over there. See if she's okay."

"I don't know." He looked at me. "I don't know if you should. Maybe let her settle down a bit?"

"That's just wrong," I said. "Why are you saying that?"

"I don't know. I'm just not sure you want to get more involved."

"Well, I'm sure I do. And you should be too."

When I called "Hi there" into the house, Alison answered, "Up here." At the foot of the steps, I said that I was just checking in. I said that I could go if she wanted me to, that I didn't mean to barge in.

"No, come on up," she called. So I climbed the stairs, trying to avoid tripping on the tattered runner as I did.

"I'm in the bedroom, toward the back. On the right."

I had been in the hall often before, every time I'd gone into her studio. But it had a different feel to it with Paul's bellowing voice still vibrating in the air. I wondered that I'd never noticed the absence of a light, the cracking plaster walls. When I reached her bedroom, I only peered around the door. She sat on the bed, leaning against a maple headboard, her legs straight, crossed at the ankles, her arms crossed too.

"I just wanted to check on you," I said. "Be sure you're okay."

She was shaking her head. "He isn't supposed to know where I am. And Nora knows that. He isn't supposed to be here. Ever."

"I'm so sorry."

She patted the bed and I stepped into the room, sat beside her. "I had no idea," I said.

"Thanks for checking on me." She reached over, laying her hand over mine.

"You had told me, I just hadn't . . ." Hadn't what? I had believed her—in a sense. I certainly hadn't thought she'd been lying about his hitting her. But there was some other way in which I hadn't given it enough thought, hadn't forced myself to imagine her being slugged, the power, the fear. The part about hitting had come up when I'd been so upset by Laine's news about Bill, and all of my attention had been on that. My own little melodrama had allowed me to glide over what she had been through.

"I didn't really get it," I said. "I should have been more aware."

"You have enough to worry about," she said. "Your father . . . everything. I don't understand how he got here. I know Nora wouldn't have told him. She doesn't . . . she doesn't know every detail, but she knows enough. I told her, 'I'd rather your father didn't know . . . ,' and then how could she not tell me he was coming?" Her eyes were starting to brim.

"I'm sure it was just a mistake. She let something slip. Or he . . . maybe something about her cell? Maybe he could find her?"

She laughed, which pushed a tear down her cheek. "I don't think even Paul is nuts enough to have her tracked on a GPS. I just . . . Oh well. It's done. And you should know . . ." She was looking right at me. ". . . well, you saw. He's awful. He's so awful. I wanted a few months' break from his rage."

"I just hate that you've lived with that." The room smelled like her, I realized, that distinctive lime perfume, but then also a little musty, the aging wood of old homes. "What was he so angry about, anyway? If I can ask."

"Money," she said. "Stupid, minor things about selling the house. But it could have been anything. It's really about me walking out on him—probably. Who knows. It's two years. More. And before I did that, it was a million other things."

The windows were open, white curtains floating in a breeze too mild to be felt. The furniture, mismatched, some maple like the bed, some mahogany, looked as though it had been in the house for eighty years or more. So did the wallpaper, yellowed, vertical stripes of tiny flowers buckling so few of the lines appeared to be straight.

She seemed to read my mind. "The website made it sound a bit less shabby than it actually is, but I don't care. I love it here."

"No, I wouldn't care either."

She sat up a little straighter. "You know, he's never been at all that way with her. Nothing like he is with me. I just hate for her even to see it."

"That's good that he's better with her."

"And she uses the religion, you know. It keeps her tied to him. 'Honor thy father,' all of that. I figured it out a while back. I'm sure that's part of why she took to it. It's a system. Rules. You know, children almost never do break off. Not really. This just gives her a reason to hang in with him, I think."

It was so difficult not to stare at her, just trying to take it in as real. Even as I could hear his angry voice still ringing in my ears, it was impossible to imagine. Her beauty had everything to do with a certain delicate quality. He must once have seen that clearly, must once have loved it in her.

Alison was staring toward the motion of the curtains, two white flags fluttering. "I know Nora spent a lot of her time here with Owen. And I was really glad for that. Your Owen is so calm and so reassuring. He seems . . . unflappable. And he was very gentle with her about her literary ambitions. I kept thinking it had to be good for her to be around a man like that. I hope he didn't mind. I hope she wasn't a bother for either of you."

"Oh, Lord. Owen enjoyed the ego boost. It's been such a rough period. Workwise, I mean."

"Well, he certainly got that." She turned back toward me, a real smile hovering. "Nora seems to worship him," she said. "She was entirely star-struck." But then the smile fell. "I just don't understand how Paul found us. And where the hell is Heather? How did the plans get all changed around? It makes no sense at all."

"You'll find out. You'll talk to her." I was pondering Owen as a father figure. A positive male influence. Maybe something like the role I had played for Laine.

"I should go paint," she said. "That's what you would do,

right? I should stop feeling sorry for myself and go make something."

"Maybe. Though . . ." Did I stop feeling sorry for myself when I worked? In a way. Often, I stopped feeling much at all. "You should paint if it will help. Or, I don't know, we could go out? It's Tuesday, you know."

"Right. That's not a bad idea." She sat up a tiny bit. "That might be just the thing."

The fact that the local farmers' market fell on Tuesday afternoons had been information haphazard in my consciousness until Alison's arrival; but by then it was woven into the rhythm of every week. We agreed to meet on the hill at two forty-five.

"I'll drive," she said, and I feigned horror, but agreed. As I stood, I considered leaning to kiss her. She would have, had the roles been reversed, I knew. But I only said, "See you in just a bit."

While I painted that afternoon, I thought about violence. I hadn't been around much in my life, yet when I'd heard it outside my window I had known it right away, known the difference between a raised voice anyone might use and the sort that carries physical weight behind it, the sort that seems somehow connected to tissue, to muscle, in a seamless continuum that could lead to impact. In this case it had been only the slam of a car door, the screech of tires, the foot too hard on the accelerator. Nobody hurt. But violence nonetheless.

I was back to working on Jackie and his chessboard that day, fiddling with the light coming in through the window—a west-facing window, so low, falling light. Violence had killed these boys, every one of them, but violence of a chillingly impersonal sort.

The paintings were tender ones, and I wondered if more evidence of violence should be found. The word *potential* came to mind. That was really what had been in that terrible voice. The potential for violence. Like the wild animal slipped beneath my father's skin, staring at me through his eyes. Was it something I wanted in the pictures? Some glimpse of the tension produced by that potential in the air? How would I do it, if I wanted to?

It was all outside my experience. Even when decimated, Owen had never shown the palest hint of a threat in his voice or demeanor. And Bill. Bill and I had been tender with each other in the way only lovers with stolen time can sustain. Even in parting, gentle, gentle, gentle, like the tedious people who must unwrap every present slowly, leaving the paper entirely intact.

I looked around the studio, at the paintings, the sketches leaning against the wall and taped to boards, and I realized that these weren't depictions of potential of any kind. Not for violence and not for love and not for happiness or misery or disloyalty or forgiveness. They were something else, something far more resonant for me. "Consequence." I said the word out loud, and went back to work.

With Alison at the wheel, I braced myself.

It was a cool day for the second week of September. We talked about the surprising early signs of fall—surprising though they arrived at this time each year. The scrubbier maples, we agreed, were always the first to turn and never made it beyond yellow. The Japanese would be the last to go out in their scarlet, phosphorescent blaze. But this summer had been a wet one, so the whole show promised to go on a long time. Well-nourished trees were always slow to drop their leaves, I said.

"I hope I'm still here then," Alison said. "I have some decisions to make. I'd been counting on being lost, I suppose. Lost to him, anyway."

"Oh, you have to stay."

"We'll see. That's very nice of you."

"Just don't think about it today," I said. "Just enjoy being here."

"Okay." And then after a silent stretch, she said, "I've had days here when I can almost forget about Paul, you know."

"Another reason for you to stay."

"Yes. If I still can."

As Alison drove, she told me more about him than she ever had before: how they had met back in London, how surprisingly happy they had been in those early days. "He was the most magnetic man I'd ever known," she said. "And romantic. Very good at the big gestures, the bouquets, the thoughtful gifts. I've never been sure how much he changed and how much I started noticing more of what he really was. Probably some of both."

By the time Nora was born, she said, they were already caught in a terrible cycle of fights and then those grand, sweeping declarations of love. "Those good moments always seemed like windows to a whole new life. I was constantly looking for the turning point. Eighteen years in, I was still telling myself that things were going to improve. And the sad part is I could read about it in any book. I would. I would go to bookstores and sneak into the self-help section, and I knew, at a certain level I knew that all couples become the same couple. There I'd be. Page sixteen. The enabling spouse. Exhibit A. I saw it. Even before he started hitting me. I knew it. I did. But I didn't accept it. Not for a very long time. To be defined by something so . . . so ultimately not about me. To see myself staring out from a page. It felt impossible in some way. I thought I should be more my own person. It sounds odd, but I found it insulting."

"That's how I feel about my father sometimes," I said. "I'm not saying it's the same, God knows. It's not. But just . . . just the way it's all taken his . . . his particular nature away. There's no conversation anymore about what he might do or how he might react.

Him: Sam Edelman. It's all how an Alzheimer's patient might react. The things Alzheimer's patients say. He's become generic."

"Maybe at the stress points we all become generic." She told me about pictures she had once seen of people on roller coasters. As soon as they were terrified, they all looked exactly the same. "That was the salvation though—in my case, I mean. What saved me was finally admitting that I was no different from every other abuse victim. There was no special skill I had that would make him change, no exemption because he was my husband and not some other woman's husband. We were just another married couple stuck in roles you could hear about on half a dozen talk shows any given week. And I couldn't stand the idea of having had my . . . my will taken away. My self. Once I admitted the truth, I had to leave. And once it became physical, I stopped being able to fool myself. Though even that . . . Even that didn't happen right away."

"I'm just glad you got out. I admire your strength."

"Well, it certainly felt like strength at the time. Like an enormous act of heroism. Which in retrospect . . ." She didn't finish the thought, but with a vigor I had come to expect swung us into the gravel parking lot and slammed to a stop.

Three o'clock on the Tuesday after Labor Day weekend was a quiet time at the market. The local mothers were back to picking their children up from school or waiting for them at bus stops near home; and the after-work rush—a country-style rush of maybe twenty, twenty-five at a time—was still a few hours off. That day, we had the place almost to ourselves, just an elderly couple; a young man; a younger couple. A little more than half a dozen of us, against the backdrop of stalls, bright signs, rough-hewn wood tables, aluminum ones, canvas roofs.

Alison always brought a list. I never did. She had particular vendors she preferred, and knew things like when the spinach was due for harvest and who was slaughtering chickens that week. She would ask questions and get advice on her own little garden patch, while I always hung back a bit, wandering from stall to stall like a child waiting for her mother to be done. I did make occasional purchases, but those were impulse buys and generally based on something visual. I loved the garlic scapes, the odd elongated green of them, the strange irregular curves, and so always bought a bunch when they were there, though I'd never found a way to cook them that I liked. And the mushrooms, driven over from Kennett Square; I loved their shadows and mysteries and swells, the sense of secrecy they carried, little embodiments of life lived in the dark. That day, I bought two zucchini largely because I felt sorry for the long-faced farmer drowning in his bumper crop; and then a dozen eggs, and a wheel of local Camembert that I knew Owen liked.

As I wandered, I thought of what Alison had said about becoming generic. It didn't just remind me of my father, I realized. It was also close to what I had felt about my affair. One day we were two fantastically, uniquely interesting individuals who had been lucky enough to find each other—even if under terrible circumstances. And then, five months later, I was that pathetic woman hoping a married man who would never leave his wife for me would leave his wife for me. A cliché. A soap opera trope. The humiliation of that had pushed me to end it, as much as anything else had.

When I glimpsed Alison a few stalls away, she was at one of the crafty ones, filled with jams and quilted potholders, handmade soaps. I watched her for a couple of minutes before approaching her. It was still difficult to process all she had endured. The image of her being hit sickened me.

When I joined her, she was asking questions in her curious way about varieties of vinegars. I admired how easily her mind could slip with genuine interest from one topic to the next. I had lived in the area nearly three years with only a minimal, outsider's need to know about the town or the life of the county, certainly no interest in chatting up the locals about their produce and home-canned goods; while she reveled in the human contact, seemed unable to imagine living in a place and not weaving herself into it.

I noticed the name on the stall. *Mayhew Farm.* I looked at the woman behind the counter. She was in her seventies, I thought, her cheeks a bit puffy, her skin lined, but still I could detect a resemblance there, in the square of her jaw, time-softened as its angles were, in the slope from her forehead through her short, slightly squat nose.

"Are you a Mayhew?" I asked. "Of Mayhew Farm," I added as though she needed me to explain.

"I used to be," she said. "Though I've been a Thompson for thirty-nine-odd years."

Alison picked up a bottle. "It must be wonderful," she said. "To feel so connected to a place . . . to be somewhere for so long . . ." She put it back on the vinyl gingham table cover. "I'm going to try the strawberry." She turned to me. "Strawberry vinegar with vanilla ice cream. How does that sound?"

"It sounds good. It sounds incredible." I looked at the woman again. "Has the family been here a long time?" I asked. "The Mayhews?"

She took a twenty from Alison and opened her cash box. "We've had the farm over a hundred years."

"I was just wondering . . . I heard about a Mayhew. From a while back. John. Jack. Or Jackie . . . He was in World War I."

She looked up at me, startled. "Jackie Mayhew? Jackie Mayhew was my father's brother." Her eyes narrowed. "How could you be hearing about Jackie Mayhew?"

"It's a long story," I said; and she looked around meaningfully at the emptiness around us, the absence of anyone pressing me to hurry through. "I'm an artist," I began. "I live with my husband in what used to be the Garrick place."

"I went to school with Emily Garrick. And her brother Freddy."

"We bought the house as part of an estate sale. I never met either of them. But we were doing some work on a bathroom earlier this summer . . ." I started to tell her about the newspapers and a little about the paintings. At some point, Alison touched my shoulder and pointed to a poultry stall. "I won't be long," she said, and walked away.

"Jackie Mayhew was one of the boys. One of the obituaries."

"You have his obituary?"

I repeated that I did. I told her my name and she told me hers, Kathleen. Kathleen Thompson, but Kathleen Mayhew before that.

"My poor father," she said. "He never got over it. His baby brother. He was there too, you know. But he took ill and never had to fight. He used to say that dysentery had saved his life."

The young couple had joined us at the stall. "I should let you work," I said, moving aside.

"We were wondering if you have any of that mixed berry jam today," the young man said.

"We give it as gifts all the time now," the young woman said. "Everyone loves it."

"Oh, sure. We always bring lots of that." And then to me, "So strange, you mentioning poor Jackie Mayhew. I haven't thought of him in years."

But then she moved back to her customers. She had been curious—but unconcerned, it seemed. He was a family myth, a sadness of the past for people themselves long dead.

I took a business card off her table as I left.

Alison greeted me by the car with the news she'd had a text from Nora. "She hadn't told Paul where we were. I knew she wouldn't have. He called her friend Heather and got the information that way. Said he was surprising Nora as a treat."

"You look much happier," I said. "I knew it would be something like that."

"I am. Much happier. Though poor Heather. She got duped and feels responsible. But that's Paul. He doesn't think twice about using people. Anyway, Nora's off with another friend now."

I looked down at the Mayhew Farm business card in my hand—white with a basket of apples in one corner. A phone number in green. An address in red. "It's so odd," I said, sliding into the car. "Jackie Mayhew's niece."

"Why odd? It makes sense, doesn't it?"

"I suppose. I just never thought. I don't know how to explain it. I haven't focused on their families at all," I said. "Parents. Siblings. Much less a living, breathing niece."

Alison laughed. "You know, where I'm from, we're used to families being in a village for a thousand years. A century is nothing. Newcomers."

"Right. I guess that's right." I wondered if I should be troubled by Kathleen Mayhew's seeming lack of interest in me and my project. Would it help to have more information? Photographs beyond the ones that had been "living" in my walls all these years? Family anecdotes? Or would it muddy things for me?

"When you paint a flower," I asked, pulling my seatbelt on, "do you care about the garden where it grew?"

"No." Alison backed out from the space with her usual vigor and both zucchini rolled off my lap. "Sorry about that. No, I don't care. Except insofar as that garden has determined everything about the flower. But then I paint flora, not sentient beings. Not people. It might be different if I were doing that."

"Right," I said, then shook the whole subject from my thoughts. "I'm really glad Nora's okay. And that you know she didn't give you away," I said. "I'm glad you can relax about that now."

Over dinner in the kitchen, Owen and I marveled at the ugliness of the morning's scene. I watched him as we spoke, looking for signs of his being in any way deflated by the departure of his beautiful admirer, but I found nothing there.

"Alison was glad Nora had some time with you," I said. "She told me Nora related to you as a positive father figure." It wasn't quite what Alison had said, but I decided it was close enough. "She described you as soothing. Alison did. Admirably unflappable."

He frowned. "Is that a good thing?"

"Well, for a girl like Nora, with a father like that, I understand the appeal."

"I suppose. Though it sounds pretty dull. There aren't many boys who dream of growing up to be unflappable."

"Well, dear, if the shoe fits. But I don't think she meant dull. I think she meant reliable. Not a loose cannon. Not a maniac. A positive influence. You know how sometimes young people need a supplemental parent to help them move forward." But then I realized that down this road lay Laine and my role in her life. "You know," I said again, "while I was working today, I thought how strange it is that my father is locked in a cell, while that man . . . I mean, it's too bad there isn't some doctor out there willing to say he has Alzheimer's just so he can be locked up. I'm sure he's more dangerous than poor Dad will ever be. It ought to be the other way around."

Owen laughed. "No one can say you don't think outside the box, Gussie."

"I'm only semi-joking. The whole system . . . how we humans

manage it. I'm having difficulty these days understanding the logic of it all. Maybe it's . . ." But I stopped myself—again. I had been going to say something about how meeting the real, live niece of one of the killed boys had made me all the more aware of the slaughter I was documenting, made that horror, too, more real to me; but the subject tumbled down another one of our rabbit holes of taboo. No work talk. "Maybe it's just the fallout from my father's condition, his move, that's got me so contemplative. And then hearing that lunatic shouting obscenities in the yard. Sometimes, it just seems like we're doing it all backwards."

"I don't think many people could look at the world and think we're doing it right."

"No, I don't suppose they could," I said. "Though it would be nice to think there's hope."

"There's always hope," he said. "Even if unwarranted."

"Well, on that cheery note," I said, "I'm turning in early tonight. How 'bout you join me?"

I was certain he was going to say no, but he said yes.

11

Here we are, Jan and I, clearing our father's belongings from the efficiency apartment he has occupied for nearly two years. Two women, sisters, similar coloring, black hair, dark eyes, tanned skin—mine from the country summer, hers from two weeks' boating and swimming in Nova Scotia. I am informal, a bit messy in my comfortable clothes, jeans and a rose-colored T-shirt; she is elegant in gray linen pants, a white short-sleeve silk blouse—straight from a morning at work. In the first moments or possibly minutes—immeasurable—we are both, together, silently overwhelmed. Not by the extent of the task, modest and meager, but by its nature.

Eventually, I say, "I can't imagine where to start," meaning that I can't imagine how this ends. I am counting on my sister's orderly mind, on her ability to see systems and methodology where I cannot. She sighs, resigned, ready to engage that brain of hers. She has boxes in her car, she says. There are categories we can use. What she will take. What I will take. What neither of us wants. What he might be able to have in his new room. I nod. It all makes sense. It sounds so obvious—though I might have stood there an hour before detecting this structural simplicity to the job.

We move quietly, rarely speaking—each of us drawn first to the meaningless objects, the things he has mysteriously acquired since our childhoods. A Lucite paper towel holder. A beer stein from Atlantic City. An afghan that looks handmade, that neither of us can place but that we decide should go with him. A pair of galoshes he will never now need. (Of all the unfamiliar things, these alone stir me. An existence spending all rainy days indoors. A life sentence. A *never again* molded into this loosely human shape, green rubber, traces of old mud still wedged in the grooves of the soles.)

Once the unrecognized objects are gone, the familiar sparkle like shards of all the memories he has lost. I find the salt and pepper shakers that sat on our kitchen table for decades, aluminum cubes I used to knock together during long family meals, and I can see that Jan wants them, so I tell her to go ahead. Into her box they go. I take the single jade bookend, its partner long vanished, the back half of a dragon carved into it. We come close to alternating, one for her and one for me; and I wonder as we do if she too is feeling the absence of the third set of hands. Neither of us mentions Charlotte. Or our mother—but that is not so noticeable an omission. Neither of us reminisces at all. Sitting on the bed, I think that we might be somehow cheerier had he died. The weight of his double captivity, within the locked room, within his own body, is heavy on us.

We haven't discussed whether or not we will visit him after the task is complete. But then I'm relieved to learn that Jan has made the decision. It's enough for one day. Let the staff bring him his things. Let us each wrap our arms around the light, half-filled boxes we will take to our own homes. Let this be over.

In the parking lot, we put the boxes down and hug, hurriedly. She is no more comfortable than I with the kind of physical affection that flows, overflows, from Alison. Like our black hair and dark eyes, like our silence on the subject of our dead sister, of our mother, our need not to see our father this afternoon, we share this reserve.

"Drive safely," I tell her.

"You too," she says to me.

"Jan," I say, just as she's leaning to pick up her box. "I was wondering. Do you ever go to the cemetery?"

She looks at me for a moment, clearly surprised. "We go on Charlotte's birthday. Once I went on Mother's Day, but we decided it was better to spend that with Letty's mother, who was clearly hurt by our opting for a grave over her. Why?"

"No reason. I don't know. Maybe it's Dad. I don't know. Nothing really."

But I want to say: *I have never known what to do with them. The ones who aren't here. I don't understand it. I have never understood it. The love I felt and didn't feel for our mother. The gash to my heart where Charlotte lived.* I want to ask her: *Do you believe they still exist?*

But instead, I say, "This was tough, I suppose. I just have cemeteries on the brain today. The obvious reasons. Plus there's some related work that I have going on."

"You can come with us any time you want."

I shrug it off with a muttered, "Thanks, but I doubt . . . Maybe sometime. Or maybe . . ." I look right at her. "Maybe instead, you and Letty could come see us? For an afternoon? Or a meal? We should spend more time together. We shouldn't only see each other here. Or at the cemetery. I mean, we shouldn't ground all our contact in misery. And we'd love to have you visit. To spend some time together among the living."

Once again, she looks surprised. "To be honest, Gus, I didn't think you and Owen were much up for having visitors. I've always gotten the sense that you're opting for total seclusion there."

There is no mistaking the irritation in her voice.

"I don't know. I suppose, we've been . . . I'm sorry if we've seemed unwelcoming. It's been . . . it's been different lately. We're in a somewhat different place. Things are . . . it's different. We would love to have you come sometime."

I'm not sure what to make of the expression on her face. Maybe there are questions she wants to ask, but cannot phrase. We always seem to be teetering on the edge of intimacy and then creeping back to the safety of something more familiar and more remote. "We'd love to come sometime," she finally says. I mutter again about finding a good day; then we both pick up our boxes and go to our cars.

Jackie Mayhew's grave is in a cemetery that sprawls in a giant circle around the old Presbyterian church, which was originally stone but then encumbered over time with additions so incongruous they look to have been made by another species, one that worships a far less picturesque deity. It was late afternoon as I pulled into the lot, the sun already low enough that every shape was shadowed. And the air smelled of a nearby farm, manure and hay.

I hadn't planned the stop in advance, but on my way back from the home that day it felt right.

A few days earlier, after the farmers' market, I had turned once again to the obituaries I'd been focusing on, but this time, my thoughts on Kathleen Mayhew, I read the lines I had been skipping as somehow irrelevant to my needs. *Services will be held at . . . Burial will take place in . . .* I looked some of the churches up online and all were within twenty minutes of my home. Doubtless, I had driven by them dozens, hundreds of times, pushing them to the periphery of my thoughts.

I had long hated cemeteries. Maybe that would have been different had our father taken us to visit our mother's grave—or maybe I would have hated them more. Either way, it wasn't in his character to march his three girls, ducklings in a row, in woolen coats, as I have always pictured us, the image fused with all those

stills of Caroline Kennedy, the mourning girl-child for a generation of us. Even if we had been allowed to acknowledge our
mother, I don't believe he would have seen the point to having us
stare at a stone, a strip of lawn, as though we could communicate
with it all somehow. As though the grave were a she who would
see how we had grown.

I did go there once with Charlotte on a summer evening when
I was sixteen. We were both a little drunk and there was the energy of a dare in the air, like children goading each other onto the
crabby neighbor's lawn despite warnings, with no real motive in
mind beyond *because we can*—or so it felt until, standing there in
the tidiness of the rows, staring at my mother's name, those dates,
it occurred to me in that sloppily acute way of tipsiness to ask,
"Wait, how did you even know where she is?"

"Oh, I just like to come here sometimes," Charlotte said, not
looking at me. "I like to say hi."

Jan is the brain of us; Charlotte was the heart; and I, I sometimes think I am the skin, not constructed for logic or even truly
for love, but designed instead for trying, always trying to keep the
world apart from my being, to prevent myself from coming undone.

We sat on the ground for an hour or so that night, and we
talked about the future, Charlotte's return to Oberlin in only days,
my dreams of art school, of a life littered and studded with all the
chaotic beauty our father seemed to fear.

"He does his best," Charlotte said. "He tries really hard."

"He can be such an asshole," I said. Something like that.

As we spoke, I thought about the woman below us—of course.
I wondered if I would feel her waft up to embrace us. Would
something in my heart flutter, expand? I so wanted it to. But she
belonged more to my sister than to me. Whatever presence Charlotte felt, I could not feel. Maybe Charlotte had taken me on this
visit to try and pass on some strand of their connection; but I was

unable to grasp the thread. I certainly never went back. Not until
Charlotte herself died and our father bought a plot for her near
theirs. And then, silently, foolishly, I was glad for their proximity.
My conviction that the dead are dead are dead are dead had hard-
ened, as had I, yet this tiny indefensible comfort at having my
mother and my sister buried so close shimmered in me like a single, dewy blade of new green grass.

At Jackie's cemetery, the graves nearest the church were the earliest, barely legible dates all beginning with 17; and then, farther
out, the 1800s. War dead. War dead in almost every generation.
But also dead of every imaginable sort. Dead as varied as the living. Babies. Ancients. Beloveds and those who evoked no eternal
adjective; nothing but the facts. And then of course the central
fact, the only fact. To walk outward in this field was to progress
through a calendar of only one date. If I kept on long enough, I
knew, I would find the place, still just grass, marking the time of
my own end, a time when the bodies of my peers-in-expiration
would begin to arrive; and then if I went farther I would reach in
some too-close grassy patch a time beyond the range of my own
life.

The late-nineteenth- and early-twentieth-century stones were
ornate compared to those before, but then notably less so during
the years of the war, the period of the Spanish flu. It seemed not
only as though the stonecutters had been overwhelmed with work,
but that the peculiar exultant joy of it had all gone flat. No more
celebration of lives well lived or the opening of Heaven's gates.
Here was a humbled bow to reality—the plain granite, the right
angles. The spirit deflated by relentless young demise. I knew I
would find Jackie soon and I almost turned back, beginning to
fear that this inescapably physical world would squelch the Jackie
of my imagination, the boy brought back to life. But something

felt important enough to me that I kept on until I found the small gray stone.

John "Jackie" Mayhew
Beloved Son
April 1901–May 1918

I read it, silently first, and then aloud. I looked away, up to the sky, then out to a distant hill. A few turning trees, the early ones, stood out among the dark green mass. As I noticed that, I felt— *something*. A truck drove by, close enough to see, but not to hear. I looked again at the name and at the dates. And I forced myself to read them aloud again, then forced myself to know that Jackie's body lay beneath my feet, his actual body—an exercise in imagining the real.

I sat on the ground and studied the Mayhews all around. His parents. His brother and brother's wife—Kathleen's parents. I imagined her visiting here, but saw no evidence, no old or new bouquets.

When Charlotte was buried, I knew I would never visit her.

Yet years later, I could feel my sister's presence as I sat among the Mayhews.

Here was the mother. Harriet Mayhew, her flat stone seeming to mimic the crush of grief. And a brother, Thomas Mayhew, whose daughter Kathleen could tell me how he had mourned for Jackie his whole long life.

And here was Charlotte too. As if buried in among them. Charlotte. The missing set of hands reaching for my father's few belongings. Charlotte, whose name could barely be spoken by her sisters, so tender were the injuries still. Charlotte. The one who would have made us stop by to see our father before leaving. She of the big, reliable heart.

Why had I come to this cemetery on this day? Not to weep

over my sister, gone more than six years. Yet I did exactly that, head in hands.

Owen had already made dinner when I got home. He told me to have a drink and just relax. If he noticed that I'd taken longer than I might have, he didn't mention it. I sent him out to the van to get the box from my father's place.

A fire burned in the fireplace as we took the odd things out. I told him sweet stories about their history and he helped me find the right places in which to set them. I gave him the jade bookend to bring out to the barn. "Dad would want you to have something literary." There wasn't much at all. It didn't take us very long. At some point, all of it dispersed, Owen asked me if I'd heard from Alison during the day.

"Or I thought maybe when you got home . . ."

I told him I hadn't. "Why?"

We were sitting on the couch, my back leaning into his chest, his arm around me. "She had two hang-up calls during the night," he said. "They seemed to have shaken her."

"For real? Was it Paul?"

"She doesn't know. They were on her cell but no number came through. Blocked." Owen stood and walked to the fire. He poked at a log. "I think she assumes it's him. But she said she isn't afraid. Still, she seemed upset."

"That's all she needs. Do you think I should go over?"

"I told her she should come for dinner if it would help, but she said she was fine. She said she thought you might need some quiet time here tonight. She was concerned about how you spent the day."

"Did you tell her to call if it happens again?"

"I did indeed. I told her exactly that."

"It probably won't," I said. "Probably a wrong number."

"I said that too. Anyway." He put the poker down. "Anyway, I slaved over a microwave and thawed us some lasagna, so let's go eat."

I looked at the emptied box on the table in front of me. "I feel bad about Alison. You're sure I shouldn't . . . ?"

"I'm sure," he said. "She knows where to find us." He reached for my hand. "Come on, Gus. It's dinnertime. Let's eat."

I let him pull me to my feet. I would check on her after dinner, I resolved.

In deep dusk I trekked over the hill, coaching myself all the while on how to comfort a frightened friend. My father had so stressed to us the importance of being brave—by which he meant fearless. He wouldn't brook worries about airplane flights or bears on camping trips or bullies at school or even illnesses, high fevers, racking coughs. The great mystery for me was always the degree to which he was like that—or in any way like the man I knew— before his young wife complained of a sharp pain in her head one morning and was dead by afternoon. Maybe his refusal to tolerate fear was part and parcel of his reluctance to talk about her, a general stance of denial. Or maybe it was closer to hopelessness. What was the point of worrying, when you could never know what bullet was aimed at your heart?

Either way, we grew up in an atmosphere of forced bravery, a condition that left me flummoxed by other people's fears, even as an adult. A part of me longed to give the kind of comfort I had never received; but undeniably a steely sliver of my father's sternness had slipped into my character. And so this strange self-reeducation as I pushed through the graying night, over the lawn between our homes.

There were people, I knew, who didn't need to be so conscious of instructing themselves on how to behave. Alison herself was a natural at interacting with other people, in a way I never would be. Charlotte had been another such. You couldn't ever detect a hitch between her responses and her true nature. A loving gesture flowed from her loving heart. But at forty-seven I still gave out kindness and warmth in starts and stutters, having to remind myself to do so all the while.

Alison and I sat in her kitchen. She looked upset, as Owen had reported, and also as though she hadn't slept at all the night before. "It was probably just a one-time thing," she said, but with no more conviction than I'd heard from the gravel-voiced nurse suggesting the same about my father.

"You look worried, though."

"I suppose so. Yes. And no. I'm a little bit shaken, that's all. Ever since Paul was here. And then the calls. I'm not afraid of him." I must have looked skeptical. "Well, I'm a little bit afraid of him."

I remembered the locked door from my very early visit to her home. "Would it help to stay with us for a while?"

She shook her head. "No. But that's awfully nice of you. I'll get past this. It occurred to me just this morning to turn off the damn phone. Funny, I think Nora would have done that after the first call, but I still think of phones as attached to the wall, not something where you just push a button and it's gone. And I don't want Nora unable to reach me."

"If you need us, if you ever want to stay over . . ."

She reached across the table, touching my arm. "I can't believe how lucky I was to land here," she said. "Truly. But now, enough about the stupid calls. Tell me how it went at your father's today."

"Oh, it was fine. It was sad. Just what you'd expect." I didn't say anything to her about the cemetery, as I hadn't to Owen either. I told her instead that I should probably go to bed, and I stood.

"But don't hesitate to come over if you need anything. Even just company," I said. "You know where I am."

Later, after I'd showered off the day's institutional perfume and its cemetery air, a glare outside the window caught my eye. Every single light in Alison's house was on.

Just months earlier this view had been of darkness, speckled at times with tiny, distant lights but more often, by this late hour, not. Now there was this bizarre, inexplicably upsetting house of light right next door, as though a spaceship had landed across the lawn.

Light. It was something I had been nurtured by my whole life. In fifth-grade science class when we'd learned the four elements, I was certain there had been a mistake. How could light not be one? When it seemed like it was everything to me?

I was still afraid of the dark then—eleven years old—and for a long time after, but my father, of course, didn't believe in such things. I would turn the closet light on each night and it was always turned off by the time I woke up, sometimes even before I was asleep.

I stared over at Alison's, remembering all those long black nights of childhood as one infinite time of unspeakable terror and loneliness. I had felt most motherless then, most lost, each darkening day an echo of the death that haunted me. Until Owen. Owen taught me to love the darkness, to view it as a necessary respite from a world of visibility, a world in which as a painter I was eternally vigilant. And that was how I first knew I loved him. That I no longer felt bereft at the nightly departure of the sun.

12

The calls didn't stop. Two or three a night. Sometimes she answered but no one was ever there. No one who spoke, anyway. Sometimes she just let it ring. After nearly a week, she agreed to stay in our house, if only once, so she could get a single decent night's sleep, but she left all the lights on at her own place anyway. "If he's watching," she said, "I don't want him to think anything has changed. I don't want him knowing I'm afraid." I didn't point out that if he—whoever—was watching, he would know from the lights themselves that she was afraid. There was no point trying to reason with her. By then, having barely slept for days, she wasn't thinking logically.

She was to sleep in the spare room down the hall, a space never occupied enough to be called a guest room. I spent a good amount of time trying to make it a welcoming space for her. Flowers. A pretty set of sheets. I dusted the old wardrobe. Took the braided rug outside to shake it clean—or if not clean, then fresher, anyway. I knocked some cobwebs off the ceiling with a broom, out of the corners, off the upper ledge of the door.

And of course she'd be using the spare bath—the one that had been renovated early that summer. I stepped into it for the first time in many weeks, a clean towel, a bar of fresh soap, in hand.

We had kept the original fixtures, the claw-foot tub, the sink with its separate hot and cold taps. The milky blue subway tile I had chosen and the pristinely painted pale gray walls gave those porcelain pieces from nearly a century before an aura of something like dignity.

I stood there for some time, not unlike the way I had sat in the cemetery, though this time it wasn't the reality of the dead in which I was trying to believe, it was the spirit of all the life that had been lived in this home. There must have been generations of children bathed in that tub, and couples who stood side by side at the sink. I had spent so much time attuned to the dead of the house. I was grateful to let the living into my consciousness as well.

Alison came by after dinner. "I'm already imposing enough," she said. "You don't have to feed me too." I took her upstairs and she said all the right things about the room. It would be like staying at an inn for the night. She was certain she would sleep well. Just as I was going to leave her alone, Owen peered around the door and said, "Why don't you give me your phone, Alison? I'll answer it. Let him hear a male voice."

I saw her hesitate, but then she handed it to him, like a child turning in a confiscated toy.

"Something tells me it isn't going to ring," Owen said quietly, as we settled into bed.

"Why do you say that?"

"A hunch. That's all."

"Well, that's a complete cop-out. Calling it a hunch. You really think she's lying? She'd have to be a pretty great actress. She looks like hell. And I'm not sure what the motive would be."

"You're assuming there's something rational going on."

I gave his arm a slap. "Yes, Owen. I am. I am assuming she's not a lunatic. Because she's not."

"Well, maybe I'll scare him away with my manliness."

"I'm certain you will. With your he-man voice." I switched off my bedside lamp. "Seriously though, I do give you points. You may not like her as much as I do or even believe her, but you're certainly helping her."

He began to rub my back. "It isn't in my nature to let the people around me feel scared."

"No. It's not," I said, savoring the darkness he had taught me not to fear. Soft, thick darkness. Velvet, loving darkness. "You know, I think you would have been an incredible father, Owen. Probably a much better parent than I."

From the long silence that followed, I knew he was adjusting to my having raised this topic, so long unmentioned—as if I had now turned on a too-bright light and his pupils needed to contract. "You have a more nurturing nature," I said. "I can be pretty self-involved, I know. But I'm just self-aware enough to understand how much is missing in me. How very much. Who knows. Maybe it's all just as well."

"I don't think it's just as well, Gus. It's not just as well."

"I don't mean . . . I'm just paying you a compliment. I shouldn't . . . I put it badly. You're just very good at taking care of people. That's all I mean. Better than I am. Even people you don't much like. I just wanted to say it. You would have been the better parent. And I'm sorry you never got that chance."

"I'm sorry neither of us did. I'm sorry I couldn't give you that."

"No apologies allowed. You know that."

We lay in silence for a time.

"It's not always easy, is it?" he said. "Having her here? All that devoted motherhood of hers. She's like . . . like some kind of monument to parenting. Like an advertisement for it."

"I've had my moments, I admit."

"Me too. I've had my moments."

There was another silence.

"But you would have left her in the dust, Gussie," he said, after some time passed. "As a mother, I mean. You would have been the best mother the world has ever known. Thorns and all. You think you're all prickles and brambles, but you would have aced it."

I felt him curve up against me. "Thanks." I shut my eyes and I raised my knees as he pressed his legs to form with mine. "I'm glad you think so," I said, forcing myself not to explain all the reasons his assessment couldn't possibly be true. He kissed the back of my head.

"I love you, Owen," I said instead.

"And I love you, Augusta Edelman. Gussie. Gus. I always have, you know. And I always will."

I couldn't remember the last time we had fallen asleep in an embrace. I couldn't imagine why we'd ever stopped.

The phone didn't ring that night.

It rang early in the morning, waking us. "It's Nora," Owen said, peering at the display. "Do I answer? How do I explain answering her mother's phone at seven a.m.?"

"Let it go. She can call her back. It's too weird." I sat up. "But that was it, right? There weren't any other calls?"

He shook his head. Alison's phone stopped chirping. "Nope."

"Any theories?" I asked.

"Nope."

"Maybe he knew she was here?"

"Whoever he is," Owen said. "If there is a he."

"Maybe it was just, you know, one of those weird things. And it's over."

"Maybe."

"You don't really think she was lying?" I asked. "Do you really?"

"Let's just hope that's the end of the whole thing."

In the kitchen, Alison, already dressed, looked confused to hear there had been no calls.

"Except Nora," I said, handing her the phone. "About fifteen minutes ago. I think she left a message. It made the message noise."

I started the coffee, my back to her, as she listened. I took three mugs down from the cabinet.

"Paul was jailed last night," she said. I turned around. "Drunk driving. Nora had to bail him out."

Owen walked in just then. I repeated what Alison had said.

"Well, that makes things pretty clear," he said. "Mystery solved. Now you just have to decide what to do."

"I have to call Nora back. Before anything." She left the room.

Owen and I looked at each other. "What the fuck?" I said. "Who the fuck does that?"

"There's a lot going on there," Owen said. "I don't think we know the half."

I poured him a cup of coffee. "What a mess. And for the record I never believed she was lying."

"Oh, come on, Gus. Half an hour ago, we both thought she might be. I still don't know. We only have her word on what Nora said."

Alison came back before I had to respond. "Nora wants to stay with him for a while. He's home. I tried to talk her out of it, but she feels like she can help him and there's only so much I can do about that. The calls will stop, though. He won't do it with her in the house."

"Did you tell her what's been going on?"

She nodded. "I tried to stop her. But I can't. She's an adult. Or anyway, that's her view. And it's . . . oh, it's all mixed up for her with that bloody religious crap. I'm sorry. I don't mean to be so contemptuous, I try not to be. But this is when all that starts really angering me. And the boy, the big Christian influence, was such a nothing. The whole thing is just unimaginable."

"I'm sorry." I threw Owen a meaningful look: *See? She couldn't possibly sound more sincere.*

"Well, maybe God can explain why Paul decided to start harassing me now," she said.

"Went off his meds?" I put a cup of coffee in front of her. "I'm really sorry."

"Oh, I'm sorry too. My guess is that my moving away made him feel like he had to up the ante to pull me back in." She laughed. "Now you know what a decade or two of self-help books does to your brain. Bloody hell. I'm so sorry to you both for dragging all of this . . . all of this mess into your lives. I know the whole point of you being here is that the worries of the big bad world are far away and now I've introduced all this family melodrama."

It was Owen's turn to look meaningfully at me.

"Don't even think about it," I said. "This isn't going to go on for long."

"Okay," Owen said. "I'm out to the barn. He's spent one night in jail. I don't know the man, but my guess is he won't want another."

Alison looked up at him. "You're right. I hadn't thought of that. Let's not waste more time on him. I vote we all get back to work."

"Meeting adjourned," Owen said.

"Meeting adjourned," I said.

"Meeting adjourned," Alison said.

Alison and Owen left together, so I didn't have a chance to speak to Owen alone right away. I could have followed him to the barn but could too easily imagine Alison seeing me and concluding that we were hurrying to talk about her behind her back—which was exactly what we would be doing. So I waited until noon, when he turned up in my studio.

"Okay, my doubter, what do you think now?" I asked.

"I think fences make good neighbors."

"No. Really."

He sighed. "Really? I think she has an abusive former husband and a freight train's worth of baggage. And I don't hate her, whatever you believe. I even feel bad for her. But I often wish she'd never moved in next door. And I don't think that makes me unfair or unreasonably suspicious."

"No," I said. "I don't think that it does."

He walked over to the picture of Jackie playing chess. He spent maybe a minute looking at it, then moved to look at the drawing of the boys in the kitchen eating eggs. "So this is the big project," he said. "It's interesting stuff, Gus."

It was the first time he'd seemed to think so. The first time he'd looked long enough to express an opinion. "Thanks," I said.

He nodded toward the sketch of Oliver Farley sitting on our front steps. "I particularly like this one. Or anyway, I like that there's one outside the house. Makes them all breathe a bit."

"I think there'll be more. I have in mind a few boys swimming in the pond."

"The detail, as always, is stunning, Gus. Not the people yet, obviously. But I assume . . ."

"No, not yet."

"That's new for you. Figures. Such distinct ones, anyway."

"I think they'll come last," I said. "I'm creating context." It was a line I had used to myself more than once.

He touched my back, just for a moment, a *bye for now* caress. He said he thought he was going to wash up for lunch if I was ready for a break. I told him that I was.

We ate deviled eggs he'd made, and a salad I threw together. I asked him if he wanted a beer and he said he thought he'd better not.

We sat for a few minutes, eating, before I asked, "When were you going to tell me?"

He made a questioning face.

"You're writing again. Aren't you? When were you planning to tell me?"

He smiled—a grin, really, those craggy lines that bracketed his lips, deepening, curving. "When have I ever had to tell you anything like that? Don't you think I know you can tell? When have we ever had to tell each other those things? Anyway, you know how it is, you're afraid of jinxing it . . ."

"What happened?"

"Jesus, if I knew that . . . I don't even want to ask. I don't really want to talk about it all. Not out loud. Let's just see if it can hold on for a bit. You know how it is. The universe decides to take pity . . ."

I nodded. I understood. After a bit he asked me if I had been in touch with the owner of the gallery in Philadelphia where I'd last been included in a group show. "She's going to be awfully interested," he said. "Knowing Clarice, she'll probably need smelling salts when she sees how good this stuff is."

"Really? You really think so?" I was surprised he seemed so sure.

"Oh, come on, Gussie. You know how good it is. You don't need me to critique your work for you."

But I had, for weeks and weeks and weeks.

"I don't suppose you'll tell me what you're working on?"

"Not yet. In a while. If it sticks."

I nodded and I said, "I understand," and we went on to talk of other things.

After lunch, I felt something absent for so long that the sensation came as a surprise and an unexpected gift. I had known I would feel relief that Owen was back engaged in his work. But I hadn't remembered the electricity that would be running between us, a rope of the stuff from my bright, sunny studio to his dusky, cool barn.

13

Maybe it was feeling that connection to Owen again that gave me the courage to take on the task I had been putting off for weeks: painting the boys themselves.

From the first, it wasn't work I enjoyed. I could never lose myself in it—because there *I* was at every turn being uncooperative, unskilled, inept. There *I* was with that strange disconnect I rarely otherwise felt between my intentions and my execution, with that heaviness in my hand, that stiffness to my lines. And there were the resulting figures, too—not people, not really, but more like paintings of soldier figurines.

"Ugh," I would say out loud, several times a day, as I stepped back to look.

Owen insisted they were better than I thought. Now that he was back at work and the subject no longer taboo, I could worry it through with him. "I don't see it, Gussie," he would say. "I think they look fine." And for a few minutes I'd be reassured; but not for long.

I was fretting over this, two weeks or so into this big push, when I answered my cell without looking at the number and heard the unmistakable cry of "Augie!"

"Laine." I instinctively turned my back to the window, to the barn. She asked right away how I was doing and I gave her a brief answer, knowing the call had to be short, hoping Owen wouldn't happen to wander in; but also feeling a guilty elation at the sound of her voice. It had been ages, maybe years. She told me just a little about a new studio class she'd started and made a few humorous remarks about her teacher. And then she said, "So, here's the big surprise. I'm actually about ten minutes from your house . . . I was driving home for the weekend, Mom is having a giant fiftieth birthday party thing and I just thought I would take a detour. I hope it's okay. Do you know it's like a century since I saw you?"

"I can't believe it," I said. "You're here?"

"I am! Surprise!"

She had no reason to know this was a problem, and I couldn't think of a way to tell her no. I couldn't think at all. For a second I imagined saying I would have to meet her at a restaurant, but nothing coherent came to my panicked mind.

"It's okay though, right? I mean, I won't stay long if you're working or whatever. But truly I just want a tiny look at you. I promise not to stay. I can't anyway. Mom's thing is like in five hours. I just need a glimpse of you."

I had no plausible excuse. "Circle the area for fifteen or twenty minutes if you don't mind. I need to get dressed, things like that. We're hermits here, you know."

She laughed. "Sorry about the bad impulse control, Augie." It was the same phrase Nora had used about her trip to see Owen in the barn. Generational code for bad judgment? "I'll give you a half hour," she said. "I could use a cup of coffee anyway."

As I walked the flagstone path to the barn, I thought of bolting, cutting her off at the driveway somehow, but I could feel the danger of that. It was one thing not to bring up our occasional contact, quite another to deceive Owen so elaborately about her coming to our home.

I didn't knock, a return to the old ways now that he was writing again. "Hey," I said, and he looked over.

"Hey, back. What's up?"

I shrugged. "Nothing terrible. Just . . . I just got a call from Laine. You know. Laine." It was shocking how rapidly his features fell, his eyes seemed to harden. "I'm really sorry. I . . . She's in the neighborhood."

"The neighborhood? Gus, we don't have a neighborhood."

"The area. I had no idea. She was driving close by, and she wants to see me. She's . . . she's impulsive, you know. She doesn't mean . . ."

"Whatever, Gus." He turned back to his computer. "Just let me know when she's gone."

"It won't be a long visit. I'm really sorry."

"Just let me know when she's gone," he said again.

"I will." I began to walk away, then stopped. "I'm not in touch with him at all. Not since his call years ago. In case you're wondering. She . . ."

"I wasn't wondering, Gus. I just want to get back to work."

"Okay," I said, and then, "Thanks."

In the few minutes I had, I went upstairs and into the bathroom, where I studied my face. What would she report to Bill? *Augie looks good. Older, but maybe like she's been working out. She's awfully tanned.*

I brushed my hair, then braided it. I thought about Alison and how she would have put on makeup, been sure she was wearing her lipstick. But I couldn't, even if I'd wanted to. The last thing Owen needed was any evidence that I was trying to doll myself up for Laine—and for any descriptions she might bring home.

Plumper than I'd ever seen her, and prettier too, Laine leapt from her VW bug and gave me the sort of hug I hadn't had from anyone in years. I thought she might lift me off my feet and spin us both around. "My God, Augie! I can't believe I'm really seeing you!"

"Laine, you look amazing!" I took a step back. Her hair, dyed purplish black, was cut into a pageboy with bangs, all very 1920s, complete with the dark red lipstick she wore. The piercings on her nose, cheek, eyebrow, lower lip, once heavy steel, now glistened with tiny gems, as though she'd been sprinkled with fairy dust. Her eyes were rimmed in heavy black makeup and she wore a short, shapeless black dress, black tights, military boots—the perennial art student uniform—and a green army coat over that.

"Come inside," I said. "What can I give you to drink? Or eat?" I made the offer instinctively, not thinking how it might extend her stay.

"Nothing. I really can't. Mom is expecting me. She'll kill me if I'm late. God, I love it here," she said as we stepped into the kitchen. "No wonder you ran away. I can't believe I've never come before. This is like some kind of paradise, isn't it?"

"Sometimes," I said. "Depending on how the work is going. Paradise. Hell. You know how it is. But yes, I feel lucky. We both do."

"Is Owen around? I haven't seen him in years and years."

"He's . . . he's out doing some errands. That's what you get for surprising people."

"My bad." She smiled, then pointed through the door to the living room. "Can I . . . ? I've been so curious about this place."

"Of course. Come on, I'll give you the grand tour."

We started upstairs.

I watched her do exactly what I had done my first time there: she walked through each room to its window and looked outside. "Oh, wow. You have a pond. Can you swim in it?"

"Someone could swim in it. I'm not much for swimming."

"I would swim in it every day."

"Not in October, you wouldn't."

"No, but summertime. Summertime it would be amazing."

When we stepped into the bedroom, I tried to squelch thoughts of how Owen would hate having Bill's child there. "Anyway," I said, hurrying us through, "the studio is the most interesting room. Let's head back down."

"It's really all perfect, Augie. And it's weirdly like I imagined it would be. A real farmhouse."

"Minus the farm. Can you imagine me tending cows?"

"Oh, you'd find a way. And I'd come help."

The biggest change I saw was how happy she seemed. Not just no longer miserable, or even pretty much okay, but positively glowing.

"You really seem great," I said, in the living room. "It makes me very happy, Laine."

She'd stopped in front of the painting over the mantel. "I never saw this, did I?"

"No. I painted that . . . you were in school by then . . . I think," I added, as though I didn't know exactly when I had painted it and that she had been in her second year at NYU, still sending me bulletins more or less weekly about her daily life.

"The light," she said. "It's so you. Dad used to call it 'Augie light,' remember?"

"It's not one of my favorites. It's . . ." I barreled past the emotions crackling in me. "Owen loves it. That's why it's there."

"I think it's kind of great."

"Well, thank you. Anyway, the studio is through here . . ."

I gave her free rein, encouraged her to move the pictures around, leaf through my sketches. What did I want from Laine's perusal of my work? I wanted her to love everything, of course. I wanted her to reaffirm what Owen had been saying, quell the doubts that I still felt.

To get a clean read on her response, I hadn't told her a thing about the project. She was close to silent for many minutes, just making little sounds in reaction as she looked. *Huh* and a very quiet *oh*. I sat at my desk and doodled until finally, I said, "Okay, so let's pretend it's a critique. What do you think?"

There was a pause before she answered. "It's interesting. I mean, I don't exactly get it, but it's this house, obviously. Right?"

"That's right."

"Huh." She looked around a little more. "I'm . . . I like them. The details are just insanely good. But I don't really understand. They're soldiers from long ago, right? I just . . . I don't think of you as someone with that kind of . . . I guess I feel like I'm missing something here. And I don't really think of you doing, I don't know, antiwar art. Is it? I mean, that would be cool, but . . ."

As she spoke I realized that something had been nagging at me for weeks. How much were the paintings dependent on the story behind them? Did they stand alone or did they need me beside them explaining about the house and the bathroom rehab and the wall?

"Why antiwar?" I asked. "What makes you think it's anything critical like that?"

"Because they're dead, Augie. Aren't they? The boys are all dead."

Over the next half hour, I forgot about Owen and Bill, both
evaporating as I explained to Laine that she wasn't wrong, but
that she also was wrong—or maybe I was. I told her the story of
the bathroom and the papers. I showed her a couple of the obituaries. "But I don't want them to look dead in the paintings," I
said. "That isn't intentional. That's . . . well, like I said. Not intentional."

"Huh." She looked concerned. "It's really interesting work,
Augie," she repeated. "And if people take it as antiwar or whatever, that's not a bad thing, is it? I mean, God, we've been at war
most of my life. And there are kids I know who barely even know
it. All these rich kids who are like, oh right, we're still at war.
And I really like that they're from some other time. It's like this
brings home how permanent death is. I mean, I look at them and
all I see is how sick it is that they were killed so young."

But it wasn't what I wanted; and she saw my distress. "I'm not
saying it's simplistic or anything. *Guernica* is an antiwar piece and
there's nothing simple about *Guernica*. Not to mention a million
other works."

"I've been . . . I've been working on them," I said. "Trying. The
thing is, I don't mean them to be like this. Dead. I mean, I want
them to be alive. To seem alive. That's actually kind of the point.
To integrate the dead into life. But you can say it, Laine. It's okay.
I know you're being polite because I'm your teacher. But what
would you say if I were one of the poser hipster wannabes?"

"Well." She bit on her lower lip, then nodded. Inhaled deeply.
Exhaled. "Okay. I'd probably say you needed to take a life-drawing
class. Except I'd find a snarkier way to put it."

I laughed. "There, that wasn't so hard, was it?"

She shrugged. "It wasn't exactly easy. But you know, you're the
one who told me that it was okay to do bad work sometimes. I

can't even count the number of times you told me if I couldn't tolerate making mistakes, I would never get better. If you can't paint the bad stuff, you'll never paint the good stuff. I never really thought about that applying to you, but it does, right? I mean, it's always true, isn't it?"

She was right, of course. Both that I had said it, and that it was true for us all. But I had grown more cautious since my days of preaching the virtues of risk and of failure to Laine. Mistakes had lost their appeal to me.

"I'm not sure this is something I can learn," I said. "Portraiture. I'm not sure this isn't more . . . something basic about me. I may just not have the life-drawing gene. Whatever it takes to make a thing look alive."

"Augie, you make *everything* look alive. Look at every brick you've ever painted. Every chair. I don't even know what you mean."

"Every*thing*. Not every*one*."

"You should just paint them, Augie. Keep going. Just paint them the way you imagine them."

I thought about that. "That may be part of the problem too. I don't paint from my imagination. I never have. You know that. I paint what I see. That's always been the point."

"Yeah. I know. But then why are you doing this?"

I didn't answer. There was no answer that wasn't better suited to a therapist. Or a husband.

"I say just go for it, Augie. And if you fail, then you fail, right? What's the big deal? Obviously, your instincts or whatever are telling you to do this. It's new ground for you. It's exciting, right? Like when I did those collages and they sucked so unbelievably, but then when I went back to painting, something had changed. In a good way." She looked at her wide black leather watch. "Shit," she said. "I really have to go. Seriously, I cannot be a minute late. Mom's been a little wacky lately. Turning fifty maybe, and then

Dad's whole upcoming wedding thing. She never says it bothers her, but she's been a wreck ever since she found out. They *'stayed friends,'* you know." The term came in giant air quotes. "I don't think she fully understood about being divorced. Until he and Miriam . . ."

"You shouldn't make her wait. Come on, let's get you on the road."

But she paused in the studio door. "I feel like I've let you down," she said. "Like I said the wrong thing. I don't want to just rush off . . ."

"No." I shook my head. "You said the right thing. The exact right thing. And the only way you could have let me down is by lying to me about this. I needed to hear it." I laughed a little. "I'm not saying I know how to respond. But I needed to hear the truth."

Outside, we ran smack into Alison, heading toward my house. Introducing them, I was aware of being in Owen's line of vision should he be near his window.

Alison was friendly and told Laine she'd heard wonderful things about her. Laine seemed excited to meet Alison, the cheery British neighbor who had finally broken through the fortifications of Augie's hideaway.

"I'll leave you two to say goodbye," Alison said after a few exchanges. "So nice to meet."

"You were coming over . . . ?" I asked.

"I was," she said. "But it can wait. Maybe stop by in a bit?"

I told her I would.

As Laine and I hugged goodbye, I said, "Thank you for all that," and she said, "I really hope you do it, Augie. You have to finish them. Just play. Don't even think of it as work." Then, "Love you!" when she got into the car.

I waved as she drove away.

"Love you, too," I said, as her car disappeared from sight.

I went for a short walk after that, by myself. Down the driveway and about half a mile on the road. I had more to process than just Laine's painting advice—and I wanted to think it through in solitude, before the scene with Owen that I knew was bound to come.

It had been Laine's description of Georgia, of how Bill's marriage had hit her so hard, that had startled me. Listening, I had expected it to be like a mirror held up to my own bruised heart, my own bruised ego, the image revealing the fragility of the truce I'd forged with those aspects of myself. After all, I too was the jilted woman, still mourning her lost love. After all, the last real mirror I had looked in had been filled with concerns about what Bill would hear about my appearance, my own face fused with imaginings of his.

But something had shifted. Just in the past hour. Or maybe it was a shift already in the works, just waiting for the right circumstance to be complete.

Laine.

Before there was Bill, before we were lovers, there was Laine. A messed-up, angry girl with talent, who needed me. Before her father and I found each other, she and I already had. Before there was danger, there had been nurturing. Caring. A kind of mutual recognition that can only be called love.

As I walked, I smiled, remembering the difficulty she'd had admitting what she thought of my work—as though she'd had to break through a barrier of some kind. As indeed she had. The barrier she knew about, the student critiquing her teacher's clumsy attempts. And the barrier that only I could see. The daughter claiming her place again in my life.

I couldn't tell Owen this, I knew. I wished that I could. I wanted to share how little her visit had to do with Bill. Not only because she had never known about us—which I had told Owen and doubtless would again, many times. But because she herself was, again, something more than Bill's daughter to me. Something different. She was Laine. Her own person. My former student. A fellow artist, now. A friend.

And it wasn't only because she had grown up, I understood, turning back toward the house. It was because both of us had.

Owen came in that evening with an expression I hadn't seen for years. As I watched him gulp his water I was unsure if it was better to say something or let it go, but decided silence was pointless given his scowl.

"I really am sorry about that," I said. "She was just trying to be . . ." I had no adjective to supply. "You know she never knew anything, right? I'm just her old art teacher, to her. This wasn't a visit about . . . about anything that happened."

"I really don't feel like talking about this, Gus. What's for dinner?"

It had been his turn to cook, but I let it go. "I just want you to . . ."

"Want me to what, Gus? What? Do you not understand that I didn't even know you were in touch with her? I really thought those people were out of our lives. And here she is. In our house. Doing what? What did you actually do?"

"I showed her my work. We talked."

He exhaled loudly as though this were the worst possible answer—as he would have whatever I'd said. "Great. You showed her your work. Did she like it?"

"Not particularly. Since you asked." I stopped short of saying that at least she hadn't just said whatever felt easiest, as I suspected he had been doing for nearly two weeks. "You never told me I had to cut her off."

"It never occurred to me you hadn't."

"You wouldn't have wanted me to. She's a kid. She still needs me. I can't believe you'd have wanted me to do that. To hurt her like that."

Something flickered in his expression, and I knew that he agreed. "I saw you out there with Alison," he said.

"We ran into her. I was . . ." I had been meaning to stop by, I remembered.

"Did everyone get along well?"

"It was all of three minutes, Owen."

"Should I assume Alison knows all about this?"

"No. Of course not."

A lie, I remembered right away, is a physical thing, like a new body part that has no proper way to fit.

"Fuck," he said. "I really did not need all of this. What happens now? Is this to be a regular thing? How did she even find you?"

It was what Alison had asked about Paul: *How did he find me?* It seemed unfair that Laine should be cast among the dangerous people, the ones from whom we needed to hide. "I don't know. I must have told her at some point. Maybe she saw the same stupid ad that Alison saw. Maybe she's some kind of pathological stalker. I have no idea. I don't remember what I told her. Or told you, apparently. She can't hurt us though. She doesn't want to."

He looked at me without speaking. He didn't have to say it: She already had.

"It won't happen again," I said.

"You have no idea. Let's at least deal with reality. Maybe she'll make it a weekly event."

"That isn't reality, Owen. She's taking classes, living in New York. She isn't hanging out here."

"I guess I'll just have to trust you about the details. Is there anything else going on?" he asked. "Anything else you may have forgotten you never told me about?"

I shook my head. "No. Well . . ."

His brows shot up.

"It has nothing to do with us. I'm only telling you in case there's some technicality and you would consider this a lie. It's just that she told me her father is remarrying. That's all."

He turned his back to me, putting his glass in the sink. "That must be tough news for you," he said without a trace of sympathy in his voice.

"It's not. It has nothing to do with me. Or with us."

"Well, you must be happy for him."

"Happy for him?" I wasn't. Not at all. It hadn't occurred to me to be, I realized with some shame. "Honestly, Owen, it has nothing to do with me. Laine is . . . Laine is . . . I have an obligation to her. Like when you save someone's life, you're responsible for them. And it isn't her fault. It's like punishing her for the stupid mistakes the stupid adults in her life made. I am so, so horribly sorry that you had to go through this. But I am asking you, as a favor, to just please understand that I can't banish her from my life." I heard myself putting it all on Laine, not describing her as any kind of daughter figure to me, not dredging up that old, unfulfilled longing. "I was ambushed. She didn't mean it that way, but I was."

He sighed, then turned around. "This isn't easy for me, Gus."

"I get that. I really do. And I'm sorry."

"Just, please, if there's a way to keep this from happening again . . ."

"I will."

"Okay. Subject dropped."

"Subject dropped," I said. "But if it ever helps you to talk about it . . ."

"It will never help me to talk about it."

"Then we never will," I said, mentally adding it to the heap.

14

~~~

Don't think of it as work, Laine had said.

It wasn't easy advice to take.

Use your imagination.

My imagination? It seemed atrophied.

I had spent so much of my life trying *not* to imagine realities other than my own, certain that my envy of other families would demolish me. And when I'd shifted my focus away from those other children and their mothers, I had only slipped deeper into a different reality. The reality of things, of light. Appearances. Shapes. Vistas. Not people.

But here were these boys demanding of me that I exercise this long-unused capacity. And there was Laine, cheering me on to give them life.

I didn't paint the morning after her visit. I drew. Little caricatures, cartoon figures really. Sitting. Running. Walking. Swimming. Fast, fast, fast. No time for me to think. Skiing. Bicycling. Dancing.

Just play, Laine had advised. So I tried to play. I worked at playing, determined to keep trying until I could play without having to work.

When I saw Alison that afternoon, we returned to the pond, our first walk there in some time. "That must have been tough for you," she said as we started circling.

"Tougher for Owen," I said, knowing immediately that she meant Laine.

"I'm sure it was tough enough for you both. Your Laine is a sweet-seeming girl. In spite of all the piercings, which I have to admit are not my thing."

"She's different from Nora, I know. She's a whole different type of kid. Of young woman, I suppose."

"Yes. But both artistically inclined," Alison said. "So not quite as different as if one of them were a titan of finance or something. Both doubtless doomed to scrape for money their whole lives. Or teach high school. Like some of us."

I had never thought of Alison envying us our financial ease. But it was hard not to hear it there, hard not to be a little startled by her tone.

"You know," I said, "Laine was so high risk for so long. Such a mess. It's difficult for me to see her as the same person. I'm used to looking at her through a veil of worry, but now . . . now she seems all right. She seems so strong. It was really good to see that. Though the whole visit was a huge problem, of course. How is Nora doing?" I asked. "I've been assuming she's okay, since you haven't said otherwise."

"Oh, I suppose she's okay."

"Any news on the job front?"

"I suspect she's let that lapse since she's been staying with Paul. There wouldn't be any pressing need. Anyway, she hasn't mentioned a thing."

"Are you angry at her?" I asked. "You sound a little angry."

"Excellent question. I don't really know. Maybe. A little bit.

Not really. I try not to be, anyway. None of it's her fault. She's just making the best of a bad lot. We're the villains in the piece."

"You're not a villain, Alison."

"Nice of you to say. But who knows? I've certainly made my fair share of mistakes."

I suddenly remembered something. "Wait, you wanted to see me yesterday. I was supposed to stop by. I'm so sorry, in all the mess of things I forgot."

She reached over and gave my arm a quick squeeze. "I was just going to tell you my news, that's all. I've decided to stay. Through the whole year, I mean. Until next summer."

"Really? That's wonderful. Amazing."

But her news had fallen on me in an unexpected way. *Months.* That was the word that came to mind. *Months and months.* It seemed like a long commitment, a weightier change in our lives than I'd ever anticipated.

"I'm glad you think so," she said. "Will Owen be able to shake this off? Is he the sort to brood?"

It took me a moment to remember the topic. "Oh, he can be pretty broody," I said. "But then also . . . I mean, he stuck with me, right? So that pretty much defines him as a forgiving type." I didn't tell her about the silence in which we had gone to sleep the night before, the cold that had seemed to emanate from his side of the bed. "We'll be okay. It's just going to take a little time. All those reopened wounds."

"Yes," she said. "All those reopened wounds, indeed."

I had the sense that she was talking about something else, not me and Owen at all; but if so, she wasn't going to elaborate. She took my arm in hers. "Come on," she said. "Buck up. We still have four more rounds to go. Think of it as penance, if you like."

Over the next few weeks, I remained cautious and undemanding
as Owen thawed—though more slowly than I had hoped. His
body remained out of reach, and I knew I would have to wait. I
couldn't hurry the timetable of his hurt or of his anger, as much as
I wanted to. Meanwhile, we lay side by side each night like figures
on paired sarcophagi, and instead of stopping for a caress or a kiss
when our paths crossed in the kitchen, or on the stairs, we muttered things like *excuse me,* and *sorry about that.*

At work, I alternated between painting the boys—humbling
for me—and painting their surroundings, which gave me a sense
of accomplishment. For every leg or arm I tried to make look less
like a plastic toy, I rewarded myself with the details of a rug, or
the bark of a tree. I didn't feel that I made much progress with the
boys, but I felt like I had struck a fair balance between pushing
myself, as Laine had advised, and allowing myself the escape my
work had always given me.

As the last weekend of October passed, I knew Bill's wedding
must have as well. I waited for my mood to plummet, but the
knowledge only made me a bit contemplative, maybe wistful, for
a day or so. Nothing more. And meanwhile, as the temperatures
outside continued to drop, Owen continued to warm. Alison and
I took regular walks, admiring the trees at the height of their
annual show; and I spoke to Jan every few days, not only comparing notes on our visits to our father, but also chatting about
other things, just a bit, a tiny glance of contact beyond the efficient absolute minimum to which we had previously held ourselves.

And then one day I heard from Bill.

I'd been staring out my window watching rain begin to fall

when a bell on my computer dinged. And there he was, his name in my inbox like a hallucination.

Dear Augie,

I hope you're well. And I hope you're happy. I only just learned from Laine that she'd seen you and told you my recent news. I should have told you myself. I apologize for that. I didn't know how to handle it, but now I see that I made the wrong call.

As I read, I imagined him writing and deleting, phrasing and rephrasing. Just as I had done, writing Laine on the same topic, those weeks before. Polite. We had always been polite. But we hadn't always been only polite, and I wondered (how could I not wonder?) what all this calm had required of him.

I know that had the tables been reversed, I would have preferred to hear the news from you. And really, Augie . . .

Right there. I could feel it, a crack in the sheen.

. . . I hope things have been good for you. Better than good. I hope everything is just how you want it to be. And thank you as always for being such a friend to Laine. She never stops talking about how wonderful you are and how you saved her life all those years back.
B.
ps She tells me your father is ill. I'm sorry to hear that and hope for the best.

I read it several times. Then I responded right away.

Dear Bill,

It's really fine that I heard from Laine, and congratulations, of course. I hope this brings you everything you want.

*And yes, my father is far into Alzheimer's. The past is gone,
the present bizarre, and I suppose the best to hope for is that the
future not drag on too miserably. That sounds glib. I don't feel glib
at all. And I thank you for your good wishes.*

A.

Without rereading it, I pushed send. Then sat motionless for
quite a time.

Outside, the rain slid over the turning leaves, watery paint
drizzling hints of gold and red from the sky. This had been our
season. Fall. September into January. Autumn days. A few winter
weeks.

I stayed there for some minutes, doing something like checking my own emotional vital signs. Was my heart still in one piece?
My mind still able to function? The answers were yes. I was misty,
a bit, like the day, but I was okay.

I looked over again at the email, but with perfect timing, my
computer set itself to sleep, the screen going black. I started to
stand, to walk away, then remembered the old rules, the old ways,
and woke it up, deleting the messages we'd exchanged, and then
emptying the trash.

In the living room, the painting of the millinery shop caught my
eye. Another marker of the end of our affair.

There I had sat, close to paralyzed with gratitude that after a
year of mute brushes, silent paints, I was able to do anything at all
again. With Bill, I had painted like a madwoman, like a woman
possessed. Possessed by him and by the intoxication of secrecy.
Secretly in love. Secretly in bed together. Secretly painting to
please him. All of it, one magic spell. And then it was gone. All
of it.

I'd been so certain that Ida would cast me away had she known what I was really doing there, that she would have been shocked and unsympathetic. But standing in my living room that day, I wondered if I had been right about that. Maybe she wouldn't have given up on me, she who could turn bits and pieces of fabric into things of exquisite beauty. Maybe she would have known how to quilt the scraps of me together, the edges still frayed and likely to come apart at whatever seams I had hastily sewn.

And I wondered, looking at that sleeve, about my mother. Would she have been the sort to make me feel worse for having transgressed, or the sort to love me harder, to help me through? Would I even have told her? Would we have been that close? I would never know. When you achieve something, a good grade, a new job, you can always tell yourself that the missing parent would have been proud. But what about when you fuck up? Arguably, that was the real test of a relationship, and as far as my mother went, I would never have a clue.

But I had been loved that way in my life. By Owen. Loved and accepted through every stumble, through every fall. I'd once assured Alison that I couldn't have done the same for him, that I wasn't as big or as generous a person as he, but standing again before that painting, I wondered if that imbalance was truly something that I should accept.

15

I told Alison about the email from Bill some days later while sitting in my usual spot on her floor, with my usual view of her legs, though with the colder weather she had taken to wearing black tights and long-sleeved shirts layered under those dresses of hers.

"Mostly, it reminded me of how I used to paint for him. How hard it was for me to claim it all back after that, to make it not be about painting to please Bill, and how easy it can still be for me to lose the thread of my own work."

"Oh, I sometimes wish it were that complicated for me."

"Don't wish that."

"Well, I do. Here I plod along. Reliable. Endlessly reliable. And uninspired. I might as well be making greeting cards. I wish I could paint the way I drive."

"It might be better if you drove the way you paint. And that isn't a criticism of your painting. If anything . . ."

"No. I understand. So, does it feel at all like a chapter closed? Was the email helpful in some way?"

I thought. "Maybe. Something has been. The chapter is closed, for sure. As closed as such chapters ever are."

Alison's phone buzzed. "Hold on," she said. "It's Nora." She stepped out from behind the canvas and left the room. When she returned, she was smiling. "She'll be here in a few days and she'll stay through Thanksgiving. Oh, she sounds so good."

"I'm really glad," I said, trying to seem sincere. I thought of adding that Owen and I never celebrated Thanksgiving, but caught myself before throwing cold water on the moment. "I know how you've missed her," I said. "And worried too."

"Yes, I have worried plenty," she said. "But she sounds really good. I try not to pester her about Paul, but she volunteered that things there have been calm. It was all, 'Oh, you know Dad, he's not exactly easygoing.' But she said there had been no incidents, certainly no more drunk driving. I think she may be in charge of the keys. And soon enough she'll be here. At which point he can drive himself off a bridge for all of me."

"It looks as though young Nora will be back with us for a while," I told Owen when he came in at the end of the day. "She's coming soon. An indefinite stay, at least through Thanksgiving."

He sat on a kitchen chair, took off his jacket. Then nodded and said, "So I hear."

"Alison seems happy," I said. "Doesn't she?"

But it wasn't Alison who had told him. "Nora emailed me this morning," he said.

Such a simple sentence really: *Nora emailed me this morning.*

"I don't understand."

He leaned over and began untying his boots. "I don't understand what you don't understand."

"I don't understand that Nora emails you her news. I hadn't realized you were in touch."

He pulled off one then the other boot before answering. "Oh, you know what young people are like," he said. "They email everyone. It's like breathing to them. Meaningless."

"You hadn't mentioned it."

"You never asked." He looked at me for just a second, then down again to line his boots up against the wall. "Anyway, there was nothing to mention. Until you told me she was coming back—and then there was. Since I already knew. So I mentioned it."

"When . . . when did this start?"

"What?"

I looked at him, searching for a challenge on his face, any sign that he was picking a fight; but found nothing exactly like that. "Never mind," I said. "I just hadn't realized. And now you won't have to email anymore, because she'll be right next door."

"I guess that's right," he said. "I think I'll go upstairs for a bit." He stood.

"Your water," I said. "You forgot your glass of water."

He looked at me for a moment, expressionless, then shrugged and left the room.

"He's been such a help to her," Alison said, as we walked the next day. I had brought the conversation around to the subject— pretending to have known all along that they'd been in touch. "I think he may have encouraged her to come back," she said. "When it's me advising her, she can't help but see it as me getting be- tween her and her father. I'm just so grateful for all Owen's doing for her."

"I'm just so glad he's been able to," I responded, for all the world as though Owen's attentions to Nora were a gift I had be- stowed.

I visited my father soon after that, alone. I felt no interest in bringing Alison, whose failure or maybe refusal to question

Nora's attachment to Owen was irritating me. And meanwhile Owen and I had somehow maneuvered ourselves into a standoff that I suspected neither of us understood or wanted. But there we were. So I didn't invite Owen, and he didn't offer to come along.

M y dad seemed especially subdued when I arrived, maybe even asleep. I sat for a while taking silent inventory: *Bad painting of mine:* check. *Afghan of mysterious origin:* check. *Photo of three grimacing girls:* check.

The first time I'd seen his new room, during that long-ago week after Labor Day, it was just as I'd imagined it would be, complete with keypad lock on the door, opened for me by an unfamiliar nurse. She'd said there were good reasons for family not to have the code, a statement that immediately put me in a foul mood. The room itself felt both clinically cold and also somehow overstuffed—as if with scratchy wool. A space in which it would be impossible to find comfort but for contradictory reasons. Too empty, too filled. Too cold, too hot. Too small but then also somehow too big, my father rattling inside like a dried seed in a gourd.

I'd visited frequently since then, though he rarely seemed to know me, and I found the visits more and more upsetting. Not only because his disease was progressing, but because he had been mild as a lamb since they'd moved him, and I couldn't bear that he was there for no reason, eternally punished for a one-time, maybe two-time, offense. At some point, I mentioned this to a nurse who said she'd pass on my concern, but as far as she knew no one ever came back from the lockup wing.

Bars on windows: check. *Guard outside the door:* check.

And then suddenly my father spoke.

"Gus," he said. "You were late."

I was well steeled for his not knowing me, but not for this.

"I'm sorry, Dad. There was traffic."

"So good with the excuses." He smiled, glints of saliva at each corner of his mouth. "It's only five minutes past," he said. "Don't look like that. I'm not going to ground you."

I wasn't late, of course. I hadn't told anyone I was coming.

"I'm just glad to be here," I said. "I like the new place." He frowned, looked confused. "Maybe it doesn't feel new to you anymore."

"No, Gus. Not after, what is it now?" His eyes focused on the distance, his head nodding, regular, small pulses, counting. "It's thirteen years, Augusta," he said. "No. It would be strange for it to feel new to me." His look was familiar now: impatience manifest as extreme, condescending patience at my failure to grasp something obvious.

"I suppose not. After thirteen years. I wasn't thinking." And then I asked, "How's the food?" and he looked at me as though I were crazy. "Never mind. Stupid question. It's really good to see you, Dad."

"It's good to see you too. You look well. Do you know your mother died? I can't remember if she told you." He leaned forward a bit. "I'm having some trouble," he said. "Remembering things. But that's certainly right. She's dead. You probably know but I just . . ." He let the thought trail off.

"I did know. I'm sorry."

He had mentioned her. My father had mentioned my mother. That fact shuddered through me.

"I thought you should be told."

"Thank you," I said. "That was thoughtful of you."

It was like some sort of natural disaster, the crash of questions I suddenly felt. The ones I had never asked. Questions about my own birth. About her sense of humor. About whether she had nursed me. How she had dressed me. What she had loved in me most.

"Would you like to talk about her?" I asked, carefully, the

whole exchange a crystal vessel I might shatter with a too-sudden move.

"Yes," he said. "I would like to talk about her. Because you see, she was my wife. So yes, please tell me everything. Tell me all about her." He sat up, like a child waiting for a story.

And I had nothing to say. But there he sat. And there we sat. As the questions inside me drained away.

After some seconds, I found Charlotte's memories crouching in a dark corner of my mind. "Okay," I said. "Well, let's see. She used to love to take her daughters to the park. Where she would push them on the swings, but she would also take turns on the swings by herself. Like a great big kid. And she tucked them in, us in, every night. With kisses. And she was very good at . . . at cooking. And also she spoke French. Or anyway, there were French songs she would sing sometimes. Songs about sheep. And one about a bird."

The expectant look remained, but I had run out of material. "And . . . and she was glad that she had only daughters, that the two of you did, because . . . because the Vietnam War was going on then, around when we were all born, and she didn't want her children going off to war. And . . . and she wasn't religious, but . . . well, she liked to take long walks and she loved to . . . to watch television because her parents hadn't had a set when she was small. And she . . . her favorite food was spaghetti. And she liked to drink wine. But not too much. Or maybe a little too much. She would dance sometimes, just around the house, when she'd had a little too much to drink, but she would never dance otherwise. And she would sometimes sing the French songs when she danced. And sometimes hold one of her daughters." The look on my father's face had changed, softened. His lids were starting to lower. "And she had a fear of elevators, not of being closed inside but of them going through the earth, of them being unable to stop. And so in elevators she would always hold your hand. And she was very intelligent too. People would forget that sometimes, but she was sharp as a tack and it bothered her just a little that because you were the schoolteacher everyone assumed you were smarter, but she knew that you didn't think so. And she was also an excellent photographer. Not of people so much, but of buildings, streets. She was never without her Brownie, always looking at things a little askew with her head tilted . . ."

His eyes were fully closed. "And you loved the way she tilted her head like that." I could hear him breathe, heavily. "And you never got over it, did you, Dad? You never did move on, did you?" I took my own deep breath. "But you're moving on now. And I suppose that's just as well."

I sat silent, listening as his breathing turned to snores, just a minute or so more.

While I drove home, I thought the world an unsteady, malleable place. What did it matter what had actually happened? My memories of my mother came from Charlotte. And now, my drifting, dwindling father might be reliving them, re-creating this woman, cobbled together of my sister's desire that her mother be shared and of my own trackless trains of association. He might well be with her on some winding road down which she walked—or danced—while singing in French.

I surprised myself by smiling at the thought. I surprised myself by hoping that they were indeed together, dancing together, as he slept.

16

Alison slammed her car into a deer the night before Nora's arrival. She was driving back from the grocery store where she'd gone to pick up a few things Nora liked having in the house. My phone rang around ten, right as I was thinking of going to bed. Owen and I were in the living room. She was somewhere on the road. It had just happened. She sounded hysterical.

"She isn't dead," Alison said. "She's bleeding. She's . . . dying, I think."

"What about you? Are you okay?"

Owen was watching me, puzzled. I reached for an ever-present pencil, a piece of paper, and sketched a hieroglyph of a car hitting a deer. I wrote *Alison,* then pushed it across the coffee table toward him.

"I just don't believe it," she said.

"Is she hurt?" Owen asked.

"Alison, are you hurt?"

She didn't think so. She wasn't sure. She felt off-kilter. The airbags had gone off. The front of the car was crumpled. "And the deer . . ."

"Has she called 911?"

"Did you call 911?"

She hadn't. "I just . . . she's still alive, I think."

I wondered if she had been drinking, but couldn't think of an acceptable way to ask. "It's just an accident," I said. "They're everywhere. Deer. It's a huge problem. But you should call 911."

"I should . . . ," she said again. "I need . . . I'm so sorry. I just can't face . . ."

I asked her where she was and signaled Owen to push the paper back to me, but then I didn't use it. I knew the place, a nasty patch of winding road. "We'll be right there," I said. "Do you want me to report it?"

But she said that she would call. "I wasn't drinking," she volunteered. "I was just . . . I was just driving very fast."

"You've never been in a car with her," I reminded Owen as we set off—him at the wheel. "It's terrifying."

"Then maybe you shouldn't be in a car with her anymore."

"Well, anyone can hit a deer," I said. "Really anyone could hit a deer."

The police hadn't arrived when we got there. Alison's car was tipped into a ditch at a crook of the road. The lights weren't on and at first I didn't see her, but then as we walked toward the car's front, I could just make out a shape, a shadowy creature, the head of a human, the legs of a beast. Closer, I saw the deer's face up against Alison's hip, and closer still saw the animal's torso, bloody, gashed, ribs exposed, crushed.

"Alison."

She turned at the sound of my voice. A rivulet of red ran from her scalp to her jaw. I reached for Owen's arm. "Call 911." It seemed obvious she had not.

"She's trying so hard not to die," Alison said. "I can't believe I did this."

"It happens, Alison. It happens all the time." Owen had stepped away, but I could hear him giving our location. I sat among the fallen leaves on frozen mud. "Your head. You have a cut. Owen," I called. "An ambulance. Be sure."

She started to sob, her face lowered into her hand, so the blood smeared her cheek, her palm. I put my arm around her shoulders. The doe was young, I saw. And seemed to be looking at me. I touched her with my other hand, just behind her ear, so that we, the three of us, made a circuit, complete, a current of life rasping unevenly through. I wanted to encourage the shattered animal to die. I wanted my touch to convey somehow, somehow, that soon the others would arrive, with lights, with efficiency, procedure, protocol. That being alive would be no gift.

Beside me, Alison's body shook with sobs.

"They're on their way," Owen said.

"Maybe she won't die," Alison said. I tightened my arm around her.

"It happens all the time," I said again.

A siren in the distance. Lights flashing at the next bend in the road. I took my gaze from the doe, and while I watched the ambulance approach, the animal died.

The moments, minutes, after that were just as I'd imagined them, except that where there had been a life, there was only the body of a deer, left on the ground while an EMT took charge of Alison. The cut was deeper than I had thought, deeper surely than Alison had known. She might have been concussed as well. There could be internal injuries. She had to go to the hospital for observation. They laid her on a cot, covered her with a sheet that was soon bloodied, small dark patches, spreading. They strapped her down.

"I'm fine on my own," she said, when I offered to go with her. "I'm suddenly so tired."

A policeman walked up to us, stern, almost angry. "You women got that close to a dying deer? You're lucky the animal didn't kick your heads right open. Those things are mean as snakes when they know that they're goners."

"I'm sorry," I said. Sincere. Like a child who's crossed the road without looking, and knows that she's done wrong.

We drove home mostly in a silence thick with what wasn't being said.

"I told her it could happen to anyone," I finally said. "And it could. But the fact is she drives like a maniac, and that has to raise the odds."

"That has to raise the odds," Owen said. "I agree."

By the time Nora arrived the next morning, I had already fetched Alison from the hospital where she'd spent the night, and set her up in our living room—not because she needed much tending, but because it seemed wrong to leave her by herself with memories, with images of the accident. There had been a mild concussion, the doctors thought, and the gash on her head had required twelve stitches. Everything else seemed to be okay, just bruises everywhere, but she was badly shaken. By tacit agreement neither of us mentioned the doe, speaking only of headaches and sore muscles, exhaustion, the sterility of hospitals, the good fortune of her injuries not being worse.

Alison had called Nora and told her what had happened, but still Nora's face jumped as if electrically shocked, at the sight of her mother on our couch, bandaged and pale. "Oh my God, Mom. Oh my God." She sat beside her, finding a space on the cushion's worn edge where no space had been before. Alison's eyes closed; her lips relaxed into a slight smile. I felt like the intruder I was and left the room.

I didn't see much of them over the next few days, and neither did Owen. After Nora and I bundled Alison up to go home, the two of them stayed huddled there together. That was how I pictured them, never apart. I dropped their mail on their porch, and it disappeared. We had our first snowfall, close to half a foot. Owen shoveled our walk, and then did theirs, cleared both cars off, but no one emerged to thank him.

During this period, a new quality of fragility seeped into my understanding of who they were. The car accident had undoubtedly been a turning point for me, Alison's bravado and daring seeming more like recklessness and desperation now. And as enviable as I found their bond to be—how could I not?—I had a far clearer sense of the shakiness of any ground on which they stood, so when I looked across the glistening white hill, I saw most clearly the shabbiness of the house, the shutters that were askew, the missing porch rails.

And as for the revelation that Owen and Nora had been in touch, that faded from my list of worries. He had used their contact to make me feel bad, a meaningless revenge for Laine's visit, to which he was arguably entitled. Maybe it had helped him get past his anger to bask in Nora's adulation a little bit. I could deal with that. Life felt both big and precious during those soft, snowy days. There was room enough for the petty to be seen as exactly that.

I kept to a regular work schedule then, trying not to get too discouraged. It would have been so easy, I often thought, just to cover up the soldiers entirely, transform these canvases into nothing more than a series of portraits of rooms in my house. But I didn't let myself.

Over time, Alison and Nora emerged and our lives began again to intertwine. Dinners for four. Walks for two—sometimes three, as Nora occasionally joined her mother and me. More often, though, I would see her heading to the barn.

And those visits to Owen didn't go unexplained. They weren't surreptitious. She had admired the space, the churchlike atmosphere—the very quality I had thought only I perceived—and he had told her to feel free to join him. She could read or she could write. She only had to be quiet. The invitation was extended over dinner at our house, this time bread and cheese and ham in the living room, nothing like our first, elaborately prepared meal.

"In the city," he said, "I always liked to work with other people in the space. It jogged my brain somehow. It's Gus who can't bear having anyone around."

"Well, it's a little different for a painter," I said. "It's all so visible. I doubt you'd have liked it if the other customers at the coffee shop had been reading your every word."

"I don't know," he said. "There were days when I could have used the critique."

"You had lots of company there, didn't you?" Alison indicated the painting of Ida's shop.

"I did. And actually I loved the hubbub. But nobody had the least interest in what I was doing. I've rarely felt more invisible in my life."

"I would feel like an intruder," Nora said. "I couldn't."

By then, mid-November, her hair was noticeably longer than when we'd first met. Like her mother, she always wore a little bit of makeup, barely visible, almost as if more a reminder of her femininity than anything else. That night, she had on jeans through which you could see her hip bones when she stood, and a long-sleeved black top, through which at moments you could see her nipples. The shirt collar fell just at the level of the cross, so the cross would slip beneath the cloth, only the occasional glint of that very fine chain remaining visible, although once you knew the cross was there, you could see that too.

As she protested that she couldn't impose, I knew that she would. And there was something about the openness with which this all unfolded that made it seem churlish to object. He was mentoring her. She was in need of a positive male role model. Alison repeated these phrases to me all the time. Owen spoke elliptically in the same terms as if it were an assessment of their dynamic to which we had long ago agreed. And I said nothing to object.

17

As Thanksgiving drew near, I knew Alison assumed we would join them and was wondering how to demur when I learned that Owen had already agreed on our behalf. They would do most of the cooking. I would bake a pie or two, if I didn't mind. "Neither of us is much of a baker," Alison said. We would supply wine. These details came out over dinner at Alison's house, and I found myself smiling and saying, "Of course, of course. I'm so glad it's all settled."

But then, as we walked home, I said, "Thanksgiving, Owen? Really? It's a brave new world, indeed. You didn't think you should consult me?"

"I can't count all the meals we've had with her that you just assumed I wanted to have."

"But we don't celebrate Thanksgiving, remember?"

"A person can cling too hard to his principles," he said, a comment that left me with no response.

I crossed paths with Jan at my father's that week and thought of inviting her and Letty. I had been serious about wanting them in our lives more; and maybe too I wanted some ballast to the gathering. But I knew they had annual plans and I couldn't stand the thought of the *no* I would certainly hear. *I thought you and Owen were too politically high-minded for such things?* She wouldn't say it, but I was certain it would be there in a raised brow, the tilt of her head. For all that we were more in touch than we'd been, I had no illusions that the lifetime of prickles between us would be magically gone.

Tuesday of Thanksgiving week was the last day of the farmers' market until spring. Only a few years before, I'd been told, it always shut down the week before Halloween, but it just wasn't that cold anymore, not usually, and the burst of shopping before the holiday made wearing some extra layers worthwhile. I'd been avoiding the place since meeting Kathleen Mayhew, sensing that if she ever did want to share family lore about Jackie, I didn't really want to hear it. I was having a hard enough time without the notion of Mayhew family members looking over my shoulder. But I needed a baking pumpkin, the big, pale, fleshy sort that the grocery store didn't have, and Alison had her usual list, though longer than usual, including a turkey, freshly killed and plucked, so we went together, just us, doubtless leaving Nora trailing after Owen.

I saw Kathleen before she saw me. She stood alone behind the old wooden table, under the worn canvas roof, arranging a set of bright quilted potholders held on a line with laundry pins. There were no customers nearby and her face, I realized, was a private one, different from what I'd seen as she'd sold Alison vinegar. Different too from the puzzled features registering my strange mention of her boy uncle, long deceased. She studied the potholders, frowning at their arrangement and changing it, noting an improvement I could not detect except in the evident approval of her unfurrowing brow, her untightening lips. It was probably how I looked as I painted, I thought. Absorbed in something others can't perceive. Aiming for some effect that doesn't yet exist.

She looked strikingly like Jackie, as she worked. Whatever the dubious quality of my portraits, I had memorized his face by then, and the resemblance seemed much stronger than the first time I'd seen her. As if by learning his features more thoroughly I had cracked some kind of code.

When she noticed me watching her, I waved, and she waved back. I hadn't been anxious to speak to her, but it seemed rude to walk away.

As I approached, I said something about the potholders looking nice. "It's an eye-catching display," I said, then realized the comment would sound more sincere if I bought one. "I'd love to have the black plaid."

"They're always big sellers at Thanksgiving." She unclipped it from the line, rearranging the others to fill the empty space. "I know I always manage to burn a few once there are enough pots on the stove. Sooner or later, I get careless and leave one too close to the flame. I suppose everyone does."

As I fished out my eleven dollars, I asked her if she made them herself, and she said she did not, that her older sister did. "But she doesn't like coming to the market. We're very different that way. I hate sitting inside sewing. She hates being out in the world."

"Sisters can be pretty different," I said.

I hadn't thought I would mention my visit to Jackie's grave, maybe not even mention him at all, but perhaps through some set of associations, the talk of an older sister changed that. "I went out to the cemetery after I was here that other time," I said, as she handed me the potholder in a brown paper bag. "Your family's, I mean. I hope that doesn't sound too intrusive. I've just felt strangely close to your uncle since starting this project of mine, and I wanted to see where he's buried. I wanted to pay my respects."

She frowned, and looked at me for a few moments, silent. Then she shook her head. "He isn't there," she said.

I thought she was going to add something religious, maybe

talk about his being in heaven; and I regretted having brought it up. She sat down on the wooden folding chair behind the counter. "He isn't anywhere. He was . . ." She closed her eyes, took a deep breath, then opened them as she exhaled. "It was a grenade," she said. "Some kind of explosion. There was nothing left of the boy to bring home."

I didn't know what to say. "I'm so sorry. I saw a grave . . . I just assumed."

"Believe me, he isn't there. That was part of the story my father told and told and told. That poor Jackie had been blown up be-yond . . . That he was everywhere and nowhere all at once. Just like God, my father would say."

"That sounds . . ." I thought of how frightening it must have been for a child. Not just young death, but the gore of it. And that conflation of a decimated body with God. I wanted to say the right thing. But another customer had appeared beside me, and I knew the subject had to be shut down. "I really am sorry," I said, once again. "And I'm sorry if bringing it up . . ." But Kathleen shrugged that off.

"It's nothing new," she said. "An old story, believe me. And truly, it isn't right for me never to remember him, if only for my father's sake. Like you said, to pay my respects. God knows, my children are barely aware he ever existed. After me, me and my sister, it'll all be forgotten."

"I understand that," I said. "The remembering, I mean. How much it matters. I really do." But I felt impatience begin to rise like steam off the other customer, now a step closer to the booth, so I just wished Kathleen a good holiday, and she wished me the same, and I went off to find Alison.

This is me, on the day before Thanksgiving:

I am making the pies, first cutting the pumpkin in half, scrap-ing out the seeds and stringy fibers around them, soaking all that in a bowl of water. I cut the halves into pieces and bake the chunks, then cool them, then scoop the soft flesh from the skin. I have done all this before, years and years before, with my father's older sister, my Aunt Anna—called Antenna by us, behind her back—at whose home in Maryland we celebrated the holiday when we were all young. She taught me to cook her specialties and though it has been years since I have done so, years too since she's died, a physical memory I haven't known I possess remains in my hands, in my arms, in all my senses. It is there as I reach into the bowl of water and strip the seeds from the muck around them, there as I fish them from the water and lay them on paper towels to dry. And it is there too as I know from the smell alone that the pumpkin has cooked to softness; as I know exactly the texture of crumbled butter in flour to make a perfect crust.

I haven't wanted to be glad we were having Thanksgiving. I've wanted only to feel angry that Owen's indulgence of Nora, or whatever I was to call it, has led us to break a pact we made decades ago. But in fact I am more than glad as I carry the two perfect pies from the oven to the marble cutting board put out for them. I am elated to have discovered this other self still dwelling within my molecules. And I am curious too, as I stand there admiring the perfect sheen of each pie, the slight fractures, lightning bolts at the centers, where each has risen, then fallen flat, curious about what other selves I carry but have forgotten. It is as though I have somehow discovered a new light in which I can detect the palimpsest that is me, the Gussies layered on top of one another, some faded, others all too visible.

"Those are beautiful," Owen says when he comes in. "Another hidden talent."

"My aunt, Antenna, taught us all how to bake them," I say. "I don't know why I never did it before. It's not the law that pumpkin pie is only for Thanksgiving, I know. I just never thought of it." It is like so much else, I realize. Another part of the past that

I have blunted or hidden or jettisoned because I lack some normal, innate understanding of how to carry experiences and even capabilities with myself through time.

"Maybe I'll bring my father some, later this week," I say. "He might like that."

Owen looks at me curiously. "I'm sure he would," he says.

On Thursday morning, I decided to set the table in white, almost entirely white. White lace over white linen. White napkins. White china—or as close as I could find among our strange collection. White candles set into old silver candlesticks. I wanted a canvas for the meal. I wanted to experience the table filling with food as I experienced a painting coming together. The only exception I made was for a handful of leaves, still moist, orange, red, that I cut into thin strips and scattered, confetti across the whiteness, ribbons of autumn itself.

By the time Alison and Nora arrived and then arrived again and then again as they carried dish after dish across the hill, I had dressed in an old, soft, gray dress that I hadn't worn in years, one Owen had long loved, and I'd brushed my hair loose, putting Charlotte's tiny emerald earrings into holes I'd half assumed had long ago closed.

I stepped out of the way as Alison, in black, and Nora, in violet, managed the business of warming or cooling their food, in my kitchen. I watched them from the doorway, mother and daughter, moving around one another, choreographed perfectly for life. I could see the beauty of it just then, just for those minutes, the warp of envy for once set aside.

"Who's ready for a drink?" Owen called from the living room.
Everyone was.

As we sat at the table, I watched Nora bow her head, murmuring the prayer she spoke at every meal; or maybe a special one for the day. I wanted to ask her about it. For the first time, I felt a genuine, nonjudgmental curiosity about what all of this praying and believing meant to her. But I didn't say anything, in part because for so many weeks I had needed to be ever vigilant that I not speak to her harshly. And though I would have asked the question respectfully this time, it was a question I might in another mood ask with belligerence, which was how I thought Owen would hear it no matter what my tone; and so I said nothing.

The meal itself was traditional—turkey, yams, stuffing, green beans—which Alison attributed to her being a foreigner. "It's all very well for you Americans to use Thanksgiving as an excuse for culinary explorations, but I had to learn to do it right. I have to prove myself."

"It's delicious," I said, and it was; though there were also moments when all I could taste was the discrepancy between this meal and the ones we'd had those many decades earlier, meals it had never occurred to me to miss, but that I suddenly longed to relive.

Across the table, Owen sat. Eating. And drinking.

The mood that had first set on me while making the pies hadn't left me yet, and so as I watched him, I thought about all the many, many Owens there, carried in that single body of his. The boy. The man he had been before I taught him wariness. The measurer of distances and plumber of pond depths.

How was it that any one of us could walk across a room without our own multitudes tripping us up?

Maybe none of us could.

We were halfway through the meal when Alison began an impromptu, tipsy recitation of thankfulness. "Well, to begin, I am grateful to have found this place, by which truly I mean the two of you." She held her glass first toward me, and then toward Owen.

"Oh, me too," Nora said, raising hers. "And I'm grateful to be learning so much every day. Though I suppose that's close to the same thing. I feel so very lucky."

"What about you, Gus?" Alison asked. "What's on your list of blessings for the year?"

"Well, all of that too, obviously." I had to say it. I thought of my father, but I didn't know how to phrase the peculiar gratitude I felt for how his ragged edges and my own now allowed us an odd new closeness; and I didn't want to expose that private sensation to the assembled group. "I'm grateful to be engaged in work I care about. Owen, what about you? Do you have a list?"

"I'm afraid we're a very boring bunch." He raised his glass. "For you all, of course. And to be writing again. Something I truly never believed would happen."

"Here's to that," Alison said.

"A roof over my head," I said. "We shouldn't take these things for granted. Food. Health. Being alive. You know those boys I paint?" I looked at Nora. "They all died years younger than you are now. Years."

"Horrible," Alison said.

"How do you phrase thankfulness for that?" Owen asked. "For not being those boys?"

"Maybe just that. I'm grateful not to be one of those boys."

"We're probably all grateful not to have died in some battle-field somewhere," Owen said. "Or anyway, we should be."

"Do you know anyone who's part of it?" I asked Nora. "The current wars?"

She shook her head. "No. Nobody from my school even thought about doing that. High school, I mean. There were some kids at Tufts who had been in the army, but they stayed to themselves. I'm pretty sure we must have seemed like babies to them. And . . ." She frowned.

"What?" I asked.

"It's so awful," she said. "But I think we were a little bit afraid of them. It was so strange to think they had, you know. They had killed people. Or anyway, they might have."

"My father was in the war. You should ask your mother to tell you the story. She knows all about it."

"A case of mistaken identity," Alison said, reaching for the stuffing. "Gus's poor father had me mistaken for an old flame from the war."

"World War II," I added, thinking it must seem unimaginably long ago to the girl sitting there. "Millicent. Millie, the English girl with the horrible mother."

"Is that why you want to paint these boys?" Nora asked. "Something about your father?"

"It was a different war," I said.

"No, I know, I just wondered. I guess I'm asking why you're so interested in them. If you even know why, I mean. Because I don't always know why I write about the things I write."

"I don't know why I write what I do either," Owen said.

"I was just wondering, Gus, if it's different for you. With a subject. With what draws you to one."

"No," I said, wary of this questioning. "No, I think it's probably not so different."

"Is it a war thing?" Nora asked. "An antiwar thing, I mean?"

"Not really. I really don't know." The same questions that from Laine had felt so like help, now felt like an attack of some kind.

"Is it something about them being local? Like part of the history of this place? Like documenting a forgotten part of history?"

"Documenting history? No." I looked over to Alison, who

showed no sign of leaping to my aid. "I don't really like to talk about my work while I'm doing it," I said, though at least two people there knew that was a lie. "I'm sorry. It's just not part of how I work. Being questioned and all. It makes me uncomfortable."

"Oh, well," Alison said, finally snapping into action. "That's completely understandable. And anyway, who ever knows why we do what we do? I can certainly give a cogent explanation for why I'm fascinated by the petal of a rose, but who knows if it's close to accurate?"

"I'm sorry," Nora said. "I'm just . . . I just think it's really interesting."

"Me too," Alison said. "But right now, I'm more interested in dessert."

Later, Owen accused me of snapping at Nora. "She's just a kid, a curious kid."

"She was badgering me. I didn't want to be badgered." We were sitting in the living room, a fire still glowing. We had spent the last hour or so tidying up with little conversation. "And I wasn't rude to her," I said, though I knew I had been. "I was just clear."

"You didn't hear your tone."

"Maybe she'll learn a lesson, then. Isn't that what curious kids are supposed to do? I don't understand why everyone is always leaping to her defense. No. That's not true. I do understand why Alison does. I'm just hoping I don't understand why you do."

"I'm not leaping to her defense. In part I'm asking you if you want to be seen as attacking her. It's, it's maybe not how you want to appear."

"Oh, please, let me worry about how I appear. What about how she appears?"

He didn't say anything.

"She's been chasing after you since the night she arrived," I said. "Father figure, my ass."

He waited a moment to speak. "We've never exchanged an inappropriate word," he said. "If that's what all this is about. I'm a model of propriety around her. I morph back into my sexless professorial persona."

"But please tell me you'll at least admit she has the world's biggest crush on you?"

"I admit that she may be infatuated, in a harmless, unserious way."

"I'm not so sure about harmless. And I don't think I was rude to her."

"Just relax, Gus. Nora isn't a threat."

"Nora." I said it as if it were a preposterous word. I stood and walked toward the fire, poked at the embers just a bit. "Perfect little Nora. Except of course she isn't little. She's more like some kind of Amazon."

He laughed and joined me, drew me to him in a hug, taking the poker from my hand, leaning it against the fireplace. "Do you know what I'm thankful for?" he asked, smoothing my hair from my face, tucking a few loose strands behind my ears.

"For an adoring twenty-two-year-old who looks at you like you're God and some kind of movie star all rolled into one?"

"Don't be a jerk," he said, and then kissed me, slowly, a little forcefully. "Let's go upstairs," he said. He slipped his hand into mine. "Let's both of us display a little gratitude for what we have."

After that, the subject of Nora felt newly out of bounds. I had raised it and Owen had reassured me. What's more, he had done so without dredging up the past. That felt like some kind of freebie to me. But to broach the subject again was to doubt his word, and to doubt his word was to drag out the whole question of whose word was and was not to be believed. And the past would never stay asleep through that, I knew.

None of this was said or even hinted at, but years of navigating these waters had given me a decent instinct for managing the nasty currents that still ran through. A certain kind of avoidance had become second nature to me.

So I watched in silence as November slid away, holding my tongue about the frequency of Nora's visits to the barn. But I began to make excuses to minimize the number of dinners we all shared each week. I couldn't imagine how Alison was letting this all go on, couldn't bear to hear from her about Owen's positive influence again, and I would have started to avoid her even more during the days, except she beat me to the punch. No more knocks at my kitchen door, no more suggestions that we run errands together or just go for a walk.

My work suffered. Even I, with my near-lifelong ability to shut out upsetting situations and isolate myself, could not achieve the necessary detachment from our daily tensions to stay productive doing what Laine had advised me to do, to *play,* to have fun with it, to stop worrying about the quality and be willing to fail. And so I shifted my eyes once again from the figures in the paintings and set about perfecting what surrounded them. You cannot fight fire with fire. You cannot fight the sensation of losing control with the sensation of being out of control.

So the interior of my house on these canvases daily took on a more and more polished sheen, while the inhabitants of the paintings, like those of the house itself, were daily more evidently out of place.

18

On the calendar in our kitchen, the words *Cape Cod* and a question mark, all in Owen's handwriting, hovered over the middle of the month. We were coming to the time he had thought might be right for our annual winter visit to his parents; but he'd said nothing about it for weeks. And I suspected that he wouldn't unless I raised the matter. And even if I did, I thought he might well trump my desire to get away for a few days with his need to keep working now that things were rolling along. But then, one afternoon when he came in from work, he popped into the studio and asked what I thought of taking a day or so to pack and then head up north.

"It's a good time for my parents," he said. "And a good time for me too. How about you?"

"I thought you'd never ask," I said.

The drive from our home up to the Cape and all the way to Wellfleet is about eight hours in the summer, sometimes even ten, but more like six and a half on a Wednesday in December when the notion of that unprotected elbow of land jutting into the Atlantic carries far less universal appeal. Owen and I—unsurprisingly enough—preferred the Cape off-season, the site of a party long ended, a few guests inexplicably remaining. His parents had first moved there from Boston nearly twenty years before, and during their early summers, we'd visited during the height of the madness and heat, a period they loved and seemed to draw energy from. But pretty soon, we began limiting our very occasional trips there to chilly days in bleak months, enduring their eye-rolling jokes over our poor timing and wrong preferences, our perverseness and also our inherently gloomy characters.

"Only the naturally lugubrious would prefer Wellfleet in February," Lillian said.

"That's us," Owen had cheerfully replied. "Naturally lugubrious and proud of it."

In general, over the years, we would spend the hours of the drive talking about his parents, as if desensitizing ourselves in anticipation of the exposure. Not that they were as toxic as all that, but there was a way in which the idea of a sudden encounter was like the idea of falling unprepared into an icy stream.

This time, though, we were quiet at the start. As I drove we exchanged only occasional comments on the traffic, the choice of Hudson River crossing. When we approached the George Washington Bridge, Owen said we must be the last people on earth to pay cash at tolls anymore and I said we couldn't be since the lines in the cash lane were so long, but that I knew what he meant. He wondered if we should get one of those auto-pay devices and I said we barely drove enough to make it worth the effort. We were a bit stiff with each other, as we had been for days, but I didn't know anything was about to shift until just as we got past the toll, Owen said, "There's something we need to talk about, Gus." And then I knew immediately what it would be.

"Right," I said. "I guess there is."

"Nora," he said.

"Yes," I said, after a moment. "Nora."

"I'm . . ." He was looking out the window.

"I know what you are. I'm not blind."

(Later, just hours later, sitting at dinner with his parents, the phrase *We'll cross that bridge when we come to it* would rattle in my head like a loose nail I couldn't shake free. How long had I been waiting for exactly this exchange? How often had I told myself not to worry in advance? That we would cross that bridge when we came to it. And then there we were, silent across an actual bridge, life laughing at us as we made our way from one shore to the next.)

"Well, I guess it's good you're talking about it," I said, reasonably—though it didn't feel good. And I didn't want to be reasonable. But it was what we had sworn after the disaster of Bill. If you ever feel tempted . . . if you feel yourself falling, fess up. Nip it in the bud. We can deal with these things together. They're bound to come up in a life. But we can deal with them. If we're honest. *We'll cross that bridge . . .*

"I know that you've wondered," he said. "And I'm not saying you're entirely wrong."

"It's a little hard to miss."

"I don't know what it is," he said. "I don't exactly know what's happening."

"She's very lovely." My voice sounded steady, detached—as though I were commenting on a photograph of somebody's niece. "It's easy to see why."

"It isn't that. It isn't that at all, really. She's . . ." He turned to me. "Do you want to hear all this, Gus?"

No, I did not. I, Gus Edelman, emphatically did not want to hear this. Nor did I want it to be true. Nor did I want to be stuck behind an enormous truck that moved with the vehicular equivalent of a series of spasmodic coughs. I didn't want anything that was happening to be happening. But I had also slipped into some other mode. An insensate autopilot mode. As though there were some emergency preparedness crew inside me ready to take over, to behave calmly, to focus on damage control.

"I want us to do whatever is most likely to help," I said. "If it helps you to talk about her, then I think you should talk about her."

He didn't respond. The truck changed lanes. I prayed to a vast imaginary power that he wouldn't want to talk about her.

"No," he finally said. "I don't think it will help."

We were silent all the way to Greenwich.

"What do you want to happen?" I finally asked. "Are you considering . . . ?"

"Honestly, Gus, I just wish she had never shown up."

He meant Alison—not Nora. I knew from the harshness of his tone.

"She was supposed to stay only weeks," I said. "Remember? It's almost funny, isn't it?"

"Almost."

We didn't speak again until Bridgeport.

"The reason I'm telling you, Gus, is because . . . because back with that other thing, back before, the part I couldn't bear was the lying. I don't want to do that to you."

Even in disloyalty, he was the better person.

"I appreciate your telling me," I said. "I would hate the lies too. I will say it again, for the billionth time, I am eternally sorry that I put you through that. But I guess, I'm just not sure what exactly you are telling me. Have you . . . ?"

"No. We haven't . . . nothing like that . . . Though a couple of nights ago . . ."

I felt immediately ill.

"We were in the barn and she . . . she told me how she feels."

I could picture it too clearly. Nora sitting on our old couch, her shoes off, her feet tucked under her. Doubtless, pages of his on her lap. That earnestness of hers in full flower. *I've fallen in love with you, Owen.*

"And you told her what in return?"

"Nothing really. But my guard was down. I couldn't muster . . . I didn't say much."

"Of course your guard was down. You've done nothing but moon over that child . . . Honestly, what did you think was going to happen?"

He didn't respond. He wasn't going to let this become a fight. And he was right. There was no point.

"Never mind," I said. "I appreciate that nothing happened. And that you've told me."

"I won't lie to you," he said again. "She told me how she feels, but she also told me she would never act on it. That she had to tell me, but not because she would ever do anything . . ."

"And you believed her? Why? Because she wears a cross around her neck? Or is it her beatific smile?"

More silence. More miles.

As New Haven slipped past, I said, "Can't you just send her away? Tell her the way she feels about you makes it impossible having her next door. Because she must have friends she can stay with. It really can't be that the property next to ours is the only patch of land on this planet where she can exist and thrive."

He didn't respond. Another minute passed by. And then another.

He didn't want her to go.

"Ah." I changed lanes for no reason. "I guess it's more complicated than that." He really was in love with her—or something like. "Okay. What do you need from me?" It was the question I had sworn I would ask if this day ever came. "What can I do to help make this better? And keep us together? Assuming that's what you want. Maybe the two of us should stay in Cape Cod. If she can't leave, maybe we should be the ones to leave. If you can't bring yourself to send her away, maybe you could bring yourself to stay away. Until . . ."

But I had lost him, I could tell. His mind was elsewhere.

"Five years ago," he said. "You told me, afterward, you told me that you had needed . . . all of it. That it was, I don't know. It was part of a journey you were on. That it had felt necessary to you."

"I don't believe I said 'journey.' I don't say things like 'part of a journey.' That doesn't sound like me."

"Let me finish, Gus. This is difficult."

"It's difficult all around, Owen. Just in case that's lost on you."

"I don't want to sleep with her, Gus."

"Oh, please." The image, sudden, vivid, seared. "The hell you don't."

"I don't mean I have no desire. I mean I don't want it to happen. And it won't. I wouldn't. She wouldn't either. But there's something I need to see through. I don't think we can fix this with geography . . . Not by sending her away or by our running off to Europe. Or the Cape—with my parents, for God's sake. You'd last ten minutes. And anyway I don't think that's going to help here. I suppose what I'm asking you to do . . ."

"You're asking an awful lot. If you're asking what I think you're asking."

"When I stuck with you, Gus, it was the hardest thing I've ever done. I don't know if you ever understood. It actually wasn't possible. That's how it felt. For longer than you know. I was doing something I wasn't capable of doing . . . And you're the one who told me this. That sometimes life demands things of you, that just the fact of being alive means allowing for possibilities that may be far from what you'd planned or even hoped."

"God, I just wish she weren't so young. I wish it weren't such a fucking cliché."

"She's young, but she's also not young."

"Oh, please, Owen, spare me."

"It isn't her youth I'm . . ."

"Let me guess. It's her wisdom. It's her spirituality."

"Gus, if you let me see this through, it will be all right."

"If I let you see this through? What does that even mean?"

He was shaking his head. "It doesn't mean sex," he said.

"Really? Can you honestly tell me that her confession of her love left you unstirred? Was she wearing one of her semi-see-through shirts? And you're telling me you felt no temptation?"

"No." His answer came with a strange purity. "No. It did not leave me unstirred. And I did not feel no temptation. But I'm not going to sleep with her."

"What is it you want, Owen? Exactly?"

"I have never regretted staying with you. Miserable as it felt. Impossible as it was."

I already knew what he wanted.

"But you didn't know I was having an affair," I said. "You wouldn't have given me your blessing for that. It was over. Long over."

"Not that long over."

"You wouldn't have put up with a neighbor, for Christ's sake. You're asking me to sit by and watch it all unfold."

"Nothing's going to unfold."

"You're not going to fuck her, you mean. You're not going to fuck her—you say. Or you are. You haven't been in this situation. I have. It isn't so easy just to decide it isn't going to happen."

"I am not going to fuck her. And I'm not going to tell her I wish I could. And I'll tell her she has to not say those things to me anymore. I can shut the subject down."

"Yet you just had to tell me, didn't you? You couldn't have, I don't know, put this down to a foolish infatuation and left me out of it?" But even as I asked, I knew he had done the right thing.

"We agreed to this, Gus. This is the plan. Your plan, as I recall.

This is how we protect ourselves, right? We see it through together. We accept that it's impossible only to be drawn to one
person for our whole lives. You told me that. That it isn't possible.
Not for everyone. So we take whatever steps necessary to work
that fact into our marriage. And we stay together. But we allow
for inconvenient feelings. We act like adults—and that one *was*
your phrase, Gus. And I did it. I acted like an adult. I don't know
if you've ever understood how difficult that was for me. But this
was your plan, Gus. So once she'd said that to me, I had to tell
you."

He was right. I had thought we could construct some kind of
behavioral flow chart to protect ourselves. If this, then that. If
that, then the next step.

"I'm afraid if she goes away, I'll stop writing," he said.

And there it was.

"So she's your muse," I said. "That self-satisfied little girl is
your muse."

"I don't know what she is. I don't think I've ever used the word
'muse' in my life."

"She's what got you back writing again, isn't she?" *Unadulterated.* The word flashed through my mind. Unadulterated adoration. My love had been adulterated. By adultery. Whatever claims
I might make, whatever devotion I might profess, it would always
carry within its DNA the memory of my choosing another over
him. Nature abhors a vacuum. I had left room for such a woman
in his life.

"It's been so fucking long, Gus. Since I could get anything but
total shit on a page."

I knew exactly how long it had been.

"You're going to want her, Owen. Sexually, I mean. It isn't
going to be enough, just the fun of feeding her your work. The
excitement of that."

"It isn't like that, Gus. I promise you."

We had reached another bridge, this one at Groton. "Has she read what you're working on?"

He didn't say anything.

"Oh fuck," I said. "Fuck you, Owen. That's just mean."

"It's not mean. It's not meant to be mean. It's . . . it's just what I need right now."

"And what will you need in a month?"

He sighed. He looked out his window and then he said, "Gus." Just that. Not even to me. Not really. But as though I were a thing or an event or a phenomenon. As though I were a problem and maybe also a solution. As though I were a fact that he alone knew and understood, a secret belonging to him.

"I can't believe it," I said.

"She isn't going to hurt us. I just want to see this through."

"You really aren't going to fuck her?" I asked—though I wasn't even sure that was the point.

"Truly not. Never."

"So if I say, go ahead, spend time with Nora, let her stir your creative embers, let her play that role in your life, that's really it?"

"That's really it."

"You'll want to. You already want to."

"I want other things more."

"Don't you feel just the least bit like a fool? It's such a cliché."

"I don't know, Gus. Yes. Maybe. I'm writing again. That compensates for a lot of foolishness."

"I don't understand it, Owen. She's religious. She believes in God. She goes to church. You've been scoffing at people like her for decades. We both have. Is it really just the prettiness? The young girl thing? And please don't tell me you find her spirituality refreshing."

"I don't know what to tell you, Gus. I couldn't write. I began spending time with her. I could. Maybe it's just a coincidence. Maybe I am an old fool and it's all . . . pathetic. I would rather be in a car with you for an eight-hour drive. But . . . but she got me back to work."

"Great. I'm the chauffeur and she's the inspiration. Since you don't like the word 'muse.'"

"It's not like I'm having an affair," he said.

But it was. Or it was worse. Very possibly it was worse. I had long ago forfeited the right to say that, though. "It's a kind of affair," I said. "You might as well be fucking her," I said.

"That isn't true. And you know that isn't true. Let's test that theory. How about I sleep with her?"

"Jesus, you can't even bring yourself to be crude about it. Is she that precious? How about you *sleep with* her?"

"The point isn't what I call it. The point is, I'm not."

"The point is . . . oh, hell. I don't even know what it is. I'm pulling over. You drive. I'm a mess."

On the shoulder, we each got out and then Owen got into the driver's seat. But I stood outside the van in the cold. I couldn't bear the thought of being back in that space with him. Cars whirred by. I looked up at the sky, light gray, relentlessly so, no break in the cover, no evident source of light.

I had no choice. I knew that. Owen knew that. He had done the right thing by telling me about her professed love—an event, I realized, that explained his sudden desire to leave home for a few days. He had done the right thing, but he had also done the hurtful thing. Here it was again. The fact that to be truthful can so often be both right and wrong.

And none of it mattered, not really. Because I had no choice but to agree.

"Whatever," I said, as I stepped into the van. "Just don't fuck her. And don't tell me about how wonderful she is. Spare me that, please."

We drove in silence for a very long time then. We crossed into Rhode Island, skirted through Providence. All in silence. We reached Fall River without our usual comments about Lizzie Borden and her axe. And when we spoke again, it was of other things, things like traffic patterns; and desolate New England towns; cranberry bogs in winter; and then his parents, of course. What dinner would be waiting for us in Wellfleet.

The empty Sagamore Bridge, so strange with no other cars in sight, seemed to have been built for us alone. I half imagined that if I turned around, I would discover it had disappeared.

By the time we reached Wellfleet, I had gone through a dozen or more moods. Rage. Disbelief. More rage. But when we pulled up to his parents' house I was gripped by a strange elation. After all, what had I really learned? That she was in love with him? I already knew that. That he was inspired by her? Arguably, I had known that too. That she had read his new work? Only that was real news and it did sting, but it did something else as well. Whether he'd meant to or not, Owen had finally given me a chance to be generous to him. Maybe even a little bit noble. And at a cost that felt bearable to me, used to Nora as I was. And so by the time we got out of the van, I felt almost exhilarated.

This was by no means my usual mood when faced with a few days of Lillian and Wolf. Often, they made me feel inconsequential, like a sapling unlikely to thrive. Both tall, both lean, they exuded an identical unflagging energy, as though all those months and years of work in sun-beaten deserts had forged them into super beings. *What doesn't kill you makes you stronger.* The first time I met them the line had stuck in my head—as had the conviction that whatever had made them stronger would undoubtedly have killed me.

Wolf answered the door with a quiet greeting, Lillian calling out from the living room, just behind him. "Hello, hello, welcome . . . don't take off your coats, because we're headed right out."

"Only if you don't mind driving," Wolf said. "Our car is in the shop."

He hadn't hugged either of us and neither did she as she emerged. That was one of their peculiarities. Not only the absence of physical affection—which I was used to in my own family—but the way they could greet us after ten months as though we'd just been over the night before.

"I'll put on a coat," Lillian said. "Though it's never really cold anymore, which would be just fine with me if it didn't signal the end of life on Earth."

They were strikingly elegant still, in that way that has little to do with anything as impermanent as clothing or as vulgar as money but everything to do with bearing. She looked like Amelia Earhart might have had she lived long enough for her cropped hair to turn white, with permanently tanned yet barely lined skin, and those loose joints of her son's, long limbs, easy motions. And even in his eighties Wolf too seemed like he'd be best suited standing beside some early-twentieth-century biplane, white scarf fluttering, blue sky beckoning—not to mention that his name was Wolf, which wasn't short for anything, his official first (or Christian) name being Edward, but was a title, an honorarium, he had acquired in his youth for quests or conquests or hungers unknown by me. Fearless. Happy. They were adventurers. By nature and in fact, putting themselves in situations time and again throughout their lives in which terrible things might have happened and sometimes did—which meant they were quick to scoff at such irritations as our impatience with having to wait endlessly at every summertime traffic light on Route 6.

I handed Owen the keys. "Tag, you're it," I said. "I could use a few drinks."

I asked if I could step in to use the bathroom and Lillian looked at me for a moment as though I had named an activity of which she was unaware, and then said, "Oh. Yes. Of course. We'll all wait in the car."

Years before, it had surprised me that they didn't share our preference for the desolation of the Cape midwinter. I'd thought
that having worked so much in empty spots, they would; but
they were as sociable as Owen and I were not. They loved the
six-month-long hubbub of summers up there, only tolerating
the winter because they couldn't afford two homes. Without the
crowds and chatter, they worked on the seemingly ceaseless project of writing up all their adventures. Of that, they spoke little,
but then, occasionally, a rather touching memoir piece would appear in a journal of archaeology and a copy would appear at our
home—both their names listed as authors. And there were reams
of typescript tucked into odd cabinets throughout their house, so
though it wasn't a topic of conversation it was a backdrop to every
visit.

As were copies of Owen's books—except the novel depicting
Lillian as a young woman. At publication, her sole comment had
been, "As fiction I'm surprisingly compelling," a response that
Owen took as a lavish compliment, given what she might have
said. "It was an assumed risk," he said. "The fact that she didn't
sue me for slander or royalties or inadequate filial affection is a
landslide victory."

The oddity of Owen's ties to Lillian and Wolf—whom he too
called Lillian and Wolf—had been a relief to me from the start.
I'm not sure I could have married a man with the sort of mother I
fantasized my own would have been, the nurturing, clucking sort,
who would love me up—as Alison might say. But I rather enjoyed
being the oddball daughter-in-law to a pair of distinctly non-
parental characters who seemed to have wandered off the set of a
Noël Coward play, brandy snifters in hand.

And they were good people, at heart. At our few early family
gatherings, I feared that these university-affiliated archaeologists,

authors of books and articles, shabbily elegant WASPs, might make my Jewish high school history teacher father feel somehow lesser. But there had never been a glimmer of that. Wolf had gone out of his way to express admiration for those who could translate what he called *the mare's nest of human civilization* to youngsters. "There isn't an archaeologist worth a damn," he said, "who can't still tell you about the history teacher who first made the past come alive."

The only truly awkward moment we'd ever experienced was when we'd all gathered for a brunch for some occasion—maybe Owen's fortieth birthday, a June event—and Lillian made a toast to my mother's memory, then began to quiz my father on the ways each of his daughters did or didn't remind him of her. He'd made a puzzled face as if to say it had never occurred to him to make any such connection at all; and it was Letty, a usually quiet presence, who'd saved the day with an abrupt subject change, asking us urgent, out-of-context questions about whether we had any travel plans for the summer.

After that, Owen must have clued them in, because it never happened again.

Since it was one of very few restaurants open that time of year, the dark basement bistro was more crowded than one might have guessed from the quiet street. Everyone there knew Lillian and Wolf, which meant endless introductions and appraisals of the degree to which Owen looked like one or the other or, as gen-uinely the case, both.

Once all of that settled down we had what was really our first chance to talk, and Lillian asked immediately after my father. I gave her the basic report, nothing good to report, nothing immi-nent either. As I looked at her face, etched deep by experience, by keen interest in the world, I wondered if she might understand the new and better relationship I had with my father now that he was no longer himself but a strange, scrambled version of a man I barely knew, full of surprises, short on rules.

The drinks flowed and the meal won us over with its simple, fine quality. I found myself thinking that life was a pretty good thing, right then. And I enjoyed, too, surprising Owen with my good spirits. *Look, I can be the bigger person also. I can let you have an adventure, let you explore something outside the close of us.*

We had sex that night in the tiny bedroom down the hall from his parents. It wasn't sweet and it wasn't particularly loving. We were both drunk by then, both unguarded and both hungry for connection. At one point when he was deep inside me, I said, "Are you really sure you don't want to do this with her?" And looking right at me, he said, "I never told you that." I wanted to hate him, maybe I did; but I could also barely stand the level of excitement that I felt.

"Fuck you, Owen," I said, for the second time that day.

19

That whole trip turned into a kind of strange sex holiday. We behaved in ways we hadn't for years. We got each other off in the van, parked in vast empty lots. We walked on the beach, then stopped to make out with his hands under my coat, under my sweater. It was as though a dam of some kind had broken, or maybe we just knew that if we didn't find the molten core of what kept us together, we would have no chance once we returned home. Or maybe he was so pent up from wanting Nora that he had endless sexual energy for me; and I was turned on by his being so turned on. Or maybe it was just the sea air. But for four days we were in a kind of haze of carnality, his usually non-parental parents transformed into strangely parental figures in front of whom we tried to behave ourselves.

"I'm so glad you and Owen are still so happy," Lillian told me on our last night, as she and I put dinner together. "You know, when he was a boy, I wondered if he'd find someone who could warm him up. He was such a serious little man. But here you are. An old, happily married couple and clearly still having fun."

When we got home on Monday evening, I half expected Alison to be on her porch waving a big welcome, but no one emerged from their house.

I hadn't really believed that the tide of physical desire would sweep us right past Nora and the issues embodied by her, but I was a little stunned at how smoothly Owen settled back into the routine of spending his days with her out in the barn. And up close to that reality, I no longer found it exciting or even remotely ennobling. I just plain hated it.

He needed her. Or thought he did. There wasn't much difference that I could detect.

Nobody outside a marriage can understand it, everyone agrees. As if people inside a marriage can. I don't know why I set myself against crying uncle, and ending what felt like daily cruelty, why I didn't beg Owen to run away with me, to admit that our sanctuary had been fouled. But for just over a week I supplied myself with reasons to stay this terrible course. Briefly, I convinced myself it was indeed the greatness of my heart. That I was a larger, more generous woman than I had thought. And that theory got me through the first day.

Next, I decided that I wouldn't give Owen the satisfaction of admitting I couldn't handle the type of suffering that I had put him through; and so a kind of fierceness got me through another few days.

And what of him?

Was he really doing this because those months and months of having no words to put on the page had made him desperate? Desperate enough to ask this of me? Or, was he just trying to hurt me? Or, was breaking my heart the only way he could restore his own creative soul?

I doubt he knew the answer any more than I did. He was kind to me when we were together, rubbing my shoulders as he passed, offering me cups of tea, cooking dinner a few nights in a row. Almost as though I had the flu. But he didn't ask how I was doing under this new arrangement of ours, and we never mentioned Nora.

On my own, I avoided her as much as I could, heading indoors with a quick wave if I spotted her while I was outside, making excuses to suspend our dinners for four. *I'm not feeling well in the evenings these days,* and *Things are going so well. I haven't been able to pull myself away from working, even after sunset.*

All untrue. Physically, I felt fine. And my work had all but stopped by then.

It was a mystery to me where Alison stood in all of this. We did try a walk together again, our first in ages, but I wanted to wring her neck as she spoke of Nora's *work* with Owen, alighting each time on the notion of *the child* needing a father figure in her life. I did not wring her neck, though, or even audibly question her view. To do so was to break my promise to Owen. So I just wondered, mystified. Had she really blinded herself so successfully to the fact that her daughter was in love with my husband and he half in love with her? Was it possible that she had? Likely that she had? I had no idea. What did I know of maternal delusions? The only person who had ever idealized me was Owen, and I could barely remember that.

"Can we talk?" Alison asked at my kitchen door, the afternoon of December twenty-first.

"Of course."

She dropped her coat on a kitchen chair. It slid to the floor and she picked it up. "Let's go in the living room," I said. "There's a fire."

"Nora and I had a conversation yesterday." She looked away while I settled on the orange chair. "I know you've been angry and I don't know if you can understand this, but I only did what I thought . . . I just, I just honestly thought that . . . I believed everything I told you all along. I wasn't lying to you."

"Alison, I'm lost." She looked distraught, and also drained somehow. Her clothes, a dark blue jumper over a black turtleneck, seemed askew, her curls, unbrushed, were a great unruly mess. And she wasn't wearing lipstick, I realized. For the first time ever. Even when I had picked her up at the hospital, her lips had shone coral, light. Even when she had stayed at our house supposedly frightened for her life. "I don't know what you're telling me," I said.

"Right. Of course." She took a deep breath. "I haven't encouraged her . . . Truly, I would never have done that. I've just wanted Nora to know there are men in the world who . . . who aren't bad."

I couldn't tell where we were headed. "I know that," I said. "You've been saying that for weeks."

"I didn't encourage her. But . . . Gus, I don't have any excuses, I just so badly wanted her to stay here."

"I don't understand," I said—meaning more than one thing.

"I saw what I wanted to see," she said. "I . . . I should have done more. I . . . I wanted her here. Away from Paul."

I didn't speak, just tried to take it in.

"He loves you so much, Gus. I knew Owen would never cheat."

"What do you mean you didn't encourage her? What are you apologizing for, then?"

"She's such a hurt person. I know she doesn't seem it all the time. Or maybe ever, to you. But she is. She's never had a steady platform. Not really. I just . . . Truly I never egged it on, I just didn't tell her to stop. Not the way I should have. And I . . . I'm not blind. But I did think it was just a silly crush. And then, yes-

terday, she told me she had spoken to Owen. Before you and he
went to the Cape. And I realized that even after she . . . declared
herself, he still hadn't sent her away. That he knew how she felt,
and he hadn't sent her away."

I stood. "I have no idea what to say." The phrase *I thought you
were my friend* came to mind; but it didn't need saying; and I wasn't
sure how recently it had been true.

"Gus, I was certain it would never get that far."

"Maybe we shouldn't talk about this. I'm not sure I can. Jesus,
Alison. You were certain it would never get that far? What does
that mean?"

"I'm taking her away. We're going to London. I told her . . . it
doesn't matter. But I told her we should go see my parents, and
we're going. She and I have to sort this out. But I know I've been
a terrible friend. Not a friend at all."

"For what it's worth," I said, feeling my own dignity make its
demands, "Owen has been straight with me. I've known that she
spoke to him. All of that. He hasn't kept anything from me. And
they aren't . . . there's no . . ."

"So you two are okay? I really hope so. I hope we haven't . . ."

"I don't know. What does 'okay' mean? Really? This is a bad
time for us. You know that. You knew that all along." I could
sense my anger rising again. "When do you go?"

"Tomorrow. Back just after New Year's. Though I'm . . . I'm
hoping she'll go stay with friends then."

"Right." There it was again: I wanted to say that I too hoped
that Nora would never return; but I had promised Owen not to
try and keep them apart. "I hope it helps" was all I allowed myself
to say.

Alison left right after that. In the kitchen, as she put her coat
back on, she said, "It won't go on. She knows that it can't go on."

I nodded. I couldn't bring myself to wish her a good trip, just
mumbled a goodbye.

The next afternoon was a cold one, the sky banded with clouds. I watched from inside as Owen carried their suitcases out and lifted them into the back of Alison's car. It was a strangely somber scene, the complexities within our quartet by now so well understood that nothing we did in any combination could be undertaken lightly anymore.

20

I didn't say anything to Owen about Alison's apology. I couldn't see how her admission changed anything between us, or between him and Nora, either. If Alison succeeded in calling her daughter off, he would have to deal with that. My hands were clean.

During Alison's and Nora's absence an unmistakable aura of suspense hung over our lives. Something had been interrupted, not ended. We both worked, or anyway I tried to, though without much success. Owen seemed more productive than that, looking content when he left the barn; and I resisted the temptation to point out that he seemed to be doing very well without his muse by his side; but then realized he was probably getting frequent encouraging emails from her. We ate our meals together. We shared our bed, uneventfully.

Christmas came and went without a ripple. It could have been any of the other days that week. And then, on Boxing Day, I got an email from Laine.

Augie, this is your conscience speaking. Are you doing the things we talked about? Are you sticking with those soldiers of yours? I have been thinking it over and I know this sounds weird coming from me and maybe I should be quiet, but I think it's really important that

you not give up on them. I mean, I DEFINITELY have no expe-
rience with this, but I'll bet it sucks to be super good at something
and then try something new. It must feel impossibly hard. Even
when I try something new, it's not like I'm giving up something I
do amazingly well, like you paint landscapes and rooms. And I'm
guessing it feels like starting over or something, which must be
awful. But it would bum me out completely if you just gave up.

I'm really sorry if that's obnoxious of me. I put off writing this
for days. But then I thought, it's not like you'll cut me off for bug-
ging you and maybe you need someone to push? So, like I said, this
is your conscience speaking. Or something like that.

Here, I'm home for the holidays. Spending a while with Mom
and then tomorrow out to Dad's new household in Wayne for a
week. Gulp. It turns out I have seriously mixed feelings about him
getting married. I didn't think I would, I thought I was okay, but
then it happened and I realized I'm just like every other kid of
divorce in the world. Somewhere in there I thought they'd get back
together one day. Unbelievable. I could see how much it upset Mom,
and I was pretty contemptuous, but it hasn't been easy for me with
the holidays and all. I haven't felt this low in a very long time.

So wish me luck, out in the suburbs, flipping out.

I soooooooo loved seeing you. Send me pictures of your pictures.

Love,

Laine

Dear Laine,

You must have been spying on me. I have indeed lost my nerve,
and been doing my old familiar work, but I promise to reread your
note until I get my courage back. And then I'll keep reading it.
You're right. Change is hard—for us all. But there's no point
fighting it. Not to go all Zen on you, but all of life is change, so we
might as well decide it's a good thing.

Let's make a deal. You try to have a decent time at your dad's
and I'll go back to painting my soldiers.

I'm really glad you wrote. Just let me know if there's ever any
way that I can help.
   I loved seeing you too. You are incredible.
   Love,
   Augie

I left for Philadelphia around eleven-thirty the next day, taking
the South Street exit off the Expressway, turning east. Once I'd
crossed over Broad, somewhere around Tenth Street, the sidewalk
grew more crowded, mostly young people, mostly in groups. It
was the start of lunch hour and the traffic was slow and impatient,
lots of honking, lots of drivers making sudden lunges to get
around stopped cars. There was a sense of too much activity
jammed in too small a space, a feeling, a phenomenon I hadn't
experienced in a very long time, this seething of people, this hive.

   At Fourth Street, I turned right, driving south.

Steinman's looked very much the same, except that instead of a
fabric shop to one side and an empty shop to the other, there was
now a used bookstore where the empty store had been and an
empty store where the fabric shop had been. Urban renewal and
urban decay, bumping up against each other. During the weeks
that I had squirreled myself in my corner of the store, I had heard
endless discussions about the fate of the street, the neighborhood,
the block, the building and also about the history of it all. That
had seemed to be the subject every customer brought in, along
with talk of colors and styles, angles of brims, opaqueness of veils.
Len's attitude had been that the area was on a fast downhill, while
Ida had taken the view that through every generation, somehow,
this street managed to survive and it would always do so.

   And in general, nearly four years after my stint there, despite
the replacement of one empty storefront with another, it looked a

little more occupied, a little busier than it had been back then. Steinman's itself, its window an array of the most elaborate, colorful, even absurd hats, still carried that air of enchantment, like an outsized Fabergé egg mysteriously placed on a gray urban block.

I peered through the glass before going in, as if afraid I might have the wrong place or maybe the wrong proprietors; but there was Len, looking thinner, his face nearly gaunt, and that was enough to propel me inside. It took him a second after the tinkle of the door's bell, but then he knew me. "Ach! It's Leonardo!" he said. "Look who's here. Ida!" he called. "Come out and see who's visiting."

"Hi, Len," I said. "It's good to be back. Good to see the old place. And you too." While I spoke, Ida emerged from behind the black drape separating the public and private sections of the shop; and it was obvious right away that something was wrong. I had studied her too intently, too minutely for too many weeks not to detect the immobility in her right arm, the stilled expression on her face.

"Gush." She said it with a slur, with that wet, loose sound at the end. "Gush." A sloppy word. As though she had always known the slosh and overflow of me, however I had tried to seem contained. She walked toward me, her left arm extended for a hug. It was the first time we had ever embraced. All through my occupation, as Len had called it, she'd kept the sort of distance a china doll ought to keep, as if for fear of being broken. But now, broken as she was, it seemed she had no fear.

"Don't let the arm fool you," Len said. "She's still the same in there. And she's still the boss. And when no one else is here, she talks my ear off. Some of this act is for show. Just to get everyone's sympathy."

She shook her head. "Don't listen"—more slurred words. "I don't. Can't. But here . . ." She tapped her head, then made an okay sign with her left hand. "Me," she said. "All there."

"She'll live forever," Len said. "They haven't invented the stroke that'll take Ida down. She'll bury us all."

It was only then that I realized it was the arm in my painting that was paralyzed, the one part of her I had felt entitled to draw. For a moment I could imagine that I had put some kind of curse on her, spoiling what I had taken as my own; or maybe I had intuited somehow that this part of her was indeed the most human, the least perfect part.

But it was all ridiculous of course. Fairy-tale logic.

"I'm so sorry to hear about the stroke," I said. "But I have a feeling Len is right. You're obviously immortal."

Ida said something I didn't catch, then shook her head with impatience. "What brings you here?" Len asked. "I'm the only one who always understands her. Tough for her, being stuck with me."

"You two seemed pretty stuck together before."

Ida rolled her eyes. "My luck," she slurred. She wore the same blue serge suit, or one just like it. A crisp white blouse. But her hair was cut short, maybe because she couldn't style it anymore. And there was something else different, though it took me a minute to realize what it was: she had flat shoes on her feet, squared toes, Velcro tabs. No more perfect, tiny patent navy pumps.

"I really just came by to say hi," I said. "I haven't been to the city in so long. And . . ." I looked over at my old corner, the chair no longer there. "I was wondering, Ida. Len, you too. I was wondering if I could do a few quick sketches, that's all. I so missed being here."

Len, rolling a bolt of lavender tulle, laughed out loud. "Last time she said that, she stayed six weeks. Remember, Ida? Gus comes in telling us it'll be an afternoon, and six weeks later, she's still in that corner, the place stinking of turpentine."

"That's true," I said. "You were both so patient and I was . . ." I let the sentence go. What had I been? Spiraling downward, in need of a safe place to hide, somewhere I could pretend I was only an observer, never an actor, never a part of any story, only a witness. "I was always sorry I hadn't drawn the two of you."

I expected Ida to shake her head no. I expected her to make it clear that the time for that had passed, but instead she nodded, looking at me, as though she had always known the request would come one day.

I told them I had a pad and some charcoal in my car. "I can sit in my old corner if I just move that chair. Only for a couple of hours," I said. "I promise you."

Years before, it had never once occurred to me to tell Ida the tale of my fall from grace. I had felt defined by shame. But that day, as I sat sketching them both, I knew, I was certain, I could have shared it all. And she would have shown compassion. Paralyzed, shorn, wearing shoes too clunky even for me, she seemed approachable. She seemed, for the first time, like a real human being.

But that view of her was also simple, I realized. She wasn't a different woman because she'd had a stroke. She had never been perfect. She had been a beautiful woman who dressed well. A woman of style who seemed perpetually in control. A person in no danger of coming undone at her seams, from whose hands sprung masterpieces. But not perfect.

So why had I needed to see her that way? Why so entranced with this notion of a perfect older woman who would reject the real me?

The question had been a long time coming. The answer took no time at all.

As I sketched, the occasional customer stepped in. Len did most of the talking now, but Ida had a thousand ways to make her thoughts known. Her face, so serene and mysterious before, now, in partial paralysis, had turned expressive, fluent in a language of necessity.

I left them with about half the sketches that I did. I hugged them both and promised to be back sooner next time. Ida nodded, and Len declared himself disappointed that I really wasn't moving back in for a month—minimum.

"Maybe next time," I said. "You never know."

I tacked the pictures of Len and Ida onto my studio wall that night. The Steinman brother and sister, patron saints of a sort for me. The drawings were undistinguished, no miracle break-throughs, though the likenesses were there and it had tickled Len and Ida to see that. But the drawings weren't on my wall as art. They were there as reminders of the example permeating every cell of Ida's body now, of her unwavering, dignified integration of what she had lost into what still remained.

There was an ice storm on the afternoon of New Year's Eve and our power went out, but only briefly. The lights came back on and the clocks did too, all blinking at 12:00—as if rushing through the last tattered scrap of the year. Neither of us reset them. Neither of us stayed up to see the year out.

I visited my father the next morning. He was talkative and insistent that I take to heart what he had to say, which was some-thing very urgent about a dog. It had run away. It had been found. Or maybe it hadn't been found. He wasn't agitated, just set on being sure that I—whoever I was—know this about the dog. I recognized the mood, familiar to me by then. It was as though all pieces of information he could detect in his own thoughts, any knowledge, anything that felt like knowledge, had to be con-veyed. The mere presence of a near-coherent thought gave it im-portance now.

"I'll be sure everyone knows," I said. "I'll tell everyone."

Out in the lot, while I was brushing the latest dusting of snow from my car, I saw the tall redheaded doctor. I reintroduced my-self, knowing that he couldn't possibly recognize me in my scarves, my wool hat; and I reminded him of my father's predicament. "It's been months," I said. "There hasn't been a sign of anything like those earlier episodes."

Was it really impossible for him to be put back into a less con-fining setting?

The doctor's demeanor showed evidence of his own months in this place. He seemed to have lost some of the enthusiasm he'd shown during the summer for the system and its rules. "It's really difficult, I know," he said. "But it's not even physically possible. Those rooms have waiting lists. I'm afraid once a person's been shifted out . . ."

"It's just so sad," I said; but I understood as I spoke that I was talking to someone who had chosen sadness for his career, who was not yet immune to it perhaps, but surely well on his way to ac-cepting it as inevitable.

"I'm really sorry," he said. "We had no choice at the time. This happens, once in a while. We err in the direction of safety and then, unfortunately, there's no way to correct."

I nodded, my lips closed tight, drawn into my mouth. I felt in danger of tears, so just muttered, "Well, thanks anyway," and turned away, trying not to notice what a miserable start I was having to the year.

21

When Alison's car pulled up, midafternoon on the second, I waited to see how many women emerged—hoping for one. But the answer was two. There they both were. I didn't want to see whether Owen hurried from the barn, so I turned my back to the windows and went to work.

Just as I was keeping my word to Owen, I was also keeping my word to Laine, though that too was difficult. I thought of myself now as staggering through the creative process, stumbling through. I continued to paint the boys though I thought the results were awful. And it made me uncomfortable, but I knew that only confirmed much of what Laine had said. I'd grown complacent over time, too willing to rely on what I knew I could do well. It had been years since my own work had really challenged me. And so I continued to slog away at this series of paintings, rarely enjoying it but convinced there must be some benefit to doing so.

I was still in the studio painting, maybe an hour after turning my back on the returning neighbors, when I heard Owen come into the house, and knew immediately that something was wrong. The volume of every motion was wrong, the door slamming, his footfall too rapid, too loud. He appeared just outside my room, his face darkened, not reddened, not flushed, but storm-darkened with emotion. He stood in the doorway staring at me.

"What? What is it?"

"The one thing I asked of you . . ." He stopped.

"What? What did I do?"

"Really, Gus? You're going to play dumb?"

"I'm not playing dumb. I have no idea."

"The one thing I asked you to do was be honest with me. Five years ago. Every minute since. That's it. Just be fucking straight with me."

"I don't . . ."

"Please. You've been mooning after him all along. You've been in touch with him. Weeping over his wedding. Exchanging private notes. What the fuck, Gus?"

I didn't ask him how he knew. "Oh my God, I'm so sorry," I said. "But really it was . . . nothing. And you were so upset when Laine came . . . I didn't want to upset you more. I just wanted the whole subject gone."

"Well, guess what, Gus? It isn't gone. And you've really fucking done it this time."

He slammed out of the room, out of the house. I heard the van start, heard him leave and was up on my feet in a moment, didn't bother with a coat, barely took the time to slide my feet into boots.

I found Alison in her kitchen, sitting at the table, a cup of tea in front of her. She looked stunned at my having barged into her house. "What the hell was all of that?" I asked. "What was that scene in my living room not even two weeks ago? What is your game, Alison? I can't believe that you told him," I said. "Did you think that apology would also cover *this*? I can't believe you would do that to me."

There was a pause while she took in my presence, my words.

"I have no idea what you're talking about. Do you mean Owen? I haven't told Owen anything. I haven't seen him in nearly two weeks."

"Don't even bother. Please. Spare me."

"I'm not bothering, Gus. I'm telling you the truth. I don't know what you're talking about, but I haven't told Owen a thing."

"Then how does he know?"

"How does he know what? What?"

"How does he know that I crashed when I heard about Bill's wedding? That Bill and I exchanged emails? That I still gave a shit? How does he know that? You're the only person on earth who knows those things."

Her face changed. She began to look nervous. Her cheeks flushed. "Oh my God. I'm so sorry, Gus. I'm afraid this is my fault."

"I can't believe you would do that to me. I trusted you. I was ready to let you off the hook for using my husband as bait for Nora. What was that speech for? What were you doing?"

"I didn't do this to you. I didn't mean to. I . . . I told Nora. Months and months ago. Before her visit. Before I . . . before she knew Owen. Or you. And then, when she came back, I . . ."

"You told Nora? *Nora?*"

"You have to understand . . . I was just . . . We were gossiping on the phone. She hadn't even met you. We were just gossiping. I didn't even use your names then. Just the neighbors. And I . . . I told her. It wasn't a big thing. It wasn't . . ."

"But you told her I emailed Bill. That was later. Nora had already been here. She was already panting after Owen."

"I . . . I trusted her. She's my daughter, Gus. I tell her things. We . . . we share confidences."

"Everything? You tell her fucking everything? Of course you do. Because it never once occurs to you that she isn't some kind of saint. Just like you've pretended all this time that she wasn't trying to wreck my marriage. That little bitch. You say you know her but you still don't get what kind of selfish, grabbing . . ."

"Gus, you have to leave. You can't do this."

"*I* have to leave? *I* have to leave? Why didn't *you* leave? Months ago. When you said you were going to. *I* have to leave? Fuck you, Alison. You and your hypocritical daughter. Both of you, just fuck you both. You and your so-called friendship and your so-called kindness. And especially your bullshit apology."

"Please go."

"She's upstairs, isn't she? Or is she out in the barn? My husband's barn. *My* barn. Jesus Christ. She told him, Alison. She couldn't have him for herself, and she fucking told him, just to ruin things for me."

I was out and heading up the stairs before she could even stand. I found Nora in the upstairs hallway. "You bitch," I said. "You conniving little cunt."

She didn't say a word. I heard Alison coming, felt her hands on my shoulders. "Gus, you have to calm down," she said.

"No, I do not." I shook her off. "Jesus fucking Christ. How was I supposed to know you would tell her everything? How was I supposed to know that, Alison? Is that the deal? Mothers tell their daughters everything? Is that some kind of fucking rule? While you encouraged this, this slut to chase after my husband, you gave her the ammunition she needed. And then you act like it's a part of the birth contract?"

"He was never going to . . ." Nora stood perfectly still, a statue speaking. "He sent me away."

"Oh, fuck you, Nora. And thank you for that reassurance. Now that you've destroyed my life."

"I'm sorry. I was . . . I was so upset and I thought maybe . . ."

"You thought it might make him leave me. What else did you think? That you deserved him more than I do? That he deserved the truth? Fuck you, Nora." I turned to Alison. "Could you please explain to your perfect little daughter here that nobody cares what she thought or how she felt? And ask her why she has ruined the lives of two people who never did a thing but welcome her. And then, would you both just leave. Just get the fuck out of our lives!"

Down the stairs, out the door, barely crossing the hill to my own door, my own home, before bursting into sobs.

Owen came back after three in the morning. Eleven long hours later.

I was sitting in the kitchen waiting, hoping, scared to death he would either never appear or return only to pack a bag and leave. But he sat down, across the table from me. Neither of us spoke for some time. The only thing I could think to say was *I'm sorry,* and the day had left me with an inescapable sense of how paltry an offering that would be.

"I have had some time to calm down," he finally said. "And I have no idea where this leaves us, Gus. Just no idea. I can't . . ."

"I'm sorry." I couldn't keep the phrase in. "I fucked up. I really did. I understand that. But it wasn't . . . There was nothing, Owen. Nothing."

He looked at me, not acknowledging my words. "At first, I didn't believe her. But there were details. Little things. I thought she was lying. At first. Because I'd really discounted this possibility. The lies. I really thought we had gotten past that part. The deceit. As humiliating as that is. How gullible I was."

I wanted to say that we had gotten past that part. But we hadn't. I wanted it to be true. But it wasn't.

"I don't expect you to believe this," I said. "But that's everything. What she told you. That I got upset when I heard he was remarrying. Because it opened up old wounds. That's all. Not because I . . . not because I want him anymore. I don't. And then he wrote me and I wrote back. Once. But there was nothing more. In years. All these years. I don't expect you to believe me," I said again.

Owen looked away, shaking his head. "The stupid part is that I do believe you. Mostly. I'm just not sure it matters. How much or how little you lied about. I suppose it does. But . . . not really."

"I don't know. It matters some. It has to matter some."

"She begged me, you know. Begged me to admit that we have something real, me and her. Something real. That was the phrase. Just, Jesus, just this afternoon. She begged me to admit what we had. And I looked at her, Gus, and I realized what I had done to this girl. How I've been using her. All along. It hasn't mattered what I've said to her, she's just been assuming. Assuming and hoping. She was staring at me as if it was obvious what would happen next. And I saw this girl, this young girl I have been using, with her deer-in-the-headlights look."

"Don't say that. Not that."

"But it's true. And I was the car that was barreling toward her."

"Jesus, Owen. You didn't kill her."

"I've had a lot of time to think today," he repeated. "And I have no fucking clue where this leaves us."

"You aren't going to . . . you don't want to be with her?"

"Have you been listening, Gus? Have you even heard a word I just said?"

"Yes. Sort of. I don't know. You're worried about hurting her."

"Well, what would any young girl think? No matter what I said to her? I played her."

"That's not my point."

"What is your point?"

"Just . . . does it matter at all that you hurt me? Or have I forfeited that?"

He shrugged. "I was desperate. Hurt. Wanting to . . ."

"Be adored? Because I adore you. I adore you, Owen."

"I was going to say, have it all. But yes. Be adored. Be adored and have that rush. That thing that happens. You know, it killed me, afterward, back then, after you told me, the big confession, and I realized how much painting you had done. All those months. For him. It was . . . it was almost as bad as the rest of it. All that work you did for him. It's why I've always loved that one." He turned toward the doorway, toward the living room. "It was the first painting you did after that. I knew it wasn't for him. All the others from the time with him . . ." He shook his head. "I fucking hate those paintings."

"I always knew you would even the score," I said. "Or the universe would."

"I wasn't doing that. Not consciously."

"I don't know, Owen. Maybe not. But I always knew I couldn't get away with what I'd done to you. Not without paying up."

"The universe doesn't work that way, Gus. Evening scores. Making life fair. I thought we agreed on that long ago."

I frowned. "Maybe. Maybe it doesn't. But . . . we're our own kind of universe. And I always knew there'd be some kind of reckoning."

We sat silent for a long time after that.

"I don't trust you, Gus," he finally said. "And I'm torn."

"Okay. But torn is a start. Right?"

"I can't imagine life without you. Not at this point. But I am so fucking angry at you. Do you understand that? Do you get it that I'm too angry even to sound angry? I am weary with it all. Wearier than I have ever been. Too weary to think about what it's going to take to glue this back together again."

I started to cry.

"This isn't going to be fun," he said. "I need that to be clear. This isn't me forgiving you. Or saying you'll ever earn back my trust. This is . . . this is something else. I thought for hours today."

"Eleven hours," I said.

"I tried to figure out why I didn't just walk out on you back then. Because that was the one upside of not having kids, wasn't it? That we could just call it quits. Nothing holding us together. Except us. And I thought today, maybe I should have."

"No. You shouldn't have." I wiped my nose on my sleeve.

He pulled a paper napkin out from the holder. "Here," he said. "Use this. I don't know, Gus. Maybe I should have," he said. "But I didn't. And that's a mystery to me. That's the mystery at the center of it all. And that's what's keeping me here still. That mystery. I just couldn't have been so wrong. And there's something else." He paused, as if I might guess. "Back then," he said, "you didn't have to come back to me. Even if what's his name didn't want you. You didn't have to come back. But you did. You did even though . . . even though it meant no children, not mine anyway. You . . . you had to love me. And that's the thing, Gus. We both stayed. Really. I just don't understand all this. Why we're still us, unless we're truly meant to be. But I am so, so . . ." He closed his eyes. ". . . So, so unbelievably sick of not being able to believe the things you say."

"I know."

He opened his eyes. "And I owe that girl an apology."

"Oh, Owen, I really don't think you do. She isn't a child. She tried . . . she almost succeeded."

"I used her," he said. "And I owe her an apology. I just don't know if it makes it better. Or worse."

"I yelled at her, Owen. After you left." I didn't want to tell him, but I wasn't going to start anew with another cover-up. "I pretty much called her a cunt and told her to go fuck herself. Alison too."

He frowned a bit, then nodded. "Yeah. I should have guessed that." He put his hands on the table and stood. "I'm going to sleep, Gus. Out in the barn. I don't know about tomorrow. I'm not making some kind of policy decision, so don't freak out. I just need a little space tonight. It's like . . . it's like all of a sudden today I realized there's this giant overwhelming task that belongs to me. To us."

"You make it sound pretty joyless."

"Do I?" He frowned. "I don't mean to. It isn't joyless. You

aren't joyless. For me. We aren't. But we are a life's work, aren't we? We are, like you said, we are a universe. You and me. Our own fucked-up, beautiful, inexplicable universe." He walked toward the door, as if to leave on that note.

"Good night," I said.

He turned back around. "You are my family, Gus," he said. "That's all. Now, go get some sleep."

I didn't sleep much that night. I went to my studio to paint. It was the only answer I could give. To try to let Owen's love be the source of more art. Good, bad, or indifferent. That was all I could think to do. Maybe I was tired—I was surely tired—and incoherent in my thinking, but I wanted to make up for the work I had done for Bill.

I had been given another chance. Again. We had been altered. Again. And we would go on. Again. Somehow.

"We are a life's work, aren't we?" Owen had asked.

A life's work indeed. The work of life.

I took the canvas of Jackie playing chess, the very first one I had started, and I began to paint a shadowy portrait of another Jackie Mayhew over the one already there. Jackie in clothes a boy his age might have worn. Long wool pants. Suspenders. I covered parts of his uniform entirely, a white buttoned shirt obscuring long swaths of khaki, but I let the uniform bleed through his clothing at other points. Then I imagined a younger Jackie Mayhew, truly a boy, and made sketches of that face to layer into the one already there.

How do any of us walk across a room without tripping over our own multitudes? I'd wondered that at Thanksgiving, my arms still alive with physical, forgotten memories of another self.

It didn't matter to me that night that the painting's message could be seen as simple. Maybe to paint young dead soldiers is necessarily a simple thing. Maybe the depiction of tragedy is just that and should never be made more complicated. There really wasn't much complicated to say about a boy being blown up at seventeen.

But the boys themselves deserved better than simplicity. They needed to be, as they were, as we all are, layers and layers and layers of selves. I doubted it would ever be a great painting, but *that* was what I could give them. *That* was what I was capable of bringing to their figures, this total and complete absence of precision. The mess and contradiction of what every human being is.

I painted until I could barely stay awake, and then I stumbled my way upstairs.

I'd only slept an hour or so when Owen woke me with the news that Nora had left in Alison's car during the night, without a word. Alison was frantic, he said. Nora had been in a state. All of it had fallen onto the girl: my anger, Owen's pity, her own humiliation. And then Alison had been furious with her, too. Whatever united front she'd constructed for my benefit, she had let Nora have it for betraying her confidence.

All this, while I still lay in bed, Owen snatching his wallet off the dresser, putting a belt into his pants. "Alison's hysterical," he said. "She's convinced Nora's going to do something stupid."

I offered to go over.

"Not a good idea," he said. "She isn't thrilled with me, but I didn't call her daughter a cunt and tell her to go fuck herself."

I asked if there was anything I could do. "She'll turn up," he said. "She's not as fragile as Alison thinks. She's not as young as all that. Not in every way."

"Good," I said. "I'm sure you're right. Where are you going?"

"I'm just going to drive around a bit. See if I can find the car. Maybe at a motel. It's cold as hell. She has to be somewhere."

"What about her father's? She could have gone there."

"Alison called. She isn't there. And not with any of the friends Alison knows. Okay," he said. "I'll be back in a bit."

"Good luck," I said. "I hope you find her. Safe and sound."

He didn't find her, and she didn't call. By nightfall Alison had phoned the police but it was too soon for anything official to be done. Maybe if Nora were younger, but a twenty-two-year-old who skips out for a day? They told her it happens all the time.

Owen went out looking again that night. When he came back, it was to our bed.

"No luck?"

"No luck."

I asked him again the next morning if he was sure I shouldn't go see Alison, certain that I really wasn't welcome, but the answer was the same. She blamed me for what had happened. She blamed herself too, but mostly she blamed me.

"She doesn't blame you?" I asked. "For encouraging Nora?"

He had been kind, maybe too kind; but kind. I had been vicious.

By the third day, the police were involved and had set up an alert. Owen divided his time between driving around every morning—to where, I couldn't imagine—and then keeping Alison company. Alison, who by his account was almost too distraught to breathe. I would watch him walk over the snowy hill to her house and then a couple of hours later watch him come home, grim-faced, somber. I wondered if he adjusted his expression to something less frightening when he was walking toward her, just in case she was watching, trying to gauge his concern. He'd told me that all he did was keep reassuring her that things would be okay, but that really he was just there to distract her for a short while, until she wanted him back out searching again. "I tell her it would be different if she had been kidnapped. She's just run away from home. And she's fully capable of taking care of herself. She's not a child."

I didn't ask him if he believed that. And I didn't ask him whether if she had leapt off a cliff somewhere, he too would blame me. I knew the answer. He would blame us both.

For three days, everything stood still. Everything except worries and searches and worst-case-scenario nightmares. And then on the fourth day, she called. Just like that. Owen was at Alison's when her cell phone rang. It was the father's number. Nora was there. She was sorry. She had needed to hide out for a while, to get her head straight. She'd been staying with a friend Alison didn't know. She knew it had been wrong. But it hadn't occurred to her that anyone would think she had killed herself. They'd been drunk pretty much the whole time. She just couldn't face anyone. Not even Alison. And she was never coming back there. Obviously. But she was safe.

The police were notified, the search called off. Owen immediately lent Alison our van to go see her. I couldn't imagine her being in any shape to drive, but I had no role to play. He knew her history as well as I did. He made the choice.

And then we were alone.

I will always remember the lunch we had that day as if it were a wedding meal, special enough for every detail to survive, though in fact it was nothing out of the ordinary. A salad and some bread. A hunk of cheddar and a cold chicken breast, sliced and divided between our two plates. Beers for us both. A run-of-the-mill kind of lunch.

But that isn't what my memories are like. In memory, each silken leaf of salad shines with a different green, new shades invented just for us; and the bread is symphonic in its textures, re-

velatory in its taste. The cheese, the chicken, each has somehow
been saturated with flavors both comfortingly familiar and exhil-
aratingly new. We share our bites, we feed each other. And each
time the scene is revisited it intensifies, becomes more beautiful,
this simple meal of ours.

The crisis had passed. Nora's crisis, yes, but more than that.
Somehow in the hysteria and the fear, our old selves had emerged,
recognizable, waiting for us like well-worn clothes into which we
could step. Owen. My husband. The man with whom I had built
a life and then destroyed it and then rebuilt it and then almost
destroyed it again. Just Owen. The man whose body had memorized my own, whose heart had expanded to match the demands
of mine. How long had it been since the last time I had felt this
peculiar, familiar sensation of being alone by being together?

I knew exactly how long.

"Do you think Alison will ever come back?" I asked.

"Just for her things," he said. "To return the car, I guess. She'll
have to. Unless she sends a friend."

I wanted to say, *It's over, isn't it? All of it. We're back to normal,
aren't we?* But I was worried that if I pushed too hard for reassur-
ances, he would feel a need to withhold.

"It probably won't be tomorrow," I said. "I can't see her rushing back."

"Who knows? I'm just glad they're both okay. And I'm glad
they're both gone."

And then we talked about the house. Our house. About a shin-
gle that had come loose over the past couple of days, flying onto
the snow where it lay, a strangely regular black square in an otherwise wild landscape. And we finished our beers. And he said he
was heading out to the barn and I said I would work for a bit and
he touched me on my shoulder as he left.

I heard the car, then saw it, but didn't recognize it until Paul got out. I couldn't think why he was there, parked in our drive, but I felt immediate fear. He left the door open and went straight for the barn, his body taut with intent. I grabbed my cell and called 911 as I ran outside. "There's an intruder, an attacker," I said. "Send someone quick."

But when I got to the barn, Owen was already down, blood flowing from his head onto the stone floor; and Paul was kicking him. "Don't you ever fuck with my daughter again. Don't you ever fuck with my daughter again." He said it over and over. I ran toward them, tried to stop him, but I was a fly, a flea he swatted away almost casually, though with a force that landed me hard on the floor. I tried again, and again hit the floor.

"Don't you ever fuck with my daughter again."

"Stop it! Stop it! For God's sake!"

Finally I heard sirens and I screamed, "Stop it! The police are here! Stop it!" But Paul didn't stop until they were practically in our yard. "Well, I guess you learned a lesson," he said, walking out of the barn, directly into the oncoming officers.

By then, I was next to Owen, on him, beseeching the heavens to let him be all right, though in my heart I already knew. There was too much blood, the back of his skull shattered, his eyes emptied. An ambulance came, but there was nothing to be done except make it official and then try to calm me down.

22

Owen was Owen. Owen was me. I was Owen. And then Owen was gone.

Owen is gone.

I remember blood and I remember snow. To those I can attest. The rest I believe, but do not remember. Not with any precision. Of course. It is a story. It is the story I tell—mostly to myself. But also to my father, who lives on and even at times emerges from his haze, like a bashful planet that has been hiding behind its own clouds.

For about two months after Owen's death, I didn't visit my father. I barely left the house at all. But then I began to go see him several times a week, sometimes many days in a row. Jan, who had taken to calling me daily, thought it was unhealthy for me to be with him so much, but I found it soothing in a way.

And no one was much in the mood to tell me what to do. For those first two months it had been unimaginable that I would ever want to do anything again. I only stared and stared out that window. And I walked around the pond—seven times, fourteen times, twenty-one times. I wept fountains. I stopped painting. For whom would I paint? I barely even ate.

And I might have disappeared entirely (I can still easily imagine that, imagine myself just fading out of existence) except for Laine, who would not let me go. She came to stay with me in the spring, *barging* into my life—her word—setting herself up in the room down the hall; and she—her word again—*mothered* me. And slowly I began to live. "It's only what you did for me," she would say whenever I sputtered my thanks. "What goes around comes around."

She didn't ask me many questions, which was just as well as I could never have told Bill's daughter the whole story. And maybe that was part of why I needed my father's company, the one person in the world to whom I could, finally, finally, talk about anything.

So now, I tell him my stories.

I tell him this story of how Owen died. The way I couldn't close my eyes for weeks without seeing the black, bloodstained stone. How I clung to him, until they pulled me by my shoulders and held me back. How I screamed as they carried him away; and then for hours more; and then for days. And I tell him about the yellow crime scene tape left across the barn for so long, how the color of it became a thing of fear for me—for me, a painter who until that day had loved every imaginable hue.

I tell him too about the summer day when I finally reentered the barn, Laine by my side, to look for the work he had been doing, but found nothing there. No files I could identify as significant. No great project. Just the same starts and stops I had known about before. Or, sometimes, when I want it to be a happier story, I tell him about the stunning manuscript I found out in the barn. In one version it's a book about a man whose heart has been broken; in another, a man who has fallen in love; or a man who strikes out on his own to climb a mountain and begins to see God around him, everywhere.

I can tell my father anything.

I tell him, only him, about the email Bill sent, formal in its composition, tender at its heart. *I'm so sorry to hear this. If there's ever anything I can do* . . . And about poor Lillian and Wolf, about the calls I still get from them, and the ones that I make, calls in which we each remember for a time that the other is suffering too, in which we all reach out beyond ourselves.

And on my darkest days, I tell him the story of the neighbor I let myself love and how, months after Owen's death, she came asking me to forgive her daughter, pleading that the girl had been punished disproportionately for what she had done. That she shouldn't have to carry the weight of her father's crime on her back for all her life. And in one version of the story I forgive them both, explaining to the child that we're none of us so innocent, that we all had a hand in what happened, that her sins, for all they resulted in tragedy, were everyday, collaborative ones.

But in another version I only shout at the mother until she becomes frightened and drives away in that reckless, wreck-risking way of hers; then I stand outside my house, just where I met her, wondering if I have become entirely empty inside, a void and nothing more, so much of me spilled out it seems impossible that anything is left.

On better days, I tell my father how Laine convinced me to paint again, to finish the pictures of the boys, so on Armistice Day that year, all the local families came to see. I tell him how very hard I worked to find a balance, depicting the soldiers not as saints but also not as ordinary boys, how I had labored to convey that death does not bestow upon its hosts perfection, yet does, must, elevate them above our muck and our worry and our pain. And sometimes when I tell this story, I say I painted my mother and Charlotte among the boys, that these are the pictures of all of the ones we loved and still love, the ones who haunt our homes.

And when the paintings were complete, I tell him, the families gone, Laine helped me crumple the newspapers again and return them to the walls, she and I working late into the night, swinging mallets and hammers, shattering tile, stuffing the paper into gaps;

then discovering when we awoke that the wall had rebuilt itself, the tile adhered itself, the mess swept itself away.

But my father's favorite stories, I am sure, are the ones in which Owen does not die, in which I do not awaken every morning looking for him in our bed, finding only emptiness. The police have come in time. Or Nora has never told her father what happened between us all. Or Alison has not revealed my secrets to her daughter. Or she doesn't lease the house next door. Or she does, but she's aloof. Or she befriends us, but not in so very intimate a way. Or I never did betray Owen's faith in my loyalty to him.

And on that January day after lunch, he and I separate for only a few hours, to work through the short afternoon, apart but together, energy flowing between us, unmistakable and necessary to us both. And then, when the sun has fallen into the pond, I thaw some stew for dinner and we share it, sitting on the couch in front of a fire, the chaos and beauty of a milliner's shop before our eyes.

Acknowledgments

This book first came to life while I was on an annual retreat with writer friends, and so to them I express my first gratitude. Thank you so much, my dear Ladies of Avalon: Carlen Arnett, Catherine Brown, Shannon Cain, Helen Cooper, Janet Crossen, Marcia Pelletiere, J. C. Todd, and Lauren Yaffe. I feel blessed to be among you.

I am blessed too by the exquisite skill and insight of my editor, Kate Medina. I have absolutely loved watching and listening to her as she turns her unmatched editorial acumen on a passage, a plot point, a character. I feel both challenged and trusting in her care.

Heartfelt thanks also to Lindsey Schwoeri, Anna Pitoniak, Sally Marvin, Avideh Bashirrad, Erika Greber, Barbara Fillon, Vincent La Scala, Deborah Dwyer, designers Kimberly Glyder and Jo Anne Metsch, and all the wonderful people at Random House who gave this book (and me) their attention and enthusiasm and expertise. Thanks also to Nina Subin for her patience through our photo shoot and for the result. Her giant talent vanquished both my habitual grimace and my stunningly bad hair day.

The ever gracious, endlessly kind Paul Baggaley, Kate Harvey, Sophie Jonathan, and Emma Bravo, all of Picador Books, U.K., are a delight and a source, always, of wisdom and support. I have learned to love the time difference between my city and theirs just because it's so lovely to find their emails waiting for me when I wake up.

While writing this book, I taught at Bryn Mawr College and at the Lighthouse Writers Workshop in Denver, two very different places connected by their seriousness of purpose and generosity of spirit. My students at both have helped me in ways they might never guess. Loving thanks to Daniel Torday at Bryn Mawr, and also to Andrea Dupree and Michael Henry at Lighthouse, for these homes away from home—and for much-cherished friendships, too.

Jim Zervanos, Bonnie West, Jane Neathery Cutler, Erin Stalcup, John Fried, Marta Rose, Karen Russell, Alice Schell, Randy Susan Meyers, Nichole Bernier, Kathleen Crowley, Julliette Fay, Jane Isay, and Steven Schwartz, you have been my readers, my buddies, my wise advisers, and are some of my favorite writers. Thank you for everything you've given me, which is more than I can say. And enormous thanks too to my Beyond the Margins blogmates past and present. I feel such respect for you all, your creative work, your generosity, and your contributions to the literary community.

Eleanor Bloch and Fay Trachtenberg, my dear friends and my hand-holders-in-chief, enormous thanks to you both.

The wonderful painter Perky Edgerton took time to help me with some of the "art stuff," and for that I am most grateful.

Henry Dunow is flat out the best agent on earth and one of my favorite people, too. Working with him has brought me not only a brilliant professional ally, but also a dear, close friend.

Lifelong thanks to my family, my siblings, cousins, aunts, uncles, in-laws, the living and the missed. Lifelong thanks, and much, much love. And a special, new-member-of-the-family thank-you to my son-in-law, Tom Faure, a writer himself, who reminds me, by example, of what dedication to this craft looks like.

All of my children inspire and strengthen me, and this book belongs to them and to my mother, who is also my first and best reader. But this time around, with my older two grown, it was my youngest, Annie, who got the brunt of having a mom in the throes of becoming a novelist. She encouraged me when I was blue, celebrated with me when I was hopeful, made me mac and cheese, and made me feel loved no matter what. I couldn't have done it without you, my girl.

For Richard, only a riddle: In a life as full and as fortunate as mine, how is it that you are still my everything? I don't have an answer. You just are.

Robin Black,
October 2013